DARE TO IMAGINE

NILZA ELITA

To Joyce & Paul
Merry Christmas &
Happy Reading

Love
Nilza

This book is dedicated to my parents
Joseph and Sidoina Pereira.

For giving me the best education, experiences (travelling the world), and for teaching me
humility, empathy and kindness.

PRESENT DAY

'*Come out, come out, wherever you are! I'm coming to get you...You can't hide from me!' Jonathan crouched inside the wardrobe in his room. He desperately tried to keep as quiet as possible by holding his hands over his mouth, but he struggled to breathe normally. His heart pounded. 'Oh Jonathan, come out little Jonathan, I've got something for you.' The last sentence took on a sing-song tone as if that would coax him out of his hiding place. Peering through the crack in the door, he dared to look, he saw a form slowly scanning his room. He started to silently cry. He closed his eyes and held his breath. Suddenly the door of the wardrobe slung open—*'

Jonathan opened his eyes and screamed. He sat bolt upright in bed, his heart pounding and he was sweating. 'Thank god,' he said when he realised it was all a dream. He scanned the room, which was blindingly bright. He squinted, realising he wasn't in his own bed. He looked around at a very unfamiliar room, on his right was a small bedside table next to a large window, the source of the light, with a scenic view of some grassy fields. Opposite the bed, he saw a writing table attached to a wall. The floors were cream vinyl or tile, he wasn't sure.

He kicked off the grey blanket, realising that was why he felt so hot. He tried to push himself off the bed and felt a sudden sharp pain in his wrists. With confusion, he looked down. His wrists were bandaged, and his left arm had a plaster with what looked like a needle in it.

A sinking feeling suddenly came over him, and he wanted to cry. Within moments the door opened, and a man in a blue hospital uniform came in. 'Good morning Jonathan, I see you are awake at last. Don't try to move too much, you will be very weak for now', he blurted out without waiting for a response. He walked around the room and began by looking at Jonathan's arm with the cannula in it. He focussed on his wrists next. He looked at his bandages to see if they were still clean, then to check Jonathan's pulse he pressed his first and middle finger just under his jaw, besides his windpipe.

The man continued talking whilst taking his pulse, 'I suppose I should introduce myself, I have been keeping an eye on you ever since you were admitted, you have been sleeping like a baby for a very long time.' He emphasised the word "very" Jonathan said nothing.

'My name is Barry, I am assigned to look after you. You are in a hospital, and I work here as a psychiatric technician. I will help you with your daily activities and provide you with any assistance you may need. Whilst you were in a coma, you were fed through an intravenous line. That's why the cannula is in your left arm. Don't worry, now that you are awake you can eat proper food again.'

Jonathan still just sat there in silence and said nothing at all, he looked as if he was in a daze.

'You will, however, be expected to behave as per our hospital rules, do you understand me?'

Barry was nearly six feet tall, well-built, had light brown hair with a medium sized black beard and he walked as briskly as he talked. Jonathan was starting to feel at ease with Barry and just looked out the window.

'Did you understand me?' He repeated slightly louder this time. Jonathan looked back and nodded his head. 'Great I am glad we are getting along, I have worked in this hospital for over ten years, and in all that time I haven't seen a boy as skinny looking as you. Would you like me to get you something to eat?' He asked curtly.

Jonathan's first words were, 'what am I doing here?' Barry took a long look at him with a mixture of surprise and sadness initially, then changed it to a more thoughtful look and then said, 'Do you know who you are?' Jonathan nodded, then quietly and almost under his breath said, 'Jonathan William Rice.'

'Great, now let's get you some food, and after some rest you will be seeing the doctor, so he can have a nice long chat with you, is that ok with you mate?' He said in a loud overly friendly manner. Jonathan nodded his head again.

'Ok, I will be back shortly with lunch and something to remove that cannula in your arm.'

Just as briskly as he came in, he closed and locked the door behind him and left Jonathan in the hospital room looking more confused than before. He looked at his body and maybe Barry had a point. He was a little skinny. However he was in good physical shape, no broken bones, or pain anywhere apart from his wrists. 'What happened to my wrists? Oh my God,' he thought. 'Did I do this to myself? Why in the world have I slashed my wrists, and how long will I need to stay here until I get out? My mum will be wondering where I am.' He couldn't understand anything or remember why he tried to kill himself. Was his life that bad?

He needed to speak to his mum and decided he would ask Barry or whoever came through that door next to let him see his mum before he was taken to any random doctor.

———

After Barry left Jonathan's room, his first stop was the 'front of house coordinators' to inform them to get Jonathan's lunch ready in half an hour. They were told to deliver it outside Jonathan's room ready for Barry to take it inside.

Once he had arranged for Jonathan's lunch, he went straight to Dr Rao's office and knocked on the door.

'Come in.' Said Dr Rao. Barry entered the room quickly.

Dr Rao's office smelt of old leather, books and a whiff of cologne. His working table with his laptop was quite tidy, and he liked it this way. However, if you looked around the room they were surrounded by floor to ceiling bookshelves that didn't have as neat an appearance as his desk did. His books weren't just for decoration.

The doctor was of Indian heritage, in his mid-forties and had done well for himself in his career. He measured about five feet ten inches tall, had a slowly receding hairline, slightly pointy ears and a large prominent nose. His eyes were dark brown and had a softness to them that made many of the patients relax when he went to see them.

'Oh hello, Barry.' He spoke in his usual calm and gentle manner. 'So, how is he?' Out of all the patients in the hospital, there was only one that caused them the most worry right now, and that was Jonathan.

'I need to sit down doctor.' Dr Rao motioned Barry to do so.

Barry spoke, 'doctor, you should see him as soon as he

has had a rest, because I don't think he can remember anything!'

Dr Rao looked thoughtful and then said, 'something I thought might happen, how do you know for sure?'

'He asked what he was doing here! And he didn't look worried or upset about anything.'

'He could be confused as he has just awoken from a coma. Another option is that he is pretending he can't remember. I will figure it out, for now, I will contact the Detective Superintendent Brown and tell him Jonathan is awake.'

Barry Fuller was one of the staff members Dr Rao trusted the most. He knew Barry was not only empathetic, but he was also intelligent, quick to judge a dangerous situation and was strong. He had all the qualities needed to look after a patient like Jonathan.

'Let him rest for the afternoon, and I will meet with him at five pm. Please take him to the secure interview room number three, it has a two-way mirror. That way if Detective Superintendent Brown wants to observe me then he can. Under no circumstances do I want anyone but you or I to talk to Jonathan for now.' Barry nodded his head, he liked being given a chance to show his dedication to his job. The doctor continued, 'I have been put in charge of that boy, and I will do the best I can to find out what went wrong.'

Barry stood up to leave, 'is there anything else you would like me to do doctor?'

'Please make sure the camera in Jonathan's room is running twenty-four hours a day. I want to know what he says and does, even when he is sleeping, or nobody is around.'

'I check on the footage all the time doctor.'

'Great well done, what would I do without you?' Dr Rao said smiling. With a nod, Barry got up and left.

After leaving Jonathan for over thirty minutes with nothing but his thoughts, Barry came back with a trolley. Jonathan lazily turned his head towards the door and looked at the food, the smells were already filling the room. Jonathan suddenly felt hungrier than ever.

On the food trolley was a bowl of soup, a sandwich, fruit yoghurt and a bottle of water. The soup smelled lovely thought, Jonathan. 'What soup is this?' he asked.

'It's vegetable, you look hungry enough to eat a horse! But I warn you, you cannot eat it all. Just have little bits of what you like so you can gradually give your digestive tract time to work again.' Jonathan shrugged his shoulders and sat on the side of his bed waiting eagerly to eat.

Barry pulled up the only chair in the room to sit on, the one piece of furniture that wasn't either fixed to the wall or floor. Whilst he watched Jonathan eat in silence his mind started wandering. What perplexed him was how a seemingly innocent boy like Jonathan could end up in this hospital.

Jonathan finished his lunch and looked tired. Barry cleared up the dishes and told Jonathan he would remove the cannula in his arm as gently as he could. Once the cannula was out, he told Jonathan to get some rest as he would see the doctor at five pm.

'I do feel a bit tired, but I just want to ask if my mum knows I am here, when will she be coming to see me?'

Barry stopped in his tracks for a moment, then gently said, 'get some rest mate, I will be back for you at five.'

Jonathan shrugged and climbed into bed, he was still tired, weak and just wanted to go to sleep. After taking one final look at him, Barry left.

2

J onathan was brought to a small interview room just after five pm. Barry, realising that Jonathan was too weak to walk, got him a wheelchair and took him there.

When they got into the room Jonathan looked around, there was only one table and two chairs. It was painted in a light grey colour and lit with 'office like' concealed lighting. There were no windows, just one large mirror on the wall to the right of the door.

Not wanting to be questioned whilst he was in the wheelchair, Jonathan told Barry he preferred to sit on one of the chairs around the table. Once he was settled, he was told that Dr Rao would be with him shortly.

A few minutes later there was a soft noise at the turning of the door handle, and Dr Rao walked into the room saying, 'hello Jonathan, my name is Dr Sanjay Rao.' The doctor looked at Jonathan and saw a boy who was taller than he expected, nearly a full-grown man. He appeared a bit gaunt. He had mousy brown hair that looked like it grew out of the shape it was originally styled in. Jonathan also had a large forehead that was partially covered by his overgrown hair. His brown eyes followed Dr Rao as he walked over to the other chair and sat down.

Dr Rao said, 'I have worked in this hospital as a psychiatrist for several years. For now, I have been given your case. I would like to add that most of our meetings will be recorded. During these discussions, I will ask you basic questions so please don't worry about anything. Just answer everything as truthfully as you can. This will enable me to make the fairest evaluation on your mental health. Are you ok with this?' the doctor finished.

'Yes, doctor.'

'Ok,' he continued, 'can you give me your full name, the street you live on and your age?'

'My name is Jonathan Rice, I live at 44 Longwood Road and, and I am 16 years old.'

'Good, now can you tell me a little bit about yourself?' The doctor asked nicely.

Ignoring the doctor's question Jonathan asked a question of his own. 'Doctor do you know why I am here? Why my wrists are hurt? Did I try to kill myself?'

'I know you want answers, but I am trying to assess your mental health and would like to know more about you. I will certainly explain everything in time, but first, you will need to answer my questions. Is that ok?'

Looking away from the doctor and down at his hands for several moments, Jonathan then glared at the mirror behind the doctor's head. He sighed heavily and said nothing. Dr Rao observed Jonathan patiently. Jonathan scanned the room then began reluctantly, 'all I know is who I am, and where I live with my parents. Frankly, I am surprised my mum hasn't come to see me. I do know she has been busier than normal. My dad has left his airline job to be with us, and he has been

8

keeping my mum occupied. I have three close friends I occasionally hang out with. I like music, I sometimes read when I can be bothered and when I do, it's always Marvel comic books— I have a large collection. I am pretty much normal otherwise. I am not sure what more I can tell you.' Jonathan finished with a direct look at the doctor.

Dr Rao smiled gently, 'that was a good start, now can you tell me a little more? Like if your mum also works and what she does for a living? Have you got any family or friends that your parents are close to, like the ones your mum invites over for dinner, for example?'

After thinking for a second, Jonathan said, 'mum doesn't work full time anymore. She sometimes helps at the local florist, but she only goes there during their busy periods or when my dad isn't around. When he left his job, he preferred her not to work, so she only goes in a few times a month. My dad took a career break from being an airline pilot a few months ago and now just spends his time harassing us!' He ended with disgust.

'What about family friends?' the doctor coaxed.

Jonathan stood up abruptly shouting, 'I don't know man! What type of questions are these? I wake up in some random hospital bed, it looks like I tried to kill myself, and I feel miserable! Who knows where my mum is, and why she hasn't come to visit me yet! I feel like a fucking prisoner for just slashing my wrists! I did slash my wrists, didn't I? Can't you all see that I am miserable? The worst thing about it is the fact that I can't remember why, when, or how I slashed my wrists! All of this is confusing the life out of me, and you are just sitting here in this fucking box of a room asking me about dinner guests? You guys must be crazy!' Jonathan finished his rant, he was shaking, and his face turned bright red.

'Please sit down, Jonathan. I know this is frustrating for you, and I promised to answer all your questions. So be patient, we were doing so well.' The doctor said calmly.

'You are doing well doctor, not me!' Jonathan snapped flopping down into his chair. 'I can't be bothered with this shit, if you want to get answers from me then let me see my mum first. Once she is here, I will then answer whatever the hell you want.'

The interview was taking a turn for the worse, and Dr Rao was expecting it. He knew Jonathan wasn't just a little kitten to be petted, he had to keep his nerve. He was a professional and he had worked with many patients like Jonathan in his career. These things took time, and Dr Rao did not have as much time as he wanted, Detective Superintendent Brown was hot on his heels for answers.

For now, it was looking like Jonathan would only answer questions if he got what he wanted. So, taking a brave step and ready to face the consequences Dr Rao whispered, 'It does appear that you did try to kill yourself. However, your mum cannot see you now, so you will just have to help me with the questions I need to be answered.' He looked at Jonathan for a reaction.

'Cannot see me? Why? Normally she comes running when I need her. Hang on a minute doctor, have you told her where I am? She might be worried sick!' He continued talking, 'that bloody dad of mine has something to do with this, I'm sure of it. They were right all along, she took his side. If my mum knew I was here, and he didn't stop her, she would be with me now. I slash my wrists, and instead of realising that it is my call for attention, she is too scared to come and see me! Great, fucking great, now I must beg her to see me instead of her being here already! What a world eh doctor, you know what I mean?' Jonathan's face turned a deeper shade of red, and he tapped his foot vigorously.

Dr Rao looked with sympathy at Jonathan thinking about the medication he was on. The anti-depressants were the only thing prescribed. The doctor was reluctant to give him anything else whilst he was being assessed, so he continued his questioning. 'When you said, "they were right" just now, who were you talking about?'

'Don't you listen, doctor? I thought doctors were intelligent, but clearly, you either aren't or have a hearing problem. I told you they were right about my mum siding with my dad.'

'You said so, but who are "they"?' The doctor persisted.

'My fucking friends, doctor.' He said glaring at Dr Rao. He was fed up with answering questions he thought the doctor knew the answers to.

'How many of them told you that your mum might side with your dad?'

'Peter said it, and they all agreed. Man, he hated my dad too, he said our dads were similar, fucking control freaks!'

'Ok so Peter did, what about the others, did they all dislike your dad too?'

'They did, they were my friends, so obviously they would support me.'

'What were the names of your other friends?'

He was calming down now from his earlier outburst, he liked talking about his friends.

'There are two others called Nick and Misty. Misty is a girl.' He said with a shy grin.

'So how did you all become friends, at school?'

'Well, actually no. I met Peter first. He then introduced me to Nick and Misty. And we have been meeting up now and again.'

'Is Misty your girlfriend?' Dr Rao asked.

'Not really,' He said shyly and continued, 'I want her to be, but I am too shy to ask her. I think she likes me, but she has a temper sometimes. My mum may not like her, and there is no point asking about my dad's opinion of her, he is a grumpy shit and likes no one!'

'Why do you think your parents won't like her?'

'Because she doesn't care what people think of her, she smokes, and like I said, she has a bit of a temper.' As an afterthought, he said, 'well she gets annoyed with Peter the most.'

'Do you think Peter and Misty have a chemistry that could lead to more than just friends?'

Jonathan laughed at that thought, 'No way, Misty can be a bookworm sometimes, and Peter is the opposite. He likes to play practical jokes all the time. That would annoy the hell out of her.'

'I see. You said you enjoy reading comics, are those the books that Misty reads as well? Is that what you two have in common?'

'I'm not sure, if she reads comics, she hasn't said. I know she reads self-help, psychology and meditation type books.' He smiled, 'actually doctor she would like you, I am sure she would want to pick your brain about the work you do. Who knows it might be something she takes up in her further education.'

'That would be nice, I wouldn't mind talking to her. Anyone interested in psychology is welcome to pick my brain.' Dr Rao smiled then said, 'so Jonathan, from what you are telling me your dad is not someone you are fond of, do you know why you don't like him much?'

He scowled at Dr Rao, he didn't want to talk to the doctor about his dad or intimate family stories, even if it was to a doctor. He said, 'I don't feel like I want to say anything else to you right now.'

The doctor realised that Jonathan was shutting him out and decided to stop questioning him any further today.

'Ok Jonathan, I think we should continue tomorrow. I am glad you seem to cope well. Your wrist wounds have been looked after by the nurse, and I am being told that they are healing well. I know you are still confused, but over the course of the next few days we should be able to ascertain your state of mental health to see what your next steps should be.'

Dr Rao was careful not to give too much away. He wanted Jonathan to express his feelings so he could find out why he did what he did.

'So that's it, you will not tell me I am going mad or something? Can't you tell me why I tried to kill myself? I feel fine, yet that can't be, right? And you know what the worst thing is, doctor?' Dr Rao said nothing, and Jonathan carried on regardless, 'the worst thing is I don't remember anything. I don't know if I did this at home or outside somewhere. Night or day. It's all a blank and making me go mad, so if you know something, please tell me, you can't keep me hanging like this.' He finished looking frustrated.

Trying to end the interview again, the doctor said, 'I need to find out everything you know, that is why we are having this interview and why I am asking you all these questions. Once I am satisfied that you are suffering from some sort of amnesia, then we can see what treatment you will need. Finding out what you are or aren't aware of is important. So far it looks like you remember everything except why, when, or how you tried to kill yourself. You are blocking out that memory, I am just trying to sort this out, we both are. I don't want you to have any cognitive reappraisals, this could affect the answers we seek.'

Jonathan raised his eyebrows, and Dr Rao explained, 'sorry, cognitive reappraisal occurs when a person alters the way they think about something and change it into a positive. And I don't want you to change anything you perceive, to fit in with what you think we want to hear.'

Looking tiredly around the room, Jonathan got up to leave. 'Fair enough doctor, please can Barry now take me back I am tired.'

As if on cue, Barry walked in to escort Jonathan away.

'Have a good evening and plenty of rest, and I will see you tomorrow.'

'Bye doctor, laters. I like you, I think you're brill.' He said smiling as he left the room.

3

W hen Jonathan left, Dr Rao gave a big sigh. He got up and turned to the mirror saying, 'you had a front-row seat detective, hope you got some of your questions answered.'

The doctor then left the room and headed for his office, where he was meeting Detective Superintendent Brown. The doctor felt drained by the interview. Everything mattered, every question he asked Jonathan was significant, every word said needed to be analysed, every expression was important. Dr Rao had to watch the interview again a few times. He would have to pose new questions from the responses Jonathan gave today. He would need to have a more in-depth discussion with him tomorrow, and he would have to be prepared for it. He could already see how unpredictable Jonathan became. But one thing was clear from it all, he disliked his father.

After a brief knock the detective came into Dr Rao's office and sat down, he was a tall man of medium build. He had a full head of black hair slightly greying at the temples, his brown eyes had wrinkles around them, just like someone in his fifties. He wore a dark suit and black and white Aztec looking tie.

The detective had Jonathan brought to this hospital due to his age, at sixteen he didn't feel that a conventional hospital would be suitable. Under section 136 of the Mental Health Act, he had the power to route Jonathan to a place of safety. Because of Jonathan's attempted suicide, the detective thought perhaps he was suffering from some sort of mental illness and in need of immediate care.

This was a high-security hospital, equipped to deal with a person deemed to be a risk on to themselves or others. Since Jonathan had attempted suicide, they needed a safe place to assess his mental health and make arrangements for his care and treatment. Keeping him here under emergency detention was compulsory for now.

Neither men said anything for a few moments. Dr Rao spoke first, 'well, what did you think?'

'You were right. You were the best person to interview him. I don't know, doctor. Do you think he is pretending or really can't remember?'

'To be sure, I will have more and longer interviews with him. For now, I am inclined to believe he is suffering from psychological amnesia. What Jonathan could be facing is a loss of memory a few days or a week before the incident and remembers nothing for the period in-between, till he woke up in the hospital.

Tomorrow I will ask him a few questions: Could he remember if he suffered from any kind of memory loss in the past or when he was a child? Did he drink alcohol or take drugs? I know the answer to the drug questions, because his blood test revealed he must have taken cannabis between six to twenty-four hours before he came into the hospital.'

'You didn't tell me about the blood test Dr Rao.'

'I have been busy, detective. Honestly it must have slipped my mind.'

Detective Superintendent Brown looked patiently at the doctor then said, 'why can't this be a simple problem? When I got this assignment, I looked at the circumstances and decided it was an 'open and shut' case. Now you are telling me we may also have to contend with psychological amnesia? God damn it, doctor, it's very frustrating!' he exclaimed.

The doctor smiled at him.

'Well, what is so funny doctor? I thought you take these things seriously, so what are you smiling at?'

'You.'

'Me!' the detective looked shocked pointing at himself.

'Yes, you detective, you sit here complaining Jonathan is suffering from psychological amnesia, but I didn't say he definitely had that problem. Like I said, I need to question him to be sure. He will undergo a memory assessment, so we can determine the extent of the memory loss. If you think you have a hard job, try mine for a change. Sometimes you have, like you say, 'open and shut' cases. For me, I can never have that. Each case is complex - granted, some more so than others. So, "patience my dear Watson"' the doctor finished with a smile.

The detective then snapped, 'this isn't a game of whose job is harder doctor!'

The smile left the doctor's face, 'I didn't say it was a game, far from it. I am saying that this is a complex case, but someone must deal with it, and that's us. There may be further issues to worry about than just psychological amnesia.'

'Oh, you mean like depression?' the detective asked.

'That too.'

'There's more?'

'There most definitely is, and I am eighty to ninety per cent sure.'

'Like what?'

'Like schizophrenia.' The doctor said raising his eyebrows.

'No bloody way! That will change everything doctor, are you sure?'

'Like I said, I am not a hundred per cent sure until I examine Jonathan, but there is a high probability he is schizophrenic!'

'Oh wonderful!' the detective said raising his eyes heavenward.

'I know, this something we seriously need to consider, it will play a major part in my assessment of Jonathan.'

'So now what?'

'Well, I need to be sure whether he is schizophrenic. And if he is, there are some other complications to be considered.'

'What kind of complications?'

'His depression and drug use, this could cause any number of difficulties for Jonathan.' The doctor said sympathetically.

The detective wasn't so soft. He had a mission to complete, and Jonathan's case was getting further and further away from the simplicity the detective wanted.

The doctor stood up and took a slow walk to his bookshelf and with his back to the detective said, 'I can't be sure at this point.' Turning back to face the detective he continued, 'I think he may suffer from the symptoms of schizophrenia and bipolar disorder, the combination is called schizoaffective disorder.

The detective looked a bit confused for a moment then said, 'wait, doctor, are you saying that Jonathan could have schizophrenia and be bipolar too?'

'Yes, I think he could. If he has a mood disorder like bipolar or depression, he can also be suffering from schizophrenia. If he has both he probably also suffers from mood swings and hallucinations.'

'So, I presume you have looked at Jonathan's records. In the past has he been diagnosed with any of the symptoms you now suspect?'

'I have looked at them briefly to check if Jonathan was taking any current medication or was undergoing any medical treatment, but there wasn't anything in his current records for me to be concerned about, especially as he has been in a coma for the past few weeks. I had requested for his full records, including psychological, be sent to me which I received just yesterday. These things take time, and as he was in a coma, I wasn't in any rush to receive it.' Dr Rao finished.

'Doctor, did you read what it said?' He asked impatiently.

'Not yet but I intend to do so immediately. I didn't expect Jonathan to wake up from his coma suffering from amnesia. The doctor raked his fingers through his hair and said, 'I thought, like you said earlier it would be an 'open and shut' case.' He trailed off his last sentence under his breath.

'We both thought the same thing. I want to meet with Jonathan tomorrow too.'

'I don't think it's a good idea detective. You might come on too strong, as it is Jonathan is already confused. If I introduce a detective to him at this stage, he may reveal nothing more. Just let me gain his trust, he may relax enough to make a mistake if he is lying to us about his amnesia.'

'No way, I want to be there. I need him to give me answers.' The detective insisted.

'I don't know. Let me go through his records which I will do tonight and tomorrow morning. I will then interview him in the afternoon again once I have a fuller picture of him.'

'That's fine if you want to do that, but I need to be there too. I think we should put him under pressure, so we can find out everything as soon as possible. All this pussyfooting will get us nowhere. Plus, my superiors want answers. I can't tell them he has amnesia and doesn't remember anything having not interviewed him myself. You owe me that doctor.' He said pleadingly.

'But detective you don't understand. You can't just charge in there and demand answers. First, you won't get the answers you want and second, he will retreat into his shell more than he already has.'

'That's debatable.' The detective interjected.

'Whether or not he has amnesia, he will still need to be handled gently, and let's face it, I don't think he is ready for your kind of questioning.' The doctor said sarcastically trying his best not to lose the ground and gains in Jonathan's trust he had achieved today.

'Fine ok, you do the bulk of the questioning, but I want to be there in the room. I want him to know this is a serious matter and I might throw in a question or two.' He held up the palm of his hand in a 'stop gesture', 'and before you say it, I will be gentle. Come on, doctor. Don't make me wait another day.'

The doctor sighed and agreed, 'Ok, you can come in tomorrow, but I am going to be the one in charge. I need you to promise to be gentle with him. Can you do that?'

'Yes, I can.' The detective said with a grin.

'Ok fine, I will review his medical records, and I will brief you on them before the interview. I plan to see him after lunch, around one or two pm tomorrow. So, I will have to meet with you at least half an hour before that. Shall we meet at mid-day in my office? We can then go to see Jonathan together.'

'Sure thing.' The detective said standing up to leave, 'I better go now before you change your mind.'

'Right, see you tomorrow. And detective, if you have any questions you need to ask Jonathan can I have a look at them as they may be like mine. We will need to coordinate our questions. Bear that in mind.' The doctor added.

'No worries doctor, you worry too much, that's your problem!' the detective said smiling and turned to leave. 'Thanks, doctor see you tomorrow.'

'Have a good evening detective, I have a feeling tomorrow will be a long day for all of us.'

SIX MONTHS AGO

4

'Hey JR, you not going to school today?' Peter asked Jonathan.

'No can't be arsed!' he said smiling, 'You got smokes? A splif would be better.' Jonathan asked cheekily.

Peter and Jonathan became friends a few months ago. Peter was about one or two years older than Jonathan and didn't seem to have parents that set boundaries like Jonathan's parents did. 'Lucky Peter', thought Jonathan. Peter was fearless, he happily climbed high fences or jumped from high walls without hesitation. Jonathan could learn a lot from him. Peter was slightly muscular, and not very tall for his age, but was very strong. He had dark wavy hair and rugged good looks Jonathan was envious of. Jonathan looked up to Peter and was glad Peter took an interest in him. Peter was like an older brother, plus there was something about Peter that seemed familiar like they met before. Jonathan racked his brains trying to figure out where, but couldn't remember. He just knew they had.

Whenever Jonathan could bunk from school, he would. On those days he wished he would bump into Peter, so he always went to the usual hangout hoping Peter was there. The same spot they had met in the park, one bus stop away from his school. If they weren't at the park, they would end up at Peter's house all day. Other times Peter just broke into the school and would entice Jonathan to bunk from classes. When that happened, they broke into an unused classroom or one of the storerooms and played silly truth or dare games. At school Jonathan didn't get much time to spend with Peter due to the busyness of the place, so he preferred to meet with Peter in the park or best case to be invited to his house.

On some occasions they went to the shopping centre and spent some time walking around, looking and pointing at girls they thought were hot! Peter said he could get any girl he liked, and with his good looks, Jonathan had no doubt that he was right. He secretly felt that Peter was slightly immature and childish. He looked grown up, but sometimes he didn't behave like his age. That didn't seem to faze Jonathan. He still thought the world of Peter, who could do no wrong in his eyes. The fact that he wasn't forced to go to school, had no limitations and could do whatever he wanted, was what Jonathan loved about him. Jonathan also thought he was self-confident and had self-esteem to match. All the things that Jonathan aspired for but didn't have!

'Yeah, I have one we can roll up but not here in the park bro, we could be arrested!' Peter said. 'Nobody's home JR, let's go to mine, relax with a splif and talk crap as usual.' He said with a wicked laugh.

That's what Jonathan wanted to hear. He was having a rubbish week. It was Thursday, and the only day he bunked off school so far. Because he was stressed, he wanted to skip school but didn't have the guts to do it till today. The conversation he had with his mum on Monday upset him and made him restless. She put his nose out of joint because she said that his dad would be back from his trip this weekend. He had taken a six-month career break which could last longer if he wished. He said he wanted to stop traveling and to be a normal husband and father for a change. His mum didn't see it or ignored the fact that their whole status quo would collapse with his dad being there. Jonathan was not happy at all, and he let his mum know it.

Whilst they walked the short ten minutes it took to get to Peter's house, Jonathan was lost in thought about his woes.

'Hey, snap out of it.' Peter said to Jonathan. 'You look like you were a million miles away. We are here, let's get in before anyone sees us.'

Peters house looked small. The main door opened on to a dingy passage with an old green floral carpet that looked like it belonged in the seventies. The corridor led to the living/dining room on the left and if you went further, to the kitchen. Opposite the front door, there were a set of stairs to the top of the house - somewhere Jonathan had never been.

Jonathan hadn't ever met Peter's parents and was glad of it. Whenever he was at Peter's place he felt uncomfortable at first, like he was somewhere he shouldn't be. Then, after a few smokes of weed he would feel relaxed.

'So,' said Peter, 'what's bugging you today JR? You haven't said two words all the way home. It's like you zoned out before our splif. If you are getting your hit from some-where else, please tell me, so I don't waste time trying to get you some!' Peter said sarcastically.

'No of course not, don't be silly.'

'Then what's going on JR? Don't you want to be friends anymore?'

'No, it's not you,' he mumbled. 'It's my dad, he is leaving his job, and now he won't travel for days on end like he used to. Life was peaceful when he wasn't there.'

'So, what made him leave his job?'

'I don't know.'

'And you don't get on with him?'

'No, I don't.' There was venom in Jonathan's voice.

'Oohhh really, now this is interesting!' He said sitting up on his chair. 'I've never asked you about your family before. So….give it up! Why don't you get on?'

'Because he is a dick! Anyway, I don't want to talk about it, Ok? So, let's drop it.'

'What? No fucking way. Come on JR tell me. You owe me that much.'

'I owe you fuck all Peter, and you're behaving like a dick, so I'm going back to school!'

'No, you're not. I won't let you leave till you give me the juicy gossip.' Peter said taunting Jonathan.

Peter seemed to be enjoying his misery which annoyed Jonathan. He decided he had enough and got up to go.

'Where do you think you're going? Not till I get the whole story.'

'Don't be a jerk, Peter, I will see you later.' Jonathan was getting grumpy.

'Go if you want, but your phone stays here.' He said laughing and running around the living room with it in his hands.

Jonathan chased him for it, but Peter kept dodging him. He was losing his temper. He lunged at Peter and took him down. They both dropped to the floor. Peter still laughing and Jonathan screaming, 'Give it back!'

'Ok, ok, fine. Here you go now keep your pants on!'

He grabbed his phone, got off Peter and stormed out of the flat. He walked fast, breathing hard. He thought Peter would chase after him to apologise, but he didn't. Jonathan continued walking fast, toward the park. He couldn't think straight, and was still angry. He didn't know whether to go back to the park or go home, but school was out of the question.

By the time Jonathan got to the park en route to his house, he had slowed his pace. His anger dissipated toward Peter but not toward his dad. For now, he felt a bit angry at his mum too, he knew his mum lacked the confidence to make the right decision for both of them.

When he got home, nobody seemed to be there. 'Thank god' he thought. He went upstairs, changed into a tee shirt and tracksuit bottoms and curled into bed. He just wanted the world to disappear. He felt depressed again.

He had been on medication for depression for a few years. His mum insisted he see the doctor regularly for it. He sometimes fooled the doctor into thinking he was ok by putting on a good mood. He didn't like to take the medicine the doctor gave him. His mum said it would make him feel better, but he didn't think so.

Jonathan's dad, Niraj, was of average height, had black hair and tan skin. His eyes were deep set, but his most prominent and endearing feature was his cleft chin. It gave him an innocent look that made him even more lovable to women.

If you asked any of the neighbours, friends or Niraj's colleagues about him, they would say he was a 'happy-go-lucky' guy. He would always stop and help someone in trouble, he could make people laugh. In social situations, he was the life and soul of the party. He liked to dance and could hold his drink well. A happy drunk. At home, Niraj was moody, grumpy, lazy and would blame his wife - Janice or Jonathan for anything that went wrong. He couldn't remember his dad spontaneously laughing at anything when they were at home alone as a family. Jonathan realised that his dad would save those laughs for an audience. His mood could change like the wind. When his dad was home, Jonathan felt he and his mum constantly walked on eggshells. He knew that when he was younger his mum shielded him from his dad's mood swings, but now that he was a teenager, his dad picked on him and his mum, at times Janice would act as the buffer between father and son.

Nothing was ever right, he got unhappy if Johnathan listened to music a tad too loud. He would yell at Jonathan to turn the music down, sometimes he pretended he never heard his dad. When he didn't turn it down, his dad would storm upstairs to shut it off. Jonathan would say, 'Oh I didn't realise it was loud.' In a nice sweet voice.

The music was a minor thing. Niraj criticised his wife's cooking, choice of TV programmes and worst of all the cleaning. Most of the arguments in the house occurred because Niraj always wanted the house spotless. He wanted Janice to do all the work, and he would go around double checking to make sure it was done to his standards. He wouldn't do any of it himself, he was just good at dictating. Niraj didn't understand that living came with its own share of mess. He couldn't understand why even one dirty tea mug should be left in the kitchen sink. He could lecture Janice for hours about the importance of a clean house. If he managed to help, he let them all know about it! For the next month or two, he would be an expert in that field, insisting his method would be the best way to get the job done.

Living like this was hard enough for Jonathan when his dad was home after his work trips. Having to live with him full time would be awful. He started feeling anxious, depressed, angry, suffocated and his dad hadn't even come back yet! He didn't know what he would do. He curled up into a ball in his bed. He relaxed trying not to think about anything at all. After about half an hour he calmed down. He could feel the darkness descend upon him, and he was warming up like a slice of bread in a toaster. His heartbeat slowed to a gentle rhythm, and he began dropping off to sleep.

Whilst he lay there, from somewhere far away he heard a voice saying quietly, 'Jonathan.' It was merely a whisper. He got scared to answer it, he wondered if he was imagining things. Then he heard it again, this time a little more loudly like it got closer, 'Jonathan.'

His heartbeat picked up speed, and he was getting scared. Then in commanding voice right beside his ear, he heard, 'Jonathan! Wake up, you wanker!'

He shot up in bed when he recognised Peter's voice. 'Fucking hell Peter, you nearly scared me to death! What the fuck are you doing here, and how did you get in?'

Peter didn't answer him. He was so busy laughing at Jonathan that he fell on the floor literally rolling around clutching his stomach. The more he laughed, the more Jonathan got angry. 'He could be such a jerk' Jonathan thought. Sometimes he wondered why he chose Peter as a friend, but then again, now was not the time to question their relationship. Now was the time to shut him up before his mum came home! She wouldn't like Peter at all. He was too common for her, and she wanted her son to associate himself with nice high-class friends, not that it bothered Jonathan.

'What are you doing here? Are you fucking out of your mind? My mum could be home at any time, and you are stomping around like you fucking own the joint!'

'Now don't be so moody JR, you know how fond I am of you. I couldn't let you go running off without apologising to you. I know I can be a pest sometimes, but I wanted to come and see your house, see if you have calmed down and generally hang out with you. I wasn't happy when you ran off.

Now can we speak about it? If I am very, very quiet. Like this?' He whispered.

He was glad of the distraction from his problems, and he was also happy that someone cared enough to come and check up on him. 'Ok fine, what do you want to know?'

'Everything' Peter said. 'Why did you say you don't like your dad?'

Jonathan got up from his bed and paced around the room slowly. 'Where should he start?' He thought then said, 'I dunno Peter, I have always disliked him since I was a child. I can't remember any one incident that stands out. I just know there is no love for that man. The more I grow up and see how he treats us, the more I don't like him. My mum knows about my feelings for him, and I suppose she doesn't like him either, but she is good at hiding her feelings. I think she has done it for years and is an expert at it.'

'So, what does he do to piss you guys off?'

'Well, he is a control freak for a start, he is also a lazy fucker. He won't do any work in the house and just dictates work for my mum and I to do. When he is due home for a long weekend, he will say 'Hi' and give my mum a peck on the cheek, then he religiously goes around the whole house inspecting it!'

'Inspecting it? For what, another man?'

'No, to check if it is clean and tidy.'

'Seriously? He sounds like he is stuck in the fifties or sixties' Peter said with a grin.

'I am deadly serious! Don't you think it's too much? He stomps around the house like a Nazi Gestapo officer inspecting a prison camp!' Now Jonathan was already smiling at the thought of his dad in a Nazi uniform!

'What's wrong with him?' Peter asked again.

'The question you should ask is, what's right with him?

My mum said that he is miserable because his family stopped talking to him when he married her. I think he was promised to another Indian girl and when he didn't marry that woman they got annoyed and stopped talking to both my parents. I don't think he ever loved my mum.' He said sadly.

'So your dad is a control freak and an asshole! Welcome to the world JR. Newsflash! The whole fucking world is filled with crap dads. Why should yours be so special?' He continued without giving Jonathan a chance to speak. 'Your dad is as crap as all the others, and the sooner you understand that, the better. There must be more to it than what you're telling me JR, come on spill. Maybe something bad happened when you were young, and you repressed it.'

Jonathan said quietly, 'I think I would have remembered something like that. Anyway, don't know, and I don't care, Peter. All I know is, I have had enough of his shit. Are you going or not? My mum will be home soon, and I know she won't like you being in my room uninvited.'

'Ok no worries, keep your pants on JR. See you in a few days.' He went towards Jonathan's window and climbed out.

'Wait, what are you doing? You can't go out from there, you could break your legs!' Jonathan said with concern.

'I came in this way, and I will leave this way. I didn't know if your folks were home, so I came in through your window. I knew you were keeping me at arm's length from your parents, and I didn't want to get you into trouble, so I thought I would come in this way.'

'Oh ok, thanks, Peter. You are a good friend. I am sorry if I was moody today.' Jonathan said sheepishly.

'No worries JR see you soon buddy.' He said as he climbed out the window, stretched his arm out to the large lead drain pipe to the left of the window. He grabbed on to that and slid down. Once he was safely on the ground, he scanned the area to check if anyone saw him and then looked up at Jonathan who was hanging out the window in awe.

'See, it was bloody easy.' Peter said with a foolish grin.

'I should try that sometime.'

'Laters, JR.' Peter said as he skipped off.

5

J onathan's mum came home half an hour after Peter left. Jonathan heard her from his room but didn't feel the need to go downstairs, he didn't want an argument with her. And because of the mood he was in, he preferred to stay away from everyone.

He heard his mum climb upstairs and hoped she didn't come into his room, but she did. She knocked quietly then opened the door. Jonathan was lying in bed looking at his phone. He was scrolling through the posts on Instagram with no real interest. He looked over at her and gave her a half smile.

Smiling back, she said, 'oh you're home. I thought you might go to your friend's house after school. Did you just come back?'

'Yes recently. You ok?'

'Yup, I'm fine. Listen, Jonathan, I am sorry that I upset you earlier today. I know you and your father don't get along, but he is your dad, and whatever the issues are, we will iron them out.'

'Mum, can we not talk about dad? It's a depressing topic

for me.' As soon as Jonathan said that he wished he could have retracted it. 'Depressing' was the wrong word to use with his mum.

'Oh my god, have you had your pills? We can go to the doctor if you have run out or if you need to change your dosage.'

'You don't have to go mad mum.' Jonathan backtracked. 'I used it as a figure of speech.'

She looked at him pensively. 'Hmmmm ok, but I will keep an eye on you.'

'You always keep an eye on me, that's the problem. Just relax whilst you can. When he comes back, trust me neither of us will have one moment's peace!' Jonathan couldn't help but sound sarcastic.

Shrugging that comment off she said, 'Fine, I'm going to make dinner. I am making lasagne, your favourite.'

'Cool.' He said and looked at his phone again. She left the room closing the door gently behind her. Jonathan sighed and threw his phone away from him and stared at his ceiling thoughtfully.

He supposed his situation wasn't the worst. Like Peter said, there were tons of crap dads all over the world. Why should his be special? What made his mind work overtime was Peter's suggestion that something bad might have happened to him when he was younger, that he could have blocked out of his memories. He thought he would ask his mum if he had ever done such a thing before.

At dinner, he broached the subject with her.

'Mum, can I ask you a strange question?' he said trying to sound nonchalant.

'Yes of course, what is it, son?'

'I know it's an odd question, but when I was a child did I have any periods of memory loss?'

Janice froze. Jonathan realised right at that moment he hit on something she was hiding.

'Not really.' Janice said as calmly as she could.

'Then why are you behaving like a rabbit caught in the headlights?'

'I'm not, I don't remember anything like that. You make it sounds so serious. You might have forgotten your books or something similar. Or if your friend had a birthday party, sometimes you would forget to tell me. But you need not worry about that, it happens to everyone.' She said in an overly casual manner.

'I am not talking about those little things, and you know it. So, from your silly attempts of pretending everything is fine, I guess I had suffered from some form of amnesia.' Jonathan said seriously.

'Amnesia is a bit over the top don't you think? Ok, you might have forgotten a few days now and again, but I took you to the doctor, and they said all children were different. They also said you were a quiet child, so there was nothing I needed to worry about.'

'A few days?' Jonathan said with a raised voice.

'Yes, but it wasn't a big deal.'

'But did my memory ever come back for the days I missed, and how many times did this happen?'

'I am not sure if they came back. If they did you didn't tell me. Plus, I was afraid to ask in case you had another episode of issues with your memory.'

'They weren't "issues with my memory", from what you are saying. I had amnesia!' Jonathan was now frustrated.

'Son,' she said in an exasperated voice, 'It's not a big deal, you may have forgotten a few days here and there, but you are turning out ok, aren't you?'

'Yes, I am in your eyes. However I suffer from depression

now and again, and I have this irrational fear of dad coming back and living with us full-time. Surely there must be a reason for that. Do you know why I get anxious knowing dad is coming back?'

'Not really Jonathan.' She mumbled.

'Then why do I feel like you are hiding something I ought to know?'

'Don't be silly, what could I possibly be hiding?'

'I am not sure mum, but I feel it. I think you know something, and you are trying to protect me by not telling me.'

'You aren't eating, and you are putting me off my food so please, can we just drop the subject?'

'Ok but only for now, at some point I will want to know what you know. I am sixteen, so I am old enough to handle anything you want to throw my way.' He ended his rant folding his hands in front of his chest in annoyance.

'Fine, can we finish our dinner in peace?'

They both said nothing else for the rest of dinner. His mum looked lost in thought, and he didn't want to have idle chit-chat.

He didn't say anything after that on the subject. He didn't like upsetting his mum, but he knew this was just the beginning. He would get to the bottom of it, If not today, then soon. But, it would be before his dad came back. He knew that once his dad got home, he had a limited time in which to talk freely with his mum. They would both freeze under the scrutiny of his dad's presence. Plus his dad was paranoid, he always thought they were talking about him.

———

Friday passed in the usual manner, nothing exciting

happened in school that day, but Jonathan started feeling increasingly anxious knowing his dad would be back home sometime this weekend. With each passing hour he got increasingly fidgety.

He saw Peter after school, both boys walked back to Jonathan's house. He was glad of Peter's company. Listening to him prattle on about random things that sometimes made him laugh, so today he hoped Peter's prattling would help him take his mind off his anxiety. Peter lived up to Jonathan's expectations as usual.

'Guess what JR, I want you to meet two friends of mine. They are fun, you will like them. Trust me you will get along with them like a house on fire.'

Jonathan wasn't up for making new friends. He already had difficulties making friends at school. Some of his class-mates thought he was a loner and a bit weird. The girls never talked to him much, and the boys always tried to show off in front of the girls by picking on Jonathan. This made him even quieter in class. He did have one or two friends he hung around with in school.

'Sorry to be a pain, but I am not sure I am ready for new friends. When did you want me to meet them?'

'Not ready? Don't be an ass JR. They are cool you will see. Shall I bring them around later, through your window quietly?'

'Are you off your trolley?' Jonathan said stifling a yell.

'No of course not.' Peter said looking offended.

'My dad is due to come back this weekend. For all I know he is probably home now. Sorry, Peter, I have that fool to deal with. Hope you realise I think the world of you, but can we defer this for now? I have been stressed because of his return.'

'Sorry JR I forgot. Yes, sure. You want me to come over

and give him a piece of my mind? I am quite strong he won't be able to push me around. Trust me.'

'No, god no. It will make things worse for both my mum and me if he meets you! Thanks for the offer though. It will stun him into silence I am sure! I don't think I know anyone that has told him to lay off us. What a great thought.' He said smiling.

'Happy to be of service JR. You say the word, and I will be there in a shot.'

'No need for now, but I will keep that in mind.' He would never get Peter to fight his battles for him. His dad was unpredictable, he didn't know what would happen if he let Peter loose on his dad. The thought made him smile, but that was all it would be, just a thought!

When Jonathan got home after he said his goodbyes to Peter, everything was silent, so he knew his dad wasn't in yet. He made his way upstairs, he heard his mum working in the kitchen. Then he heard her say, 'Jonathan are you back? Wait a minute, I want a quick word, can you come in here please?'

Jonathan halted and gradually turned around. He walked into the kitchen plastering a big smile on his face so that his mum didn't know how anxious he was. 'Hey mum, what are you cooking? I don't think I can wait till seven.'

His mum smiled, she looked relaxed he thought, which was a good sign. He could hear Jazz music in the background on her digital radio. He knew that meant one thing, his mum was happy and jovial because his dad wasn't coming home this weekend, or at least that was what he hoped.

'You will wait till dinner. If you are hungry already have some olives with bread and butter. I bought it for the salad we are having with the pasta later.'

'Ok yeah, I will.' Jonathan said as he made his way to the jar of olives, he opened it, put an olive in his mouth then rummaged around the bread cupboard for the bread his mum said he could have.

'Wash your hands first.' She said when she saw he was already touching the food. 'I got some news for you if you're interested.'

He continued making his snack and said, 'oh yeah, what is it?'

'Your dad isn't coming home this weekend, and at the rate he is going, he may not be back next weekend either. He had work setbacks, so they asked him to stay a few weeks longer.'

Jonathan halted his actions for a moment then said, 'oh ok, at least we can have a few more weeks of peace and quiet then.' Secretly Jonathan was elated but pretended to sound calm and matter-of-fact in front of his mum. She realised he would be happy with the outcome, and she looked pleased with the news too. How wonderful life would be if it was just the two of them rather than having to deal with his pathetic dad too he thought.

'I knew how anxious it was making you. This way you have more time to digest the fact that your dad will come to stay for good.'

'Great, let's not think about it.' He didn't want to face that music yet or even deal with the thoughts. For now, he was happy.

'If there is nothing more can I go up to chill mum?'

'Ok but don't play your music too loud please.'

'No worries, laters mum.' He said practically running out the kitchen and up the stairs.

The next few days passed uneventfully, Jonathan and his mum went about their business as normal.

Jonathan now had time to meet Nick and Misty. He had called Peter to tell him the good news and arranged for them to meet two nights later. Whilst Jonathan was asleep, Peter shook him awake a few minutes after midnight.

'Peter, what the fuck? It's late.' He said half sleepily half scared out of his wits, trying hard to whisper even though he got a shock from being shaken awake!

'JR, ssshhhh.' Peter said putting his finger over Jonathan's mouth. 'Stop shouting, your mum will wake up. I thought you would like to meet Nick and Misty. I told them to wait outside till I woke you up. Shall I call them to come here? We can have a party in your room.' Peter said excitedly.

Jonathan looked at him like he was crazy. He was still a bit dazed and confused, but he managed to say, 'I'm in my boxers, can't I meet them at yours tomorrow? It's fucking late, and I am not sure I want anyone in my room at this hour. Really Peter, sometimes you don't think. You just do whatever the fuck you want.'

'Hey, hey, calm it JR. I knew you were stressed by your dad coming back home I thought we could get together with the others to have fun too. Plus, Misty is kinda cute, if you know what I mean.' He said winking at Jonathan.

'Big deal, you can have her, if you like her that much.'

'No way, she is boring sometimes, like you! That's why I thought you should meet her.' Peter said smiling. 'And Nick is funny, you will definitely think so too. So, shall I ask them up?'

'Stop being an arse. I don't want to meet anyone tonight, including you! I got school tomorrow, and I don't have time for your crap!' Jonathan said in a strop.

'Tomorrow is Saturday JR, so you can stop being a big baby. Come on, say yes. I got a few splifs for all of us.' He said pleadingly.

Jonathan couldn't understand his hyperactivity. Peter would not worry him for days on end, then all of a sudden, he got full on and wanted undying attention. Now he wanted to bring his friends around too. Good thing his parent's room as on the opposite side of the house or his mum would have heard something. Jonathan's room faced the back of the house, and their garden wasn't exactly overlooked by neighbours, so he was lucky in that respect.

'Ok fine, I will come down. I don't want them in my room, and it's not that cold outside. There is a park nearby. If we are quiet, we can smoke there. My mum would surely smell weed in my room if she came in, and I am not risking that.' He said.

'Aaaaww, ok. I suppose that's fair enough. The smell from four of us smoking is a risk.'

'Finally, now you make sense!'

'Ha, ha, very funny. Ok get dressed then and meet me outside. I'll go and tell them.' He said making his way out the window.

Jonathan was glad he fobbed Peter off, he was hard work, but at least he cared.

After finding a pair of jeans and a hoodie in the dark, Jonathan put his trainers on, and made his way out the window, easily getting hold of the lead down-pipe. It was cold to the touch but felt secure, and he slid down. Halfway down he was wondering how he would get back up again, but he dismissed that thought almost immediately.

When he was safely down, he couldn't see anyone there. Jonathan thought he was dreaming for a second. 'Peter?' he whispered as loud as he could trying to find out where he went. 'Peter, stop playing games. Where are you, you dick?' he called out again as he made his way to the gate at the back of his garden.

There was darkness everywhere he looked, and the night air smelled fresh. Jonathan liked that smell, quite earthy, the smell of rotting mouldering leaves. Jonathan's eyes got used to the darkness of his garden. When he got to the gate, he realised that it was locked. 'Peter' he called again. The gate was only about five feet high, and he realised he could peer over it if he stood on an upturned plant pot. After scanning the garden, he saw an empty terracotta pot a few feet away. He turned it upside down, then stood on it to look over the gate and just as he did so he heard, 'BOO' deafeningly in his ear. Peter jumped up from where he was crouching behind the gate, so he could startle him. Jonathan gave a yelp as he fell back from the fence and on to his bottom. He stood up quickly brushing off the dead leaves and dirt from his body, he wanted to scream but then realised it was night, and he wasn't meant to be up at this time.

'Peter for fuck's sake, what's wrong with you? I nearly died!' he growled.

Peter didn't respond at. First, Jonathan could hear him laughing from the other side of the fence. A real belly laugh, and the fact that he was trying to do that silently made it even worse for Peter. The more he tried to stop, the more he laughed.

Jonathan stood there with his hands firmly on his waist and contemplated going back home. He got on the pot again to peer over the fence, and he saw Peter holding a tree for support as he continued to laugh. 'So childish' thought Jonathan.

Peter saw him and slowly stopped laughing. 'Hey JR, you know why I love hanging out with you?' Without waiting for an answer he continued, 'for moments like these. Man, you crack me up!' He said still giggling.

'Good for you Peter. I am not some kind of pet you could

entertain yourself with whenever you feel the need to! I have feelings.' Jonathan said, as his anger dissipated.

'Sorry JR, at this time of night it would be rubbish if I didn't do that. You know it's funny so stop making such a big deal about it, let's go meet the other two. They have already headed towards the park.'

Jonathan needed convincing and wasn't about to jump to Peter's tune. Especially now he made Jonathan look like a fool. 'You can join them, I am going back to bed.' He said sulking.

'For god's sake JR, it was a silly little joke, now come on, don't be a baby.'

He wanted to go to the park now that he was here, he was just playing hard-to-get, and he felt a bit annoyed at Peter's stupid games, but then he sighed and said, 'fine, but cut the silly childish games. I'm not in a mood!'

'Ok, no worries, now hop over let's go, I'm dying for a splif.'

It was only a short walk to the park. There was nobody about at that time. The air smelled even crisper, and Jonathan took a deep breath in to get a lung full of the smell. He loved it, he felt alive and free, being out at night whilst the whole world was sleeping. The tranquillity, the smells, the swish of the swaying leaves all made him glad he was out here and pleased that Peter coaxed him out.

When they got to the park, he could see two figures from a distance. They were in the darkest corner of the park, sitting on a bench under a tree. As they got closer, Jonathan saw Nick who was wearing a hoodie and tracksuit bottoms. It was still dark so Jonathan couldn't make out his features, he did, however, notice that Nick was tall for his age. Nick spoke first, 'so you're the elusive JR. Hi, you want a splif? We just rolled one.' Nick stretched out his hand to offer the rolled joint to Jonathan.

Extending his hand to take it, Jonathan said, 'Hi Nick, yes please.'

'Hi JR, I'm Misty.' The girl sitting next to Nick said.

'Hey Misty, you ok? You can call me Jonathan. For some unknown reason, Peter insists on calling me JR.' He said as he looked at her.

Wow, he thought, even in the darkness he could make out some of her features. She looked mixed race, with a mass of black semi-curly hair. Her eyes were light brown, wide and almond shaped, like a Disney princess. She wore tight black leggings with black boots and a leather jacket on top. She was pretty, Jonathan surmised.

'Here is your light, now stop gawping at her.' Peter said giving Jonathan the lighter and sat down between Misty and Nick on the garden bench. Jonathan took it saying, 'thanks, I was just saying hi.'

'So, it's a nice fresh night, now what do we do? Just look at each other?' Said Nick.

Jonathan took a few drags out of the joint and passed it over to the bench as an offer. Misty took it off him and drew in a lung full of smoke from it, she was looking relaxed. Nobody answered Nick, they were just happy with the joint they were having.

'So, what are you guys doing tomorrow?' Peter said breaking the silence.

'Nothing much as usual.' Nick responded.

'Lazing around looking pretty.' Misty said giggling.

Peter, looking over at Misty said, 'That won't be too hard for you darling. And you, sleeping beauty!' he said turning to Jonathan.

They all burst out laughing, this time Jonathan joined in

too. 'Good one Peter.' He said happily. The weed relaxed him, and he felt less uptight. 'Well I got homework to do this weekend, I will finish the new Marvel comics I got and just watch some movies on Netflix.

'Awww, what a good boy you are.' Misty said with humour in her voice.

All the three boys laughed.

'That's me, good boy Jonathan.' He said giggling.

They stayed in the park for under an hour laughing at silly jokes they made up. They then left and agreed to meet up at Peter's house at some point but didn't set a specific date.

Jonathan walked back home alone, he climbed over his garden fence effortlessly knowing where he kept the upturned garden pot so he could get over the other side with ease. He got to the lead downpipe that he slid from earlier and hoped he could climb back up just as easily. Hugging the pipe, placing his hands and foot on it like a koala bear on a tree he tried to climb up. He realised his upper body strength didn't help him, because it wasn't strong enough to lift his body up the pipe. He slid down several times. 'Oh, my days,' he thought, how did Peter make it up and down so easily? The last thing he wanted to do was wake his mum up, or the neighbours.

After five minutes of trying, he looked around the garden for something that would get him to one of the top notches of the pipe where there was a better foothold. He scrambled around for what seemed like ages, but he still couldn't find anything. In desperation, he looked at his back door and thought if he were to get in without breaking anything that would be amazing. He saw the little side window to the left of the door. If he could open that he could put his hand through and unlock the double-glazed door. He went over to the little window and tried to open it, but it was locked and wouldn't budge. He then looked at the door and thought he better try that too. What could he lose, he was getting desperate. He turned the handle, and as if by magic it opened! Effortlessly, 'Oh my god, how jammy' he thought. His mum must have forgotten to lock it.

He couldn't believe his luck, he got in as soundlessly as he could. Locked the door behind him and made his way up to his room. The house was dark, it was two am, and he didn't want to be caught in the middle of the landing with his jeans and hoodie on. His mum would then know he had been out. Thankfully, he got to his room with no issues. He changed into his night clothes and dived under his covers. His electric blanket was still on the low setting, and he was glad he forgot to turn it off. He felt relaxed, warm and cosy. He thought about his antics trying to get up the lead pipe and giggled. He wasted all that time, and nearly fell off and broke something when the back door was open all along! Too funny. The last thing he remembered was Misty's pretty face, and soon after that, he dozed off with a smile.

FIVE MONTHS AGO

6

J onathan met Peter, Nick, and Misty several times after school over the next couple of weeks. He expressed his anxiety with his dad coming back home. It seemed to be a topic that the group got excited about. Each of them had opinions on how Jonathan should tackle the situation. They had a few laughs, many joints of marijuana between them, and long conversations about nothing. The only discussions he remembered were ones about his family, mainly his dad, he found talking to them about his issues relaxing. After a few conversations where they slagged his dad off between them, he went home happy knowing he had good friends on his side.

The weekend his dad would be back home, his mum started her excessive cleaning rituals. She also looked worryingly at Jonathan when he came back home from school. She constantly nagged at him to finish tidying up his bedroom. Over the course of the week the nagging worked, and he started cleaning it. He didn't have the energy to do it all at once. He got fed up and angry at how they had to change the way they were to suit his dad's rules. Couldn't they just be a normal family? Couldn't he have a regular bedroom with clothes here and there? Leave his comic books wherever he wanted, and shoes strewn in random places? But no, the books had to be in the bookshelf and in order of height! The clothes (all of them) in the cupboard, or in the wash basket if they were dirty, and the shoes kept together as a pair in his wardrobe. Well, that's just the way his dad wanted it, and he had to conform! He knew his mum would get an earful from his dad about it if he didn't do his room, and he didn't want his mum to get the blame for his mess. So, like a dutiful son, he slowly cleaned it. By Friday evening it was nearly spotless. Jonathan looked around and thought, although it looked lovely, it was more like a show-room rather than a real teenage bedroom.

Jonathan's dad Niraj enjoyed his job. As far as Jonathan can remember, he was always away from home flying around the world. His dad loved the attention he got when he put on his pilot's uniform to go to work. He was quite good looking, and his cleft chin gave him a John Travolta look, he said women mentioned this quite a few times. That always put him in a good mood, being compared to John Travolta.

Despite loving his job, his dad wanted to take a career break for a few months. He said he wanted a long rest and felt he could afford to take some time off. When he got back home in a taxi at seven pm that Friday evening Jonathan was in his room, he heard his dad come into the house, but he didn't bother to go downstairs to welcome him. 'There was no need to roll out the red carpet for a dictator!' He thought.

He heard his mum and dad talking, but he preferred to stay in his room. He was as quiet as a mouse so that he could listen to their conversation, he wanted to see if his dad started his usual tactics early. But to his surprise, he heard them laughing downstairs and thought his mum said, 'Don't be silly Niraj,' and giggled. 'Wow,' he thought, this was a change from his dad's normal behaviour, he never made mum giggle like that, well not that he could remember.

Usually, Niraj inspected the house for tidiness and then opened a bottle of wine, which he wanted to share with Janice, or he went straight for the whisky on ice. That was his drink of choice, it made him grumpy and moody the next day, and Jonathan didn't like it when he drank that, but he had learned to keep out of his dad's way. His whisky hangovers were the worst ones.

Janice didn't drink much alcohol, sometimes Niraj forced her to have a glass or two of wine, and she drank it to keep him company. Jonathan knew she didn't buy or drink anything alcoholic when his dad was away. If Janice refused to drink with him, he would accuse her of being "high and mighty," or "Miss Goody Two Shoes." Now she just accepted the glass of wine without complaining.

Jonathan hated that, his dad's psychological manipulation. For a long time, he thought his mum was dumb and stupid. That's what his dad always called her when she didn't do things according to his standards. If she dared say something in public to embarrass him, he would shout at her in the car back home.

'Janice, you are really dumb sometimes, aren't you?' He would say. Most times my mum knew his mood would only get worse, no matter what she said, so she said nothing at all, she just listened. He once said, 'You can't keep your stupid mouth shut, can you? Who told you to tell Sam's wife I can't cook? Now they will think I am lazy.'

'No, they won't, I was trying to say…'

He wouldn't let her finish her sentences.

'Say what? For all I know, you slag me off all the time.

Don't you even think about what comes out of your foolish mouth?'

'I say nothing bad about you Niraj, I was just talking about cooking.' She continued to defend herself.

'You can say what you like, but I know what I heard, and you clearly said, "Niraj doesn't like to cook".'

'Well, you don't do you?'

That was the worst thing she could say to him. He then went off the rails completely. 'Oh really? So now the truth comes out. And here you are sitting like an angel saying you don't say anything bad. Ask Jonathan who cooks the best breakfast in the world on Sunday's? Go on, ask him?'

'Please Niraj, don't bring Jonathan into this.'

Jonathan had to pretend to be asleep at the back of the car, so he didn't have to get involved. If he said anything, it would be in defence of his mum, which would annoy his dad even more and would result in his dad accusing them of ganging up against him.

'Ok fine, we will ask him in the morning. You didn't tell them about my amazing breakfasts. All you did was show off about how good you were and how lazy I was. Now they will think we are a family that belongs in the fifties!'

His mum knew not to speak anymore the whole way back home. Sometimes that journey could last more than an hour. If she didn't talk, he would get angry at her silence and try to pick another fight with her.

'So now you're going to give me the silent treatment? Just because I told you, you were out of line?'

'I am not giving you the silent treatment. I am tired, and it's late, and I am just listening to the radio.'

During those journeys home, Niraj always insisted on driving even if he was just over the drink driving limit. Jonathan would rather his mum drove back. That meant his dad slept for the whole journey. When Niraj drove, he chose the radio station to listen to, and it would be very loud. He didn't care that Jonathan was at the back trying to sleep. If he was arguing with Janice, he turned the volume down to ram his points across.

The night they argued about the cooking, he turned the radio down but forgot to turn it up. It disturbed Janice's peace when he accused her of sulking, however, she got used to it. He then turned the radio off just to annoy her. She would either look straight ahead or through her side window for the rest of the journey. If Niraj was particularly harsh and continued to harass her for the whole journey, Janice would apologise for things, just so he could calm down and drive less erratically. Those apologies were affirmations to Niraj that he was right, and she was wrong. He then had leverage, which he used to his full potential. Why else 'would someone apologise if they weren't admitting their guilt?' Thought Niraj.

As Jonathan grew up, he realised that his dad, in his eyes was, 'All shades of wrong'! Those were the words he would mutter to himself whenever his dad picked up random fights with either his mum or himself, 'all shades of wrong.' He loved that phrase. That summed up his dad perfectly.

Now here he was back home playing the loving husband. Jonathan was yet to find out if he would play the loving father as well. Eventually, he would have to face the music by going downstairs.

When Jonathan was hungry, he made his way to the kitchen. When he got down, he saw his dad was sitting calmly watching TV with a glass of red wine in his hand. He noticed his mum wasn't around, so he guessed that she was in the kitchen finalising dinner. Niraj didn't hear or see him come down the stairs. He then calmly but reluctantly said, 'Hi dad, you're home.'

Niraj looked over at Jonathan and smiled. 'Aahh, so you're awake son.' He got up and went over to give Jonathan a hug. Jonathan felt awkward and stiffened up but tried to hug him back. 'Your mum said you came home with a headache and was sleeping. I came up to see you and you were curled up like a bear hibernating, so I thought I would leave you to it.'

First, his mum lied to cover up his lack of enthusiasm in seeing his dad. Janice knew he wasn't asleep. And secondly, his dad was now lying by saying he came up to see him and found him fast asleep when he was wide awake! He knew why his mum lied, and it was a white lie. His dad, however, blatantly lied to his face. Anyway, Jonathan didn't care about anything his dad said anymore!

'Oh yeah, I came home with a terrible headache. I had a busy week at school, which probably didn't help.' Jonathan said smiling. Then he thought, he would be brave and tackle his demons. He asked, 'mum said, you wanted a break from work. So, you want a bit of a rest and be at home for a few months?'

'Yes, I fancied a break. Find out how my family operates in the real world and, I want to muck into the daily chores. Support you if you need help at school. Re-connect with friends. So much I have missed out on, travelling here and there. Mind you, I don't know how long I would last! I might get bored after two or three weeks and want to fly again!' He laughed.

Jonathan laughed too, 'I'm sure you will find something to be occupied with!' Although Jonathan meant that comment sarcastically, his dad didn't realise it.

'Sure, it will just be a matter of what would be interesting enough to sink my teeth into.'

Jonathan wished he would get bored and leave. That would be the best result. He wasn't sure how he would cope with his dad staying at home full-time.

They had dinner that evening with no arguments or strain. Janice seemed to be relaxed and surprisingly, Niraj was too. 'Who knows, this might work,' thought Jonathan for a few moments, but then he dismissed it. A leopard doesn't change its spots. He knew in time, his dad would revert to his bastard self. It was just a waiting game.

To Jonathan's surprise, a few days passed with no issues, and for the first time, he saw a funnier, happier, and energetic side to his dad. He thought things had changed, or were changing, and even complained less about his dad to his friends.

Peter was as surprised about the change as Jonathan was. Nick and Misty were extremely sceptical about it, they didn't want to believe such a transformation could happen after all the temper tantrums that Niraj put Jonathan and his mum through. They were adamant that Niraj would revert to his old self and even suggested ways that Jonathan could get back the memories he had lost, so they could find out what happened. Why were those memories so bad that Jonathan forgot them?

Peter said to Jonathan, 'like I said before, maybe something happened when you were young, and you repressed it. That's why you don't like him. What if you found him in bed with another woman! Or he touched you or something!'

'Don't talk crap, do you think I would have forgotten something like that?'

'It's possible, many people do it and choose to blank the whole episode. Think clearly JR.'

Jonathan responded, 'I don't think so.'

'Maybe, but now I made you think, haven't I?'

'No, you haven't, you are just trying to cause trouble. Fuck off with your shit.'

One day they were in Peter's house talking about random things. Their favourite subject came up, 'Jonathan's issues with his dad.' Out of the blue Misty said, 'What about hypnosis?'

The three boys turned and looked at her.

Peter laughed and said, 'hypnosis? What are you talking about? Have you had too much weed?'

'I mean what about hypnotising Jonathan, so he can remember what happened to him? Fill in the gaps he can't remember.'

Peter answered, 'and how are we supposed to do that? We know nothing about it. For all we know we might make things worse for JR!'

'Actually, it might be a good idea. We could learn more about hypnosis, then one of you could try it on me.' Jonathan said suddenly realising this could work.

Nick piped in, 'I like that idea, don't be such a baby Sparker.'

Jonathan looked at Misty and mouthed, 'Sparker?' And Misty whispered, 'tell you later.'

For once Peter was the responsible one amongst them. 'This is not something you could learn off a book. It may be dangerous.'

Nick continued to defend the idea saying, 'sounds like fun, whilst we are at it why don't we put Sparker under too and find out when he suddenly became a granddad?' He said laughing out loud. Making Misty and Jonathan laugh too.

Peter glared at him. 'Very funny Nick, I say it's a crap idea. But, I am happy to go with what JR decides.' Then he addressed Jonathan, 'JR, you're in the driving seat. What do you want to do? But before you answer think carefully, maybe let's research it before you make your decision. What do you say?'

Jonathan raked his fingers through his hair like he was making a life and death decision and then said, 'yes I think it's a good idea, but we should look into it first, that way we know what it will entail for one of you, because I obviously can't do it by myself. So, who wants to do the actual hypnosis?'

Before anybody said anything, Peter quickly responded, 'definitely not me, that shit freaks the hell out of me.'

They all looked at Peter and laughed.

'My god you're such a fucking baby.' Nick said teasing him.

'I have to do it.' Misty commanded. 'I am already interested in psychology and psychiatry. I know I could try and influence Jonathan to delve deeper into his mind. I have his trust and can put him at ease, and I know what we need to get out of him, so I feel I am best placed to do it.'

'Cool, ok you do it then.' Jonathan added quickly, not giving a chance for Nick to volunteer. He liked spending time with Misty. Maybe this way they would get to spend time alone with each other, instead of as a foursome.

'Great, now that's settled who wants to watch Bates Motel on Netflix?' said Peter.

'Hang on a minute.' Misty interjected. 'This is just the beginning. We need to do some research on the topic. Watch some YouTube videos, and who knows what else we might have to do to learn hypnosis. I need to get more books on the subject and practice with Jonathan. We haven't got all the time in the world, his dad could return to his old self at any time.'

'Oooohhh, someone's got to protect our sweet, cute Jonathan!' Said Peter smiling in his usual mischievous way.

'Don't be silly Peter, do you really need to create a mountain out of a molehill!' Misty shot back

Jonathan realised it was getting late and he had to get home. 'Anyway guys, think about how we can do this. I should head home, or he might get annoyed if I come in late!'

'Ok cool, see you tomorrow?' Said Peter

'Yes, of course, bye guys. Bye Misty,' he said shyly to her.

Misty had already started researching about hypnosis on her phone. She barely looked up at Jonathan when he said bye. 'Yeah, laters, JR.'

He left Peter's house with the anticipation of getting one-on-one time with Misty. He was feeling excited, he might finally find out the memories he had repressed. He thought a lot about it all the way home and realised he didn't feel as anxious as he was before. Especially now his dad's moods had improved, he hoped it would last.

―――――――

Over the next few days, Misty and Jonathan spent a lot of time together trying to understand exactly how to get Jonathan into a hypnotic trance. They read articles on the net, watched YouTube video's and tried a little meditation, so he could relax into a trance. They decided, if they practised on each other, it would give them more experience, and without realising it, they were having fun too.

Misty was constantly reading books on the subject of hypnotherapy, on one occasion she exclaimed loudly, 'Jonathan listen up, I found this article that sounds interesting from a hypnotherapist in America. Can you hear me?'

Jonathan looked at her, drinking in her enthusiasm, her eyes were sparkling with excitement. 'Yes, I can, what does it say?'

She read some of the article to him, 'He says, "*There are many kinds and degrees of hypnosis. Nobody hypnotises someone else, a person hypnotises themselves. All hypnosis is really self-hypnosis.*

Having said that, any person can help another person get into a hypnotic state. That person is a hypnotist. It is extremely easy to do. Hypnosis is a powerful tool and needs to be used as such." So, I feel confident I can help you get into that deeper trance. We have to try.'

'That's interesting, and I have confidence in you Misty.' He said giving her some reassurance. He felt glad she was that passionate about helping him out.

Whilst they were researching and practising hypnotism, Peter and Nick were in a world of their own. They would either be smoking, watching Netflix, annoying each other with pranks and giggling or laughing about jokes that seemed funny only to themselves.

A week later, Misty told the group she was ready to hypnotise Jonathan. Nick looked like he didn't care, Jonathan looked excited, and Peter said, 'wow so soon, I thought you had to go to university or something to do that!'

'For god's sake Peter, it's not that complicated. We have researched it to the hilt, and I am fed up with just researching and trying it out a little. I want to do the real thing, and Jonathan is ready for it, aren't you?' She asked turning her attention to him.

'Yes, I can't wait. But let's start with simple stuff like we discussed.'

'What simple stuff?' Asked Peter.

Misty replied, 'Oh, things like, what Jonathan did last week after school, or what he ate for dinner yesterday. Something not too in-depth.'

'Great, I can answer that, and I don't even need to be put in a trance. Jonathan was with us!' Peter liked annoying her.

It was working, Misty was getting annoyed with his negativity on the topic. 'What's your problem, Peter? You have been against this from day one. Whilst all of us thought this was a good idea, you make fun of it. I thought you were Jonathan's friend. What other way do you suggest we find out what happened to him?'

'I am his friend, if it weren't for me, you wouldn't have met him at all. So, don't get on your high horse.'

Jonathan interjected, 'Hang on you two. There is no need for tempers to flair. Let's just get this over with and see if it works first. For all we know, it might not work, and we will be getting het up about nothing.'

Misty and Peter stopped glaring at each other. Jonathan couldn't understand why Peter was so negative about hypnosis, he was happy that Misty took this seriously. 'Finally,' he thought, he would get answers to what had happened to him when he was younger. He knew deep down that something went wrong with his relationship with his dad, but he wasn't sure what. Once he gets some of those gaps filled in, he could question his mum further and get definite answers.

Jonathan started getting closer to Misty. He had difficulty talking to girls at school, a lot of them thought he was very odd. Sometimes he felt like some of them were afraid of him. Most of them stayed away from him like he was a freak of some sort. Occasionally he even heard them sniggering, then giggling whilst looking at him. Other times conversation would stop if he walked in on a group of them talking. He wasn't sure if he was paranoid about it or not. Either way, he got on well with Misty. She didn't shy away from him or make him feel inadequate, she was approachable, funny, and the best thing he liked about her was that she was very smart. Misty picked up information at lightning speed and often read text very fast.

Misty broke his thoughts, 'So what about doing it tomorrow guys?'

'I don't give a shit, do it whenever you want.' Nick said sounding like he didn't care.

'If you must.' Said Peter feigning interest in the idea for fear of Misty giving him another tongue lashing.

They all looked at Jonathan.

'Yeah, I am up for it. After all, it will get me closer to the mystery of my memory lapses I didn't even know I had until recently. I say bring it on. I will come here after school tomorrow, and we can try it.'

They all seemed to be content with that idea. Jonathan then headed home.

7

Whilst Jonathan was going home, he started feeling excited about the prospects of being in Misty's company. The hypnotherapy sessions ensured he would get to spend time with Misty again. Lately, he couldn't stop thinking about her, he wanted to get closer to her. Although he knew she liked being with him, he wasn't sure about her romantic feelings towards him. Did she feel the same as he did about her or find him attractive? He knew she didn't have a boyfriend because she said nothing about him, if she had, he would have been introduced to the three of them. He was still thinking about Misty when he got home.

He could hear his dad talking to his mum in the kitchen, their voices were raised as if they were arguing about something, but he couldn't make out the whole conversation. His mum's voice was as loud as his dad's, which led Jonathan to think it was a serious topic. If it wasn't, then his mum would have listened to his dad without responding. When she replied this passionately, he guessed it was because the subject was close to her heart. They didn't hear him come in.

He tried to edge closer to the kitchen, so he could eavesdrop. He wanted to make it look like he just came home if they suddenly came out, so he kept his book bag on his shoulder.

Jonathan heard Niraj saying, 'like I said before, you should have sorted this by now. It's unacceptable.'

She replied, 'and do you think I haven't tried? I am telling you Niraj, this is a recent development. No one knows apart from me, and I am only saying this just in case you stumble upon something odd, because I don't want it to freak you out.'

'Freak me out? You are only telling me because I am back home rather than flying off here and there. This might have been going on for ages, and with me not being around, I probably wouldn't have known about it at all. Have you confronted him?'

'I haven't, I don't want to make it worse. Have you got any ideas?'

Just then a phone rang. It was Niraj's mobile phone. Jonathan pretended he was walking towards the kitchen when he heard someone coming out, it was his mum.

'Oh, hello love, you're home. Just got in?' she asked.

'Yeah. I want to grab a cup of tea and a biscuit. You ok?' He said moving past her, so he could get into the kitchen. His dad wasn't in there, he had gone out the back door to finish his conversation. Jonathan could hear him talking outside.

His mum followed him. 'Let me make it, you keep your bag in your room, wash your hands, and when you come back, it will be ready.'

Jonathan knew how kind his mum was, and thoughtful too. He wondered why kind and gentle people got stuck with mean and miserable people. He thanked her and as he went up to his room, he heard his dad come off the phone and his mum whispering to his dad, 'Jonathan's home, I don't think he heard anything, so we better change the subject till we are alone.'

'Fine, but I am not comfortable with this Janice.'

He heard nothing more from them, so he skipped up the stairs quickly. He wondered what they were talking about. They wanted to hide something that worried them, so what now, he thought, were they going to gang up against him? This wasn't normal, it was usually Jonathan and his mum against his dad not like this: his dad and mum against him!

The good mood he was in was dampened slightly, so he didn't say much at dinner and decided to have an early night. He told his parents he was tired and going to bed.

The next morning, he woke up and excitedly got dressed for school. All he could think about was meeting up with Misty. He wasn't that bothered about their hypnotherapy session, he just wanted to hang out with her. Jonathan felt close to her somehow this morning, and then he remembered he had dreamt about her last night, racking his brains as he tried to think of what the dream was about, but couldn't remember. Getting annoyed with himself for forgetting, he left the house and walked to school. Just as he passed a local park, he remembered the dream. The trees in the park reminded him.

In his dream, he was in a thick dark forest. He was walking around lost and looking for a road he could follow. He heard noises, and when he looked around him, he thought he saw a shadow of someone, who darted behind a tree when Jonathan looked in their direction.

Jonathan got scared, but he approached the tree saying, 'hello, is somebody there?' Silence, not even the wind moved. He got to the tree, but there was nobody behind it. He then heard a rustling noise and looked in the direction of the noise. Again, he saw someone run behind a tree quickly. He shouted a bit louder but didn't go to see who ran behind that tree, 'Hello, is anybody there?' Nothing. He got even more frightened. Just then he heard a voice calling him from the opposite direction that sounded distant, 'JR.' He looked around and could see Peter waving to him from about forty feet away. The forest was dark, and he could barely see him, but he knew that was Peter. He smiled and walked quickly towards him waving back saying, 'Hey Peter, thank god I saw you.' But as he neared the tree, Peter laughed and dashed out and ran behind another tree. 'Aw, Peter come on. This isn't funny.' Jonathan headed toward the tree, but once again Peter ran out from behind the tree and stood a short distance away smiling at Johnathan. And then right before his eyes Peter just vanished into thin air.

He stopped dead in his tracks not knowing what to do, or where to go. He felt lost, alone and confused, and he walked around for a while trying to find the way out, then he heard someone laugh in the distance. A girl, he turned to look and saw a clearing in the woods. Misty sat in the middle of the clearing with the sun shining only on her. It looked surreal because everywhere else was dark. She was reading a book and laughing. He approached her cautiously, afraid she would vanish like Peter did a while back. Without looking at him, Misty stopped laughing and said, 'hi Jonathan, come closer my darling'. As he started to move in closer, he saw the title of the book. It was on hypnotism. He sat down opposite her cross-legged and looked at her beautiful face. Her olive coloured skin looked so smooth. Her curly hair was just wildly resting around her shoulders. Sitting there, she looked primitive but exquisite. Finally, she looked up from the book and gave him a big wide smile that made his heart quicken. He leaned over to touch her and like Peter, she suddenly vanished, and the clearing was dark again.

Jonathan fell back and scooted away. His head turned left and right as he frantically scanned the trees to find her, but she was nowhere in sight. Completely freaked out he stood up. 'Misty! Where are you?' He spun in a circle still scanning the trees. 'What in the hell is happening?'

His eye finally caught some movement, but it wasn't Misty. It was someone with his back to Jonathan hitting a tree trunk with his fist. The skin and muscle on his hand were in bad shape, and blood was streaming from his knuckles. 'Hey, you! What are you doing? You're really going to hurt yourself.' As Jonathan ran up to him, he realised that it was Nick. 'Nick! Stop it! Come on!' He reached out to grab Nick's arm when he too vanished into thin air.

Jonathan couldn't remember more about the dream. He wasn't sure whether the dream meant anything at all, he was just happy that Misty was in it. He liked that, although he would have preferred a less confusing dream.

As soon as his school day ended, Jonathan got out as quick as he could and ran to Peter's house. The first time he knocked on the door nobody answered, he pounded harder the second time, but still nobody came to open it. Peter was always home to let Jonathan in. He wondered if something happened to Peter. After loitering around for about ten minutes he gave up waiting, and as he got ready to leave, Misty opened the door.

'Ah there you are, we were wondering what happened to you.' She said dragging him in.

'What happened? I was waiting outside for ages. Why didn't anyone hear me?' Jonathan complained like a sullen child.

'That's because we were busy nattering in the back, in the kitchen. I thought I better look to see if you got here, and there you were, standing like a lemon!' She giggled at him.

His heart melted, 'why does she have to be so pretty?' His mood changed, and he cheered up.

After greeting everyone, Peter offered him a joint, which he gratefully accepted. They talked about general things whilst smoking, then Misty changed the topic of their conversation, 'Ok so I thought that Jonathan and I will go to the living room alone to start our session. It's better if we are alone, because Nick will just make silly jokes, and Peter will try to stop us. You know how he gets scared about the whole thing, like a big baby.' She said and laughed at him.

'Fuck off Misty.' Peter said. 'You do your voodoo mumbo jumbo on JR and see if I care.'

'Voodoo mumbo jumbo?' Misty shouted at Peter. 'God, how ignorant can someone be? Is that why you're scared? Because you assume it's supernatural?' She said finally realising what Peter's issue with hypnotherapy was.

'Well, it's not normal is it? In that case, we might as well consult an Ouija board! You think you are so clever, Misty. Have you thought what you could be doing to JR's mind? He could be possessed with all kinds of spirits and shit!' Peter ended his rant.

'What makes you the judge of Jonathan? His mind, that's what we have already been studying. By using hypnotherapy, we are going into Jonathan's state of mind to uncover information he might have forgotten, that he has experienced, and hopefully will recall. What you are suggesting is that we will consult a spirit blowing in the surrounding wind so we can ask it questions about Jonathan! It's absolute bullshit.'

'I don't want to be involved, whether or not you are calling the spirits! I don't want JR to be forced into anything, just because you gave him one of your sweetest smiles!'

'You can fuck off.' She said aggressively. 'You think I

want to experiment with his mind, so I am seducing him into it? You got a healthy dose of imagination that's for sure.'

Jonathan listened to them argue. Nick started walking around in circles, something he did when he was stressed. He preferred to laugh off stressful situations, but this time the conversation exasperated him, and this manifested in him pacing around. Looking down at his feet intently whilst doing so.

Jonathan couldn't get a word in whilst Misty and Peter were arguing. The last thing he wanted was for them to get angry and fight. He liked their little group the way they used to be, not like this. Finally, he heard her say to him, 'Come on Jonathan, let's go, or else we will argue with Peter forever.'

Grabbing hold of Jonathan's upper arm, she pulled him into the living room. All the while glaring at Peter.

'Ok we've read topics on hypnotherapy and watched YouTube video's, so we can do this, right?' She sounded confident.

'Misty are you sure we should do this now? Peter is upset, he is already mad at you, and I don't want him to be mad at me too, so maybe we should do this tomorrow instead when he has had time to get used to the idea.'

'He will never be used to it. I thought you would be so up for this. If you don't want to do it at all, just tell me. I don't want both Peter and you telling me I am forcing you into it.' She said looking slightly annoyed.

She was already annoyed with Peter, he didn't want her getting annoyed at him as well.

'Ok fine, you're right, Peter will never be comfortable with this idea. Let's try it and see if it works, at least. Who knows, it may never work. If it does then– Great!'

Misty gave him a big smile that lit up Jonathan's world. He went to lay down on the three-seater sofa, and she sat beside him on a chair. She then asked him to concentrate on his breathing and relax into a meditative state.

Misty started coaxing him in a very soft and soothing voice, 'keep breathing slowly, take a breath in………... and out………. keep your breathing steady. Listen to the sound of my voice. Now try to go into your inner soul, go down deep into a place you feel safe and secure. It is warm and comfortable there. You are relaxed.

As Misty was saying this, he was relaxing more, he was starting to only hear his breathing and Misty's voice. A few more seconds passed by, then in the same soft, soothing voice she said, 'now, every time I touch your shoulder, you'll go deeper and deeper into a hypnotic trance.' She then touched his shoulder very gently so as not to wake him.

He didn't move, then she said, 'you should allow yourself to enjoy this level of trance. Give yourself permission to continue deepening your relaxation. Know you are becoming a positive person as a result of this trance.'

Misty let Jonathan continue for a few more minutes saying periodically, 'keep breathing, you are going deeper and deeper into your mind.' Misty occasionally touched his shoulder to make sure Jonathan was responding to her.

After a while, she asked him, 'Jonathan can you hear me?'

'Yes,' He mumbled.

'Ok Jonathan, when I count to three, I want you to tell me all the months in the year starting from January.'

He didn't respond. Misty started counting, 'one… two… three.'

Jonathan said, 'January, February, March,…' till he got to December.

'Cool.' Misty thought this is working a treat.

'Ok now, can you tell me your full name?'

'Jonathan William Rice.'

'And, who do you live with?'

'My mum and dad.'

'And what are their names?'

'Janice and Niraj Rice.'

'Jonathan, can you remember what you did when you got home from school yesterday?'

'I overheard my parents arguing about something they didn't want me to hear, I then had dinner and went to bed.'

'You are doing really well, now tell me what your dad does for a living?'

'Airline pilot.'

'Jonathan, when did you first begin hating your dad?'

'A long time ago.'

'How long?'

'When I was small.'

'Can you tell me why?'

'I don't know.'

'Ok try to think of a time when you were small, and your dad made you furious or scared? Can you remember an incident that brought out those emotions in you?'

Jonathan was deep into his trance, he started to recall what happened that first time he was scared:

'I am asleep in my bedroom. A noise wakes me up. It is dark, and I am afraid of the dark. I realise my little night light isn't on, so I get out of my bed and run into my parent's room. When I get there, I see my dad jump off this woman. I think she is my mum at first. I call out to her, but when they hear me, she screams and hides under the covers. He just shouts at me to go to my room. I am angry and scared.

I start to cry, I am upset that he is shouting at me, so I run to my room. I can't understand who that woman is and what she is doing here. All I know is that she isn't my mum. I cower in my room for a few minutes, and then my dad comes in. He is furious with me, he grabs me by my shirt and shakes me, saying I must never ever leave my room in the middle of the night. He says I must forget what I saw and not say anything about that woman, or he will make my life a misery. He says if I ever tell anyone he will take my mum away from me. He keeps repeating that I must forget what I saw, or he will take my mum and leave me all alone on the street in the dark somewhere. Whilst he is saying this he is shaking me like a rag doll. I am terrified! I never told my mum what happened that night. I didn't want him to separate us.'

Misty was shocked but tried to sound calm, she could see he was getting distressed with her questioning. A few tears had rolled down the side of his face, and she didn't want to stress him out anymore, so she wanted to take him out of the trance. But first, she needed to make him feel better.

'Ok Jonathan, can you tell me when was the last time you laughed and why?'

'Yesterday when Nick lost his joint, and he went mental because he couldn't find it. Peter, Misty and I knew it was behind his ear, but we didn't tell him. The more we laughed at him, the angrier he got.'

Jonathan was smiling. Satisfied by his mood, Misty decided that would be the last question for the session.

'Ok Jonathan, I will count from twenty down to one. As I do so, you will slowly come out of your trance and get back into the real world. Ok, twenty... nineteen... eighteen...' And she continued till she got to one. She then said, 'Jonathan open your eyes.'

He opened them seeing Misty right above him, looking at him with her big brown Disney eyes, he smiled at her. 'Hey,' he said.

'Hey, you, welcome back Jonathan, you did very well.' She added smiling.

He sat up and couldn't remember what he did well for a second. He drank in her smile and was smiling himself. That lasted for all of five seconds. Then he remembered what had happened, and his smile disappeared. He stared at Misty, her smile vanished too. For about a minute neither of them spoke. She then said, 'can you recall what you said when you were in a trance?'

Jonathan took a deep breath in then said, 'yes I do, I'm not in a mood to talk about it right now Misty. Can you tell Peter and Nick I am going home?'

'You can't go like this, let us discuss this together, then it will help ease your mind. If you go home now upset and angry, you might start a fight with your dad. God knows what might happen. Please stay for a while. I will make you a nice cup of tea.' She said pleadingly.

All the while she was talking Jonathan got up and started getting ready to leave. He went out of the living room to put on the jacket he left on the banister. Misty followed him. 'Jonathan please.' She said in desperation.

'Misty don't worry I am fine, I want to be alone.'

'But promise me you will go to your room. Please say nothing to your parents, until we discuss this ok, promise me?'

The way she looked at him made his heart melt for a second, but he was too upset to think clearly, so he hastily promised that he wouldn't cause any issues when he went home, he then left.

Jonathan walked quickly, pulling the hood over his head when he noticed it was raining. He didn't really look at where he went, he just headed in the general direction of his house, walking onto the roads without checking if it was safe to do so. Many cars sounded their horns at him in anger, but he didn't care and walked on. It was a miracle he got home in one piece.

At home, his dad was sitting on the couch watching TV. Jonathan ignored him and made his way up the stairs to his room. 'Jonathan, are you ok? You look like hell.'

He stopped and turned around and gave his dad a dirty stare. 'Yes, I'm fine.' He said rudely and walked up again.

His dad got up from the chair and shouted, 'what the hell kind of look is that Jonathan? You come down this very minute and apologise.'

He didn't even acknowledge that request, he continued going up faster. His heart was racing, he ran into his room and banged the door shut behind him. He locked it and rested his back on the door. He heard his dad following him.

'Jonathan, what the hell is wrong with you?' He said trying to get into Jonathan's room but realising it was locked he said, 'open the door, are you fucking mad?'

'Just go away dad, I had a crap day, and I want to be alone.'

'Fine, fuck you. Like I give a shit anyway.' He said, and Jonathan could hear his dad walking away.

Jonathan breathed a sigh of relief that his dad had finally left him alone. He slid down the door and held his head in his hands, it was throbbing, and before he knew what was happening, he began to cry.

8

J onathan couldn't remember how long he stayed on the floor crying. His head started hurting, and he wanted to take his painkillers and his depression tablets. He didn't want his parents to come into the room and see him that way or to answer questions from them, his friends or anyone. After what seemed like ages and because he was feeling cold, he crawled into his bed, put the covers over his head and cried his heart out.

After the hypnotherapy session, he remembered new things he had previously forgotten. His mind tried to make sense of it all. How could his dad be so shameless by having an affair with some woman? To make matters worse, his dad then threatened to leave him alone in the dark somewhere if he said anything to his mum! By shaking him, it frightened the life out of him. He was only six. He now remembered his dad not talking to him for days after the incident and being overly nice to his mum. His dad also kept coming into his room at night under the guise of tucking him into bed and repeating his threats. This may have continued for a week or so, then he forgot the whole incident, probably because his dad went to work, and the episode wasn't mentioned again. Jonathan forgot about everything until now!

He realised that from around the age of six he wasn't happy to hear that his dad was coming back home. That trend continued still. Jonathan thought, for a dad to manipulate his son like that from such an early age was disgusting. It's no wonder he hated him. His mum was so lovely, how could he do that to her! While he lay there thinking about everything, twisting and turning the situation in his head, he concluded there was more to this than just that one episode. He remembered his conversation with his mum. She was aware he had memory lapses, something must have happened during her watch too. As far as Jonathan knew, his mum had never found out about that other woman. Well, at least not from him. But he wondered if there were other things he had forgotten to recall.

When he initially got back home, he didn't want to see or speak to anyone. He just cried and wanted to die. He knew death would mean peace. No headaches, no pain, no suffering, just peace.

Jonathan now realised his dad cheated on his mum and threatened to leave him in some cold dark place. He was angrier than ever before, he just couldn't understand his dad's behaviour. Now he didn't want to see his friends, but at some point, he had to face them and have further sessions with Misty to unlock those memories. He was scared to find out what they were. In the scheme of things, he understood people had extra-marital affairs all the time. And yes, he was angry with his dad for his affair and the excessive threats he made to him. He finally figured out why his feelings for his dad were so strong.

Later he heard his mum knock gently on his room door, calling out to him. He didn't answer her for a few minutes.

But when he realised that she wouldn't go away, he said, 'leave me alone mum, I am fine, I had a bad day at school and now have a throbbing headache.'

'Ok, I will bring you a painkiller and water. Dinner is ready, will you come down to eat?'

'No, just get me the painkillers and leave them outside.'

'Shall I make you a cup of tea Jonathan?'

'Whatever.' he snapped.

She left, and he wondered why he was annoyed with her. She had done nothing wrong. All he knew was he wanted to be left alone, and his headache to go away.

After a while, his mum knocked on the door to say she placed a tray outside. He heard her wait a while to see if he would open the door to get it, but when he didn't, she left and went downstairs. After she'd gone, he got up and tried to make his way to his door. Immediately he felt his head swimming, and he was feeling giddy and nauseous. He waited a moment to let his head settle down and then he went to the door and put his ear to it to make sure his parents were still downstairs. He then opened it and brought the tray inside immediately locking the door behind him.

'Bless his mum' he thought. There was a cup of tea, a bottle of water, two painkillers and a buttered scone. He realised he was hungry and fearing his tablets wouldn't work on an empty stomach, he quickly ate the scone and drank the tea making sure he had the tablets after his last sip of tea. Remembering he needed his depression tablets he looked in his bedside drawer and found them. He took them with some water, put the tray back on the floor near his bedroom door and climbed back into bed. It was still warm, he snuggled to get comfortable and as he fell asleep he noticed it was only seven pm. It was too early to go to bed for the night, but he hoped that he didn't get up till the morning.

Jonathan woke up with a start, he looked at his phone for the time and saw that it was 11.14pm. Wondering what had awoken him from his sleep, he strained to hear, propping himself onto his elbows and wondered if it was Peter trying to get in his room again. He looked over to the window, and although his curtains were ajar, his window was still locked, he hadn't opened it when he came home earlier. He sometimes opened it about an inch to get fresh air into his room even in the winter. Looking around, his eyes got accustomed to the darkness, and then he heard what woke him up.

His dad shouting downstairs, but he didn't hear his mum. Ok so that was it, his dad getting up to his old tricks, and his mum just taking his abuse without retaliating. Jonathan wondered how long it would take him to revert to his usual self. 'Not long at all,' he thought. He tried to listen in but couldn't make out exactly what his dad was irritated about. He guessed it was because he was rude to his dad earlier. Jonathan knew if his dad got annoyed, and wouldn't get any joy harassing him, he would turn his anger towards his mother or the other way around.

He got off his bed quietly and tiptoed over to the door and put his ear to it. Something startled him, and he jumped back when he heard a crashing sound. His dad then shouted, 'I don't care if he can hear me, I don't give a shit if the universe hears me. I am fucking fed up with you and your fucking son. Do you think money grows on trees? For all these years I have been a model husband to you and a perfect father to that son of yours. I can't continue this forever. That boy has serious problems, no son of mine would behave like him.'

'I have told you a million times, it's our son.'

'Really, well then why doesn't he look like me or behave like normal people?' Niraj answered his own question, 'That's because he is a fucking freak. And I can assure you that he is not mine.'

'I know he is, because not only was I newly married to you, we were so in love when he was conceived. At that time, I wouldn't have looked at another man or worshipped anyone like I did you.' She said trying to talk sense into him.

'At that time? So now you will, or should I say are ready, to worship someone else?'

'Don't create drama where there isn't any Niraj. You know I only have time for the two of you.'

'Oh, so I am the drama queen here, am I?'

Janice didn't respond.

Niraj continued, 'If I knew when I married you, you were a simpering, washout I wouldn't have done it. And what have you given me? A retard of a son! I am embarrassed to call him my son! I am ashamed every time we go out as a family. Do you know how people look at me, an airline pilot, when I introduce the two of you as my family? They look at me with pity in their eyes! I even overheard someone saying what a simple and plain wife I had! This is the disgrace I must face when I go out with you. You have no 'get up and go,' everything is gone with you! No spark, no life, no passion. You just exist!'

Jonathan cried at what he heard his dad saying, his mum started crying too. But she never replied to his dad's rant. She just listened and cried, and this broke Jonathan's heart. He had never realised that his dad thought he was a 'retard,' what a horrible word Jonathan thought. He knew his dad found out about his depression, but he didn't know this would cause his dad to think of him in that way. And now, his loving mum was being called 'simple,' 'plain,' and 'a disgrace'? It hurt Jonathan more than ever. He hated his dad even more, if that was possible.

Niraj said, 'I am done talking to you, it's like talking to a brick wall. You can't even respond to me or defend yourself. Look at you crying there pathetically! What a waste! Why do you think I don't even want to touch you in bed? Who wants to touch a lifeless, soulless, waste of space? Anyway, there is no point wasting my breath on you. Go to bed so I can watch TV and finish my whisky in peace.'

Janice said nothing and got up to leave. Then Niraj said, 'Oh and Janice, sort that son of yours out. If he is rude tomorrow, I will fucking slap that look off his face.'

Again, Janice said nothing but Niraj wanted an answer, 'did you hear me, Janice?'

'Yes,' she said quietly.

Jonathan went back to bed not hearing the last part of their conversation. He threw the covers over his head and tried to sleep.

Downstairs, Janice went to the kitchen to get a broom and spade to clean up the vase Niraj smashed. She made a mental note that he had smashed vase number twenty-two. He always broke the vase that sat on that side table. It was always similar to its predecessor, the same side table vase ended up shattered every time he was annoyed.

Janice would have to go to the shop to replace it with something similar, a transparent glass vase. That's what she did every time, she always replaced it, and she cleaned up the mess. She listened to his abuse of her, and she was always reminded she wasn't worth anything. In the beginning, his family said he was too good for her, and now over the last ten years, from Niraj saying he was the better half in this marriage.

Janice was now numb to this abuse, all she cared about was her son. She wanted to provide him with a stable life, a roof over their head, food on their plates, a father and husband so that they fit into society, and nobody thought they were strange. He always hurt her with his comments, and she was getting deadened to his harsh words, because she wanted to keep their status quo. She would put up with anything Niraj threw at her, if Jonathan got as normal a life as she could get him.

After cleaning up the broken vase, she went upstairs, making a mental note to buy another one this week. She walked silently, stopping at Jonathan's door to check if he heard anything Niraj said to her earlier. After putting her ear to the door to listen, she was satisfied Jonathan was fast asleep. She went into her bedroom and shut the door, she knew she would continue crying in there, knowing Niraj wouldn't come into the room, he would sleep in the spare bedroom tonight. She also knew he would be all 'sweetness and light' tomorrow and would act like the whole thing never happened. That was the cycle of what went on in the Rice household, and she was used to it.

The next morning Jonathan awoke with a start. 'Oh crap,' he thought. In all the confusion of last night's argument, he forgot to set his alarm. He got dressed quickly, grabbed his book bag and remembering he didn't have dinner last night, he stopped by the kitchen. His mum had made him some tea with toast.

Janice looked tired, but she smiled when she saw him and said, 'morning love. I heard you making a racket upstairs, so I knew you were up. I thought you may want to have something to eat before you go, you didn't have dinner last night. Here is some breakfast.'

He was so grateful for her thoughtfulness. 'Thanks a lot,

mum, but I am late. I can eat the toast on the way to school, but I don't have time for tea. Why didn't you wake me?'

'Your dad said you came back in a bad mood last night. So, when you didn't open the door for either of us, I thought you might not want to go to school today, and I let you sleep in. Are you getting depressed again?'

'Don't be silly, mum. It was just a bad day at school, nothing major. Anyway, I don't have time to talk about it. I will see you later.' He said leaving his mum in the kitchen.

'But what about your tea?' She shouted after him.

'You drink it.'

Jonathan rushed to get to school and surprisingly, he wasn't as late as he thought he could have been. He thought about yesterday's argument between his parents, the hypnotherapy session with Misty, the way he ran out of Peter's house soon after his session, his pain as he thought about his dad's lady friend and lastly, his dad giving his mum grief last night. 'God what a mess'! He decided he wanted to have a joint and relax with Misty, Peter and Nick. He also wanted Misty to do another hypnotherapy session with him, because he realised he had many more lapses in his memory he needed to get out of his mind. What he needed most was to remember and find out everything, his days of running away from his dad would come to an end, he was feeling strong and empowered this morning. He had to take control.

He didn't stay at school for the whole day, feigning a headache, he asked to be sent home. The school knew he was on medication for depression. His mum told them in case they wondered what was wrong with Jonathan. Janice decided that if the school was aware of it they would be kinder to Jonathan. At first, Jonathan wasn't happy she told them, but he soon realised he could use his depression as an excuse to get out of school earlier!

After leaving school, he walked towards Peter's house and knocked on the door, but nobody opened it. He knocked, for a further ten minutes. He assumed they were at the back of the house again, talking in the kitchen. Ten minutes later, there was still no answer. He went up close to the living room window to look inside, but he couldn't see anything. He was getting frustrated, but he then realised he was far earlier than he normally visited, so he guessed they weren't expecting him. His only other choice was to go home, but he didn't want to run into his dad, so he went to the park to kill some time.

Jonathan bided his time in the park, hoping to see Peter or Misty, but he saw none of them. After he lost patience waiting, he went back to Peter's house. As he got closer, it looked strange, like nobody lived in it. It looked dark and even scary. He didn't remember the house being that shade of green either. The house today looked like a dirty emerald green. He thought it was light and bright green yesterday. He felt strange knocking on the door, and he had an even stranger feeling that nobody was inside. Getting totally confused, he stepped back to check if he was looking at the right house and he concluded that he was.

He got worried; he remembered his mum talking to the doctor about him when he got diagnosed with depression. Jonathan overhead them say the word 'prodromal phase of psychosis', and believed his depression tablets would stop the depression, and any issues with anxiety which he sometimes felt. He remembered taking his depression tablets yesterday. What if those tablets were making him confused? He couldn't make sense of anything. After standing around for another five minutes, he gave up and went home. He would have to check the side effects of those depression tablets before he took anymore. The last thing he wanted was to become paranoid and muddled because of them.

When he got home, luckily his parents weren't in. He ran up to his room and fished out his box of depression pills. The name of the medication given to him was called Haloperidol. Jonathan began reading the side effects, but none of those symptoms applied to him, so he decided it wasn't the medication after all. In fact, he had a great night sleep last night, despite the issues he had at home. Jonathan sat on his bed thinking about his three friends, wondering where they might have gone, and why they weren't at Peter's house as usual.

He got annoyed, he thought they were a team, but then a thought struck him. Maybe Misty told them about his hypnotic trance, and they decided that he was weird and strange, and they wanted nothing more to do with him. Maybe they thought he was a 'freak' like his dad suggested last night! Nothing made sense. They weren't there today, but they should be there tomorrow. Jonathan decided getting unnecessarily paranoid didn't help and scolded himself for thinking like this.

That night he took his usual headache and depression tablets in combination like he did the night before. Firstly, because he wanted to forget why his friends weren't at home today, so he would stop speculating about where they went, and he needed a good night's sleep. And secondly, he figured that if he continued to take the tablets, it would stop him from getting depressed again.

Over the next few days after school, Jonathan went to Peter's house and the park to look for them, but they weren't there, they just vanished! Something told him it was the hypnotic session that changed everything, or Misty told them something that scared them off. Now they didn't want to be friends with him either! He understood why his school colleagues weren't his friends, but he valued the friendship he had with Peter, Misty and Nick, he didn't want to lose them. He began getting even more depressed. Jonathan wanted to take more of his depression tablets than the dosage required on the packet, but he decided taking more of the medication wouldn't make his friends come back.

At home, his dad was back to his usual antics, drinking late at night, and then verbally abusing Jonathan or his mum. Janice took the late-night abuses. If Jonathan ever heard it, he wanted to go over and punch him. Jonathan imagined going downstairs in a rage and smashing his dad's head into the nearest wall! He wanted nothing to do with the man, and he didn't want his mum to suffer at his dad's hands. The only thing that stopped him from acting out his fantasies was his dad's daytime behaviour. His dad was ten times nicer in the day than at night, his parents even shared a joke now and again. Another thing that helped was the fact that Jonathan's dad wasn't violent to either of them. For now, he only became an ogre for the odd few nights a week, so both Jonathan and Janice put up with it patiently.

He told his mum he had started taking his depression pills, and he began feeling much better. Janice was happy to support him and suggested they go to the doctor to have him checked out again. She knew that he was bipolar, and the medication was for more than depression. The doctor suggested that they tell him it was only depression until he was better, that way he could more easily handle that infor-mation. Going to the doctor was the last thing that Jonathan wanted to do. He didn't want to answer the doctor's ques-tions, he found they were too invasive and made him feel uncomfortable. His mum didn't seem to want to spoil Jonathan's mood, so she left the topic alone.

After a month of Peter, Misty and Nick's disappearance,

Jonathan believed he would never see them again. He stopped looking out for them in the park or going to Peter's house after school to aimlessly knock at a door that was never answered. Jonathan decided he wasn't depressed anymore. He started getting used to his warped home life, although he was secretly angry at his dad for sleeping around on his mum and threatening to leave him in a cold dark place, Jonathan still kept his nerve.

THREE MONTHS AGO

9

Two months after his friends mysteriously disappeared from his life they reappeared once again. One evening when Jonathan came back from school, he went to his room, and sitting 'as cool as a cucumber' on his chair in his room was Peter, he got the fright of his life. He shouted, 'what the fuck?' and Peter smiled at him and said, 'Hey JR, ssshhhh your mum will wonder why you are shouting. Shut the door quickly.'

'Jonathan, what's the matter?' Janice shouted from the bottom of the stairs.

'Oh, nothing mum, I just dropped my bag, and all my books went flying everywhere. I'm picking them up now. See you downstairs for dinner.' Jonathan then quickly shut the door and spun around to face Peter.

'Ok, I can explain.' Peter said apologetically to Jonathan.

'Explain? Explain what Peter? That you and the gang abandoned me? That after my hypnotherapy meeting with Misty nobody wanted to know me and just left me without an explanation? Explain why there was no one in the house when I went to see you? That maybe you were in but didn't want to talk to me? What can you explain exactly? This will be interesting!' While he ranted at Peter, he paced back and forth in his room.

'JR you got every right to be annoyed, but please keep your voice down, or your mum will come up. After your session with Misty, she explained what had happened. I am sorry to hear about your dad being a total jerk, but we always knew something was off with him. We were still shocked and upset for you. We decided that Misty was right, you would need to go under again to find out what else you blocked out from your memory. As you know I am not a fan of all this hypnosis business, but I see its uses, I will turn a blind eye to it when Misty and you both try again.

Anyway, the next day, Misty found out her dad was sick, so she had to go up north to see him, and she told me she wouldn't be back for a while. Nick and I decided that because she was upset, we would travel up with her, after all, we weren't doing anything here. So early the following day the three of us went on the train together. We couldn't contact you, but we figured we would be home in a few days, so it wouldn't be a problem. Unfortunately, her dad looked terrible when we got there, he was admitted to hospital, and Misty didn't want us to leave her all alone. She had no family apart from him, so we stayed, she needed our support. He passed away a month ago. We then helped Misty sort his stuff out before we came back. Misty stayed on and won't come down for at least a week or two.

Nick wanted to come here as well, but I figured you would be angry with us. I know we owed you an explanation, so I told him I would see you first, then he could come over tomorrow. Please JR, don't be annoyed.' Peter pleaded.

Jonathan said nothing for about thirty seconds. A lot of things were flying through his mind. He stopped being angry with Peter, then he shifted his thoughts to Misty, he felt concerned for her. He wished he could have gone with them to support Misty, but he knew with his parents around he couldn't just leave. They knew that too, so there was no point in asking him to join them when they went to support her.

'Fine.' he said at last. 'Next time at least come and tell me. I looked like a complete fool going to your house everyday looking for you. God knows what the neighbours thought.' Jonathan said smiling and happy to have Peter and the others back in his life.

'I have no neighbours. They have moved out ages ago.'

'Oh, I didn't know that. So now what? And how did you get inside? My window is locked.'

'Yeah it is, but not the spare bedroom window. Isn't that where your dad sleeps when he has a fight with your mum? I came in from there and snuck into your room.'

'Wow, you are a chancer, aren't you? Yes, my dad sleeps there so he must have left the window open when he had a cigarette. Anyway, it's safe around here so nobody's worried about break-ins. Plus the window isn't close to the bottom of the house, how you manage to climb up is beyond me. I tried once and couldn't do it. Good job the back door was open the night I went out to meet Misty and Nick the first time.'

'I am quite fit you know JR.' Peter said smiling. 'Anyway, I am sorry for leaving you in the lurch mate.'

'No worries, I survived. Although it was kinda lonely without you and the others. It doesn't feel like two months though. Well, now it doesn't, but a month ago I felt abandoned. I was left alone to face that monster without my friends' support.'

'Now don't milk it!' Said Peter raising his eyebrows.

Jonathan chuckled.

During the next two weeks, whilst they waited for Misty's return, life went on the usual way, with Jonathan going to Peter's after school, spending some time there with a few smokes of weed and making silly jokes. Sometimes neither of them would talk for ages. They would just sit there staring into space. Nick always paced the floor to relax.

When Misty got back, all the boys were pleased to see her. She looked very well, thought Jonathan. He had not realised how much he had missed her until he saw her. It was as if nothing had changed, their group dynamic was the same as before. Nobody talked about Jonathan's hypnotic session with Misty because nobody wanted to upset him. They were all just re-acquainting themselves with each other and having fun.

One week after Misty's return, she found herself alone with Jonathan and brought up the subject of the last hypnotic session. She wanted to conduct more sessions, but she also did not want to upset him, so she approached the topic with kid gloves.

'So, Jonathan, how did you manage after you left me that day? Peter told me your dad still doesn't know you got some of your early memories back. So, I guess you had time to come to terms with what we found out that day.'

'Well, I don't think I will understand how my dad ever behaved in such a devious manner. Ok, I get that people have extra-marital affairs, but how he could make me so scared and threaten me is beyond my understanding.'

'That is why we still need to do more sessions, there is more I just know it.' She said.

'I think so, my mum knows I suffered from some memory loss too. I didn't tell her about that incident I discovered, and

I know my dad wouldn't have told her about it either. I also realise there may have been other things will need to dig up from my memory.'

Misty nodded her head and agreed with Jonathan. 'So, when do you think you will be ready for your next session? Bearing in mind that Peter has already warned me about pushing you too hard. I will not push you. Just tell me when you are ready, and then we can go for it. Neither Peter nor Nick wants to be around, and it's pointless having an audience anyway. You have to feel totally relaxed for it to work as you know.'

Jonathan wanted to do the next session the day after the first one. He was eager and ready then, but nearly three months had passed since that session, and he was getting cold feet. He feared what he would find out, he didn't know if he could deal with it without confronting his parents. Then again, living in the dark wasn't ideal either. He had to find out everything at some point.

Misty reading his facial expressions then said, 'I know you fear finding out more. Heck, I would be too, but we both know it needs to be done. I am happy to do it when you feel prepared, but I would suggest you confront it as soon as possible. Rip it off like a plaster. Ok, that sounded violent.' She smiled.

'Oh my god,' he thought. He had forgotten how beautiful she was when she smiled. Her eyes lit up and sparkled like a Christmas tree. Jonathan smiled too.

'Yeah, you're right. The sooner we get it done the better.'

'Ok but let me warn you that we might not find out everything in the next session. Just thought I would tell you.'

'I know. But let's see how it goes.'

They agreed to do the session the following day. They told Peter and Nick about their plans and asked them to make themselves scarce. Peter scowled at them, but he was mainly staring at Misty.

'Hope you didn't force him into it Misty?' Peter said glaring at her.

'Don't be a fool, you know he needs to know the truth about his past, so don't throw a spanner in the works now.'

'Fine, but if he is a mess afterwards, then you better be ready to deal with it and not run off like the last time.'

'What the fuck do you mean? You fucking know my dad was sick, I didn't run away.' Misty shouted.

'Hey, you two. Stop it.' Said Jonathan trying to break up their argument, so they wouldn't get into a full-blown fight.

Peter and Misty stopped talking and stared at each other. Then Peter said, 'Sorry Misty, I didn't mean that.'

Misty was still annoyed, she grunted at Peter and said she was going home and would see Jonathan the next day for his session.

When Jonathan got home, he realised nobody was in. He remembered that his parents had a dinner party to go to, so he had the house to himself. His mum rang him up to tell him his dinner was in the fridge, and all he had to do was heat it up. He said he would be fine and asleep by the time they got back.

Jonathan watched TV for maybe an hour or two, he didn't know. He sat there channel hopping without paying much attention to anything. When he realised he was hungry, he went to get his dinner. After getting tired and dozing off several times on the couch, he called it a night and went up to his room.

That night he got woken up by a noise, and he guessed it was his drunken dad and ever suffering mum. He tossed around to the other side of his bed hoping they went to bed quickly. He didn't want to be disturbed by his dad again, but he heard him shouting at his mum. 'Again!' Jonathan said out loud! He wondered why his dad didn't realise that his drinking made him into a monster. Why couldn't he see that? Jonathan didn't want to know what the issue was tonight and no doubt by tomorrow his mum would have forgiven him. So, it was pointless.

The next day Niraj did his usual thing, he was nice to everyone to make up for his behaviour the night before. Jonathan wondered if maybe his dad just couldn't remember how he had behaved. Anything was possible!

'Listen to the sound of my voice and only my voice. You will go into a deep, deep sleep. Concentrate on your breathing. Taking your breath slowly in through your nose and out through your mouth.' Misty said soothingly.

Jonathan was lying on the three-seater sofa like he did the last time. He tried to clear his mind of any thoughts, and he relaxed into the trance listening to the sound of Misty's calming voice.

After thirty-seconds, and in the same quiet, and soothing voice Misty said, 'now, every time I touch your shoulder, you'll go deeper and deeper into a hypnotic trance.' She then touched his shoulder very gently.

'Ok I will count from one up to twenty, and you will go deeper into your sleep. You will respond to only my voice.' Then Misty said, 'One… two… three…, very slowly until she got to twenty.

He was just breathing, and Misty looked at him lying there peacefully. For a moment she thought he had gone to sleep. So, reassuring herself, she asked, 'Jonathan, can you hear me?'

'Yes.' He replied.

'Ok Jonathan can you tell me what your favourite pastime is?'

'Reading Marvel comics and hanging out with my friends.'

'And what are your close friend's names?'

'Peter and Misty.'

Misty smiled to herself. He didn't say Nick, but then again Nick wasn't as engaging to Jonathan as she and Peter were.

'Jonathan, what did you do last night?'

'Watched TV, then I went to bed.'

'Can you remember that time you feared your dad after you found your dad in bed with his mistress?'

'Yes, I can.'

'Was there another time you feared your dad?'

'Yes.' Jonathan was quiet for a few seconds, still deep in his trance, he then recalled the next time his dad scared him:

'It was two or three years after the first incident I think. I am thirsty, I get up for some water, I don't know what time it is. Everything is dark, and the landing light is off. I open the door and hear my dad talking, I think he is talking to my mum, so I walk downstairs. I am half way down, then I hear him say, "I love you, and can't wait to see you tomorrow." to someone on the phone. I know he isn't talking to my mum, I stop on that stair to hear some more, I need to be quiet, I need to stay hidden. I wait on that step eavesdropping, and I think he is talking to another woman, but I don't know who, what shall I do? He is laughing, he sounds so relaxed and happy, and I wonder why he can't behave like that with us. I think I will have to tell my mum about this, but I don't want to. She will be upset with me, and she might hate me for making her sad. I don't want to make her sad.

I need to go back up before he catches me here. I turn around, but the stair creaked, and I think my dad heard me. Oh nooooo! He is running up the stairs!

He is very annoyed with me, his face looks like a monster, he is pulling my ear and dragging me downstairs… he is hurting me.

"Dad please stop you are hurting me." I try to talk to him, to make him stop.

"What did you hear boy?"

"Nothing, please leave my ear."

He lets go of my ear, "what did you hear Jonathan?"

I start crying, I am confused, and he is still looking at me like he is going to kill me, his face is contorted in anger, and he asks me what I heard again. I can't say anything, I am too scared. He is getting more annoyed with me, he squeezes my mouth and asks me again what I heard. He lets go of my mouth so I can answer, I am so angry now, so I shout at him, "you are a horrible dad! You were telling someone else that you loved them, and it wasn't mum!"

I think I have stunned him, and he lets go of me, he says nothing. Suddenly he slaps me hard across the face. My cheek hurts, why is he hurting me? I didn't do anything wrong.

I wish I didn't say that, now he drags me into the kitchen. I am not sure why, I think to leave me outside the back door for the night. No, he isn't, he opens the pantry door and throws me in. Oh noooo, it's dark and cold in the pantry. I hear the key in the lock. I try to open the door, but it doesn't budge.

"Please dad don't leave me here, it's dark. Please don't do this dad! I am sorry! I am sorry!"

He isn't listening or doesn't care. I continuously bang on the door to ask him to let me out, but he isn't letting me out.

Then I hear him say, "That will teach you for being nosey you little shit. You can stay in the dark till you learn your lesson."

I continue to cry and bang on the door, but he isn't opening it. I look around me, the pantry is dark, and I fear bugs that might be crawling around. I can't understand why he is so cruel, and I don't know how long I must stay in there. I start shouting for my mum. I know she will rescue me, but she doesn't come or can't hear me!

After a while I quiet down, I try to hear if my dad is still around, but there is no noise coming from the other side of that door. I can hear random sounds, or maybe it's my mind, I don't know.

After what was an age, my dad finally opens the door to let me out. At first, I am too scared to even look at him. He asks me if I learned my lesson, and I nod a yes. He grabs my shoulders, and coldly states that if I ever tell anyone about his phone call or being locked up in the pantry tonight, he will take my mum and leave me in the middle of the woods by myself. When I look at him he repeats his threat and adds that he will beat me first before he leaves me alone in the woods.

I stare at him completely frozen, I am too scared to say the wrong thing in case he locks me back there again. When I get to my room I change my clothes, I feel dirty from being locked in the pantry, I start to cry, at some point I go to sleep. The next night he comes into my room, and he says "You have to forget what you heard me say on the phone and that I locked you in the pantry. If you don't, I will take you and leave you in the woods forever, and you won't see your mum ever again. Do you hear me?"

I nod a yes. He comes in the next night and the following few nights to say the same thing. I don't like him. He is not nice.'

Misty listened letting Jonathan do all the talking. Once he

stopped, she realised she had to take him out of the trance. He would be further distressed by recalling this incident, and she knew this was enough for today.

Like the last session, Misty took Jonathan out of his trance.

When he awoke, he sat there silently. Misty tried to soothe him with some kind words, but he was lost in his own thoughts. He then put his face in his hands and cried. Misty came and sat beside him, awkwardly holding his shoulders trying to soothe him, but he didn't register her there, he was lost in his misery.

10

The few days after Jonathan's session with Misty was a blur to him. He didn't talk much at home or at school. He avoided going to Peter's house because he wasn't ready to face his friends. He answered questions asked of him monosyllabically at school and at home. He hid in his room, lost in his thoughts. When he came back from school, he would plod up the stairs to his room ignoring his parents. Once in his room, he locked the door and put his headphones on. The last thing he wanted was a confrontation with his dad about his music being too loud.

A week later Jonathan decided he was ready to find out more of what he could have forgotten, so he approached Misty to ask her to take him into a trance again.

'So, you decided to come back to the land of the living! Thought you wanted to sulk forever!'

'Don't be like that Misty, you know how upset I got finding out what that bastard did to me the last time you hypnotised me. I needed to digest and process what happened when he locked me up. To be honest with you I don't think I am ready to find out more, but the sooner I do, the better. I just want it out in the open.'

Misty felt sorry for him, he didn't deserve a rotten father, so she agreed to hypnotise him again. 'Shall we do it tomorrow after you finish school?'

'Can't we do it today?'

'What's the rush?'

'Please Misty, if I don't do it today I might not have the courage to do it tomorrow.'

'Fine, fine, keep your hair on.'

'Where is Peter and Nick anyway?' Jonathan asked looking around the living room of Peter's house.

'They are out, don't ask me where. I don't know, and anyway it's peaceful when they aren't here so let's start. Go and relax in your usual spot.'

Jonathan took his place on the settee and made himself comfortable.

'Are you sure you are ready. You don't know what you might find out!'

'Stop trying to scare me off. Let's do this, I need to know everything.'

Misty took Jonathan back into a trance the same way she had done twice before. Jonathan was eager to get hypnotised which made her part easier. She felt confident in her newfound abilities of hypnosis.

Once in the trance she started asking her usual questions of Jonathan like what he had done over the past few days. When she was satisfied he was deep in the trance she asked him about his dad's behaviour towards him.

'Jonathan, when you were younger did you dad ever lock you up?'

'Yes he did.'

'Where did he lock you up?'

'In the pantry.'

'Apart from that incident, did he lock you up again in the pantry?'

'No, not there.'

'Somewhere else?'

'He didn't lock me up, he abandoned me. I think I was nine or so.'

'Can you tell me what happened?'

'It's summer, and my mum is in hospital. I am not sure why she is in there, she told me it was a routine operation, and she would stay there for a few days. I told her I don't want to be alone with dad, but she said I have no option. I am not happy to stay with him alone, and I am scared for my mum. I hope her operation goes well.

The first night she was in hospital it was calm and peaceful at home. My dad feeds me dinner, he makes a pizza, I cheer up because I like pizza. I never know what to say to him. He shouts at me for no reason sometimes then other times he is jovial. I think the best thing to do is stay in my room as much as I can.

The next day my dad says I can go to my school friend Anthony's house for a sleepover. He calls Anthony's mum who agrees I can stay the night. I don't want to go to Anthony's house, why didn't he ask me first? Anthony isn't always my friend in school. Sometimes he makes fun of me and teases me in front of others. I pretend to be happy with the idea, and to keep my dad satisfied, I go to Anthony's house.

After dinner in, I ask his mum if I can come home because I can't sleep there. I tell her I am worried about my mum and want to be home in case something happens to her overnight. She is nice about it, she calls my dad to tell him, but he doesn't answer the phone. I tell her my dad will be home, he never goes out in the evening. She reluctantly agrees to take me but warns me I have to come back with her if my dad isn't there.

Their house is only a ten-minute drive from mine, and when we get to my house, I see my dad's car in the driveway and the lights on inside. I thank Anthony's mum. She smiles at me, and I tell her I will be ok to get inside, she doesn't need to drop me to the door. It's raining.

When I get to the front door I wave and tell her I am fine, she can go. When she drives off, and I go inside. I immediately feel something is wrong, there are clothes on the floor, and I hear some strange noises coming from the living room. I walk in there apprehensively, I then see a lady in her underwear on top of my dad. I recognise from somewhere but I'm not sure where. She notices me almost immediately and tells my dad, "Your son has returned home, as if by magic!" She glares at me whilst getting off my dad. She isn't very friendly.

My dad gets up and is very angry at me, he too is in his underwear. I am terrified. I know I wasn't' supposed to see that. I turn to run to my room, I start to race up the stairs. I know he will try to hit me, and I don't want that woman seeing it. He catches up with me and drags me the rest of the way up the stairs. He throws me on the bed telling me, "you are in deep shit, just you wait! When I come back you better be ready for a massive punishment! You are a waste of space and a little bastard!"

He slams the door, and I hear him going downstairs. I am too scared to go to the door to hear what they are saying. I don't know what his punishment will be. He shouldn't be with that lady whilst my mum is in hospital, that isn't right.

I can't cry, I am just scared he might beat me. After some time, he comes back into my room. He tells me to put my shoes on and take my heavy coat from the wardrobe. I don't know why, it's summer I won't need my heavy coat, but I can't question him. His face is like thunder.

He forces me in the car and tells me to shut up, he doesn't want to hear a word out of me. It's late, nearly ten pm. He drives for about an hour, we are getting further and further away from the city. I doze off for a while, it's late, and I'm tired. My dad is strangely calm for the journey. I thought he would be angry with me, but he isn't shouting at me.

I wake up with him dragging me out of the car. I am confused, it looks like we are in the middle of a lot of trees. He dumps me on the ground and throws my coat next to me. He then looks at me with anger.

"What did I tell you before? Not to sneak up on people, didn't I say that?"

I can't speak to him when he is in this mood.

"Can't you hear me? I told you not to do that but, you can't sit still, can you? God, what did I do to deserve you?"

I look around me, everything is dark, and nobody is around.

"The last time you sneaked up on me I told you I would leave you in the woods if you did it again. And guess what, I am a man of my word! You will stay here tonight, on your own!" He shouts, I stand up immediately.

"Dad, please don't, its dark here, and there may be some wild animals. I don't think it's safe. Please take me back. I won't ever come out of my room. I will stay there till you let me out, but please don't leave me here."

"I don't think so, my boy." He has a strange grin on his face. "I may be back for you tomorrow, or what's left of you!"

He looks happy I was in distress. I start crying and I try to hold on to him, but he pushes me away with such force I fall to the ground. He almost runs to the car, he locks all the doors as soon as he gets in. I get up and try to open the car door but can't. He doesn't even look at me, I bang on the glass and beg him to take me with him. He doesn't listen, he starts the car and drives off.

I continue crying, I can't believe he left me here like this. It's dark, but my eyes get accustomed to it after a while. There is nothing to see, just lots of trees. I can hear them swish and sway. I was not cold when he left me, but after a while I am glad I got my winter coat with me. I make some space to sleep near a tree. At first, I sit against the tree and look around me, to familiarise myself with my new surroundings. I can't believe my dad would bring me to a place that has dangerous wild animals. I suddenly remember I don't like snakes. What if one slithers by? I won't even know. It might slither over me when I sleep. I am crying again.

My mum won't be happy when I tell her he did this to me. If I get back in once piece. I can't stay awake forever so at some point my eyes begin to close. I lay my winter coat down and snuggle it around my body like a sleeping bag. I feel warm and secure in it and doze off almost immediately.

I wake up in the morning, it must have been early, five or six am. The sun comes out early in the summer. I look around me, the trees cover most of the daylight from coming through. Luckily for me, it hasn't rained. I feel very hungry, I look at the spot where my dad's car was. There are tyre marks, but he didn't leave any food for me. I am only nine years old. How can I fend for myself? I need to stay here, when he comes to collect me he will come to find me here. But, I want to wander around, I want to follow the car tracks, so I can get to the road. If I find the road someone could alert the police, and they could take me to my mum. I won't go home to him.

I start following the car tracks, but after ten minutes I

can't make out any tracks, the leaves that he drove over have moved around in the wind. I stop and look around me. It looks the same as where I slept for the night. But I know I need to go back, that spot was safe for the night. It will be safe in the day too.

I walk back to my tree. I wait there for ages, I walk around the trees, I hum to myself. I think I am trying to cope with a nightmare of a dad. I can't understand what I did so wrong to be left here like this. I am getting hungrier and hungrier, but there is nothing to eat. I have been thirsty for a while too, but there is no water. If it rains, I might get some water. I think it's afternoon, the sun is bright. I decide to go for a little walk and to try once again to find the road my dad came from. I keep a mental note of the tree I stayed under for the night.

I start walking to look for the road, I hear some noises, when I look around I think I see something, a shadow of someone behind a tree. Now I start getting scared, but I approach the tree anyway saying, "hello, is somebody there?" There is no sound or movement. When I get to the tree, there is nobody behind it. I then hear a rustling noise and look in the direction of the noise. Again, I see someone run behind a tree quickly. I shout a bit louder and go to see who ran behind that tree, still nothing. Just then I hear a voice calling me from the opposite direction that sounds distant. 'JR!' I look around and see a boy waving to me from about forty feet away. The woods look darker than normal, I can barely see that boy, but I have a feeling he is friendly. I smile and walk quickly towards him waving back saying, 'Hey you, thank god I saw you.' He comes right up to me. We introduce ourselves and sit by my tree and talk for hours. It feels so much better to be with someone else, and I like Peter. He is funny.

We wait till nightfall, and just as it is getting dark we hear a car coming, it is my dad. It must be around nine pm. He pulls up, gets out of his car and looks at me like I was dirt.

"So, you survived eh? I didn't realise you were this strong!"

I am so angry with him, I can't speak.

"Fine don't talk to me, that's better for me. Now, I brought you a sandwich and water. I figured you must be hungry. Unless you found food, which I doubt. Go eat that right now whilst I take a piss. It's a long drive home. I don't want crumbs in my car so eat quickly. You hear me?"

I nod my head and grab the sandwich, I find Peter hiding from my dad behind the tree and offer him half even though I am starving. He declines, so I down almost all the water in one go and wolf down the sandwich. Peter says he must go, so we say our goodbyes, and he runs off. I get in the back of the car and wait for my dad. I am thrilled that I won't spend another night in the woods even though I will miss my new friend Peter.

When he came back he opens the back door and looks straight at me and says, "now, let this be our little secret, boy. I don't want you to tell anyone about what happened at home with that lady and your little trip to the woods, do you understand me, boy?"

I nod a yes.

"Good, and when we get home have a shower and brush your teeth, you stink!"

I think he hates me. I don't understand why. I sit there the whole way home glad to be away from the woods, even though I enjoyed my talk with Peter. I will not say anything to anyone because he might take me to the woods and leave me there forever. Then nobody will find me, and I will die there!

When we get home, he grabs me and tells me to repeat what he said to me in the car on the way home, and I say, "nothing to anyone about that woman and the woods." He looks satisfied.

"If you ever tell anyone, I will leave you to rot in the woods, you hear me, Jonathan? I will take your mum away from you, and nobody will know where you are. So, keep your stupid mouth shut!"

I say okay under my breath.

He beckons me to go and get cleaned up, he says he doesn't want to see me again till the morning, which is fine by me. When I get into my room, I feel like I'm in heaven! My bed looks so soft, and I feel safe again.'

Misty looks at Jonathan, he cried through this trance again reliving his ordeal with his dad. It's no wonder he blocked it all out. She decides to get him out of the trance.

Once he is out, he sits up confused. He looks at her strangely, and she says, 'Jonathan what is it? I know that was a bad session too. Leaving you alone in the woods like that. You were only young. I could kill him myself.'

'Misty wait a minute, I know he is a bastard by now, but I am so confused.'

'Why?'

'I didn't remember meeting Peter back then. That's why he looks so familiar. I wonder why he's never said anything about it.'

'I've no idea. You'll have to ask him.' Misty replied.

'Fuck it Misty, I don't know about what Peter was doing in the woods that day, but I do know what my dad did was real and nasty. That bastard, as soon as I tell my mum what he did she will leave him, I am sure of it. I blocked all this shit out, and he got away with so much. It was that same lady I saw when I was five. I couldn't remember her clearly because

I blocked out the memory, but now that I have all my memory back I know it was her. She looked at me like I was a piece of shit as well!'

'I am sorry Jonathan, I don't know what else to say.'

'Nothing I guess, what can anyone say? I won't tell my mum anything yet. I need to figure out a plan of action. I need to watch that bastard. He is satisfied I can't remember anything, but now I know, I want to watch what he gets up to. He was nasty from the beginning I just blocked it out, but now I know I am older and stronger. He can't push me around like he did when I was younger.'

'Be careful Jonathan, I don't trust him.'

'I don't either.'

11

———

Jonathan was restless over the next few days, he couldn't eat or sleep properly. He told his mum he was coming down with something and wouldn't go to school. She brought him Paracetamol and tea. He said he wanted to stay in bed and rest. Once she had gone, he threw the tablets out and drank the tea. He paced his room deep in thought. He tried to fit the pieces together, his dad's behaviour towards them, his time away from the house, his domineering nature, everything now made sense. He realised that since the first time he caught his dad with that woman his dad despised him. Jonathan was always a threat to his dad. He knew now what he couldn't understand before, the amnesia and stress he suffered were caused by his dad, and everything was his fault.

He stayed put for a while, he had to tell his mum every-thing. That was inevitable, but when would be the right time? Then a thought struck Jonathan, if his dad hurt him he must have hurt his mum too. Maybe that's why she was intimi-dated by him. He tried to think, could that be why his mum went to hospital that time? No, it couldn't, she said it was routine, and he can remember her telling him she was waiting for an operation date. There must be something, his dad couldn't have only been mean to Jonathan and not his mum.

He would have to ask his mum about it, but he was too scared to open something she may want to keep shut. He would have to reveal to her his unsavoury episodes with his dad. Was he ready to explain it all to her? He thought he would ask Misty, she was so insightful.

When the coast was clear, and his parents went away, he snuck out to go and see his friends. Peter opened the door for him.

'So here you are, we've missed you.'

'Sorry Peter I had a lot to think about, so I stayed home. Hope you don't mind.'

'Of course not, here at Peter's house we aim to please!'

Jonathan looked heavenwards, 'don't be so melodramatic Peter. It was only a few days!'

'You know I like harassing you, don't you?'

'That's your favourite pastime! Anyway, where is Misty? I want to pick her brain.'

'I don't know, do I look like her keeper?'

'Oh, never mind. Nick ok? I haven't seen him in a while.'

'Yup fine, you want a smoke JR?'

'Not for now, did Misty tell you about our last hypnotherapy session?'

'She did, your dad is a royal ass, you were right.'

'I saw you when I was younger, I thought I remembered your face when we first met. You were in the woods that day he left me there. Don't you remember?' Jonathan asked him.

'Not really JR, you're not high already are you?'

Jonathan eyes clouded over, 'no of course I'm not high!'

'Hey Jonathan, you ok?' Misty came into the room interrupting their conversation.

'Hi Misty, yeah all good. I wanted to pick your brain.'

'Shoot.'

'I realised if my dad was a bastard to me he must have been one to my mum, too right?'

'Go on.'

'So, what if we are hiding stuff from each other and he is getting away with it all quite happily?'

'True.'

'So, what do we do?'

Peter spoke, 'why don't you just ask your mum?'

'Because then I will have to tell her all the things my dad subjected me to, and I am not ready to hurt her with that information yet.

'But it's not her fault JR.'

'She will feel like it is, I know her.'

'I could always hypnotise you again to find out more.'

'Ever ready to hypnotise aren't you Misty? Well, you won't get anything out of JR, not if it happened to his mum.' Said Peter.

Ignoring Peter's jibe at her Misty said, 'yes true.'

'But what if I was there and it happened to both of us, and I forgot it happened? Remember that time I asked her at dinner? She knew something had happened but didn't say. Whilst we were trying to get my memories back, we concentrated on my dad and me. What if we concentrate on my mum and me? Maybe I forgot an incident there too.'

Misty nodded her head, 'You got a point there, Jonathan.'

Peter looked worriedly at them, 'haven't you both found out enough? Why can't you just ask your mum and be done with it? This is carrying on like a soap opera!'

'You are never involved in it, so why are you so bothered about it.' Misty glared at Peter.

'Because as I said previously, I saw what it's done to poor

JR. Look at him, he is skinnier than before. He looks constantly worried, his mind is now confused because he is now seeing us in his trances and he turned down a smoke earlier. Classic signs of stress.'

'Dr Peter to the rescue!' she said.

'You can mock me all you like but you know I am right.'

Jonathan begged Misty. 'Please let's do it one last time, and if I find out something about my mum, I can ask her about it. If I tell her, I found out something she is more likely to open up. Otherwise she will dismiss me and say, "everything is fine." I can feel it, I know something isn't right between them.'

'Ok but let's do it tomorrow. Come here earlier and well rested. Peter has a point you look like a skeleton so eat well.'

Jonathan went home glad they would try again tomorrow. As usual, he was dreading it, but he had no choice. He had to find out the truth.

'Ok Jonathan, can you remember a time that caused you any stress at home that involved your mum?'

'I can't remember.'

'Were your parents a loving couple?'

'No.'

'Why not?'

'Because she feared my dad.'

'Do you know why she was scared of him?'

'She thought he would hurt her again.'

'Again? What do you mean again? Did your dad hurt your mum before?'

'Yes.'

Misty could see Jonathan getting agitated and breathing quickly.

'Jonathan, what are you seeing?'

Jonathan starts reliving an argument. 'I can see my dad hurting my mum. I come in from playing outside, and he is choking her. Nooooo stop it, you are hurting her. Stop it!

I punch him, but he doesn't stop choking her, he can't do that to her, I love her. He has her pressed against the wall whilst I can see her struggling to get his hands off her, and I scream when I see them. I then try to pull him away from her, but I can't, I am not strong enough, so I get up on the couch, I take the vase on the side table to smash it on my dad's head! I raise the vase over my head and hit him! The vase hits him hard but doesn't break, it bounces off his head and onto the floor. It breaks on impact, my dad immediately left my mum when he gets hit by the vase. She slid down from the wall coughing, trying to catch her breath. Oh no, I am scared! He turns around to look at me, he is shocked, and he isn't happy at all. He left my mum alone to come after me.' Jonathan was crying.

'He was a bit dazed and wasn't really running. He tries to walk fast or run but wobbles, he can't catch me because I run back outside. I am so relieved. After a few minutes, I return to see if my mum is ok. She is alright and just sitting on the sofa like a zombie. She looks like her entire world came crashing down. When she sees me, I go over to her, we both hug each other crying. I don't know where my dad has gone, but after a while, he comes over with a cup of tea for my mum, looking apologetically at both of us. He says he is sorry, and everything got out of hand, but neither of us says anything, then he goes away for hours.

That evening my mum gives me a light dinner. She is reading to me from one of my comic books trying to mimic the characters, but her voice sounds sad. I can tell she is trying really hard to seem happy.

I think I must have dozed off at some point, but then I wake to someone coming into my room. It is my dad. He comes in quietly and shakes me, then he says in a whisper, "Jonathan don't you ever tell anybody what happened today, you hear me?" I was still half asleep, so I say nothing. He says it again, a little louder this time, "Did you hear me, Jonathan? Don't you ever repeat this to anybody or I will tell the police it is all your fault, you tried to kill me with that vase. They will send you away to prison, and you won't see your mum ever again. Now you don't want that do you?" I was terrified. I shake my head. "Good, don't you ever speak of this to anyone, this includes your mum and I. Just forget anything ever happened here today. Do you understand?" I reply that I did and turns and walks out the door closing it behind him.'

Misty was crying, but she wiped her tears and decided to take him out of the trance. She then said, 'Ok Jonathan you are safe, when I count to three you will be lying on a warm beach relaxing in the sun.'

'One…Two….' She waited for around 10 seconds, and she said, 'three.'

He visibly relaxed.

When he came out of the trance, he opened his eyes and saw Misty again and smiled as usual and like his previous trances, his smile almost immediately vanished. He sat up and looked sadly at her.

'Can we talk about it? You remember everything about that incident, right?' She asked.

'Yes.'

'What led up to it?'

Jonathan had a faraway look as he recounted his now

regained memory to her. 'We had a lunch party that after-noon, that woman in bed with him was at the party too, and I think my mum was unhappy she was there. After they had all gone home, my parents had a big argument, and I think it was about that woman. I was outside playing, then I heard my mum scream, so I ran inside. When I got there my dad had his hand around her neck….' Jonathan paused for breath and looked sadder than ever.

Misty then gave a massive sigh, 'What happened the next day?'

'Nothing, everything went back to normal. My dad went on a job a day after that incident. My mum wore a scarf around her neck for a few days to cover the bruising he had caused, and I didn't talk to her about it. I remember not wanting to talk to anyone and being terrified of my dad.'

'God Jonathan, so you remembered just after that inci-dent, but at some point, you must have removed it from your memory, again just like you did with the others.'

'I don't know when, but it must have been soon after, because I can't remember anything more about it.'

Jonathan thought for a while. 'I need to know if it happened again. If I blocked some other stuff out. Clearly, my mum won't say anything about it to me and I know I was a little child then, but if I tell her I found out new stuff, she will open up to me. I'm sure of it. She has lived for so long with that burden telling no one yet.'

Misty interjected, 'How do you know she hasn't?'

'Because she isn't that type of woman. She is very humble and shy, has also got an upper-class background, and wouldn't talk about personal family matters to anyone who wasn't family. Typical English, 'stiff upper lip'!'

Misty said, 'don't bring it up with your dad whatever you do!'

'No, I won't, let's see what my mum says first.'

'Ok whatever she says, you come and discuss it with us, and the four of us will try to get a solution together, or at least talk about what she said. "All for one, and one for all" just like the Four Musketeers!' Misty said smiling. 'Is that a deal?'

'Fine ok, but it's the Three Musketeers' Jonathan said. He resigned himself to accept her demands. After all he thought, he would need advice anyway, and he wouldn't know how to handle it by himself.

'True, but there are four of us so forgive me for improvising!' Misty said laughing.

Jonathan laughed too. He looked relaxed, but he wasn't. He knew there were dark clouds of despair in the background looming, and he would have to deal with it very soon.

Over the next few days, Jonathan didn't get any chance to speak to his mum. His dad, Niraj was around most of the time either watching TV in the daytime or 'watching TV and drinking whisky, his favourite pastime, at night. His mum still worked in the flower shop part-time. Niraj wasn't very pleased about this, but Janice needed to be out of the house and away from him sometimes.

Janice was proud of many things: herself, being a good mother to Jonathan, a good wife to Niraj, having a lovely house that she kept clean and tidy for her family, having family friends that thought she was an efficient mum, wife, and woman. She was also proud of showing how well she coped despite Niraj's treatment of both Jonathan and her. And she was glad she could smile through the pain of her emotionally upsetting marriage to Niraj, and she didn't retaliate when he was horrible to her. She hid her suffering well from Jonathan, for he was the only one that knew what Niraj put them through. She was also glad that the entire world didn't know how miserable she had become, and she showed no one (including Niraj) how much she hated her husband. Janice had a lot of things to be proud of she thought and smiled to herself.

She was, however, getting increasingly worried about Jonathan. She knew he always hated his dad. When he was younger he was already scared of him. But he despised his dad even more after the incident where he threw the vase at Niraj's head. Janice thought Niraj would have killed her if Jonathan hadn't intervened! Luckily, they both survived it.

After that day, she thought long and hard about leaving Niraj. She was even ready to beg forgiveness from her dad and go back to live with him with Jonathan in tow. Janice knew after a good apology her dad would have taken her back. However, he was a stubborn man and would have insisted she live her life his way, and she hated that. She liked the freedom she found after he cut her out of his life. Janice knew, enduring life with her dad would have been preferable to enduring Niraj's tempers. But after weighing the pro's and cons of her situation, several factors made the decision for her. Firstly, Niraj was 'sweetness and light' after the incident. And luckily for all of them Jonathan had a memory lapse and forgot about the whole thing. He couldn't remember what happened to her neck a few days after the incident when he saw her come out of the bathroom. He asked her if she was ok and how she hurt her neck with a bruise like that. Janice could have cried with relief, he didn't remember! She gave him some excuse of tying her scarf too tightly around her neck and not realising it would cause her such a bruise. Luckily for her, it wasn't as purple as it had been a few days before.

Because Jonathan couldn't remember, and Niraj started being decent to both she stayed. She knew Niraj's job took him away most of the time, so it was something both could endure. She just had to be on her best behaviour when Niraj came back home, and she had to keep Jonathan away from his dad as much as possible. Although Jonathan forgot the incident, he disliked his dad and that confused him, because he couldn't remember why he felt that way. He remembered the usual 'day to day' meanness that Niraj subjected them to, especially to Janice, the emotional blackmail and abuse, but he couldn't remember the traumatic ones. Janice would tell him when he was older but not until then. It wasn't fair he had psychological amnesia, and it was all Niraj's fault. She hated Niraj for doing that to her son, but because of the way he treated Jonathan he didn't deserve to be called his father.

Lately, Jonathan became increasingly distant. Janice acknowledged as a teenager he would become moody and reserved, but she couldn't help but think he got moodier than most of the other boys his age. She looked online at mum's forums, she knew Jonathan wasn't as bad as some boys that joined gangs or stayed out on the street all day bunking off school. She felt lucky that he wasn't like them, however he did suffer from depression and anxiety, and that always got worse when Niraj was back. Considering how worried she was knowing Niraj was home full-time, things were going quite well. Niraj was nicer than she had expected but she still hated him for what he had done to them over the years. The love she had for him he chipped, and chipped away at, till there was nothing left. His constant emotional abuse took care of that! Janice was struggling to remember why she had married him. She thought what she felt was love, but maybe in hindsight it was escapism, a chance to belong to someone that would love her unconditionally, the usual reasons people fell in love.

Janice wanted to escape from the clutches of her dad's

possessiveness and from a life of being lonely. She was an only child, who had lost her mum at the age of thirteen. That was a turning point in her life which got worse when her dad became even more possessive about her. He wanted to know where she went and what she was doing and that really annoyed her. Because he was rich, he always had the means to keep an eye on her. When she realised it, she confronted him and told him as soon as she was old enough she would go her own way. He threatened to cut her off from all her belongings and wealth, but she didn't care. She was still grieving the death of her mum. She wasn't that close to her dad who was always busy with work and the businesses he owned, so her gran was her main carer until she died too. He tried taking her on expensive holidays to re-connect with her, but that wasn't enough. When her gran died that threw her out of sync, so she left all her rich friends behind and took a job in London in a flower shop. She then realised London was a lonely place for a girl with no friends or family.

When she met Niraj, she fell in love with the promise of a better life. She knew he had a big family that would be preferable to her one parent family. She discovered soon after she married Niraj 'how wrong she was'! It became a nightmare she couldn't get out of, it wasn't what she expected. Over time, she realised how naïve, gullible and young she had been.

Niraj had 'the gift of the gab' as they say. He was a charmer that knew how to do all the right things if he wanted something. And he wanted Janice, he made that clear. She got swept up in the excitement of it all, so after less than six months of dating him he proposed to her, and she was over the moon. Janice said 'yes' immediately, and she couldn't wait to start the next chapter in her life with him. She expected to be engulfed into the fold of Niraj's large family, and she thought it would be amazing. Niraj insisted he didn't want a long engagement, he said they should get married within the month, after all, what was the point of waiting? Janice didn't want a large wedding or even a medium one, she didn't care about the size, but she thought just one month after the engagement was rather soon. When she voiced her concerns, he became moody accusing her of having second thoughts. Janice suggested they marry on their one year of meeting anniversary, but he said that was way too long, so they planned to get married three months after the engagement. They would have a simple court marriage with just two witnesses. Janice chose the flower shop manager Irene to be one of the witnesses, and Niraj suggested Janice invite the owner of the shop Maisy as the other witness. She was surprised that Niraj didn't want to involve his family or invite some friends to the wedding, but he said he didn't like a fuss and Janice accepted that explanation.

She did not know the real reason he wanted a wedding, but later, she discovered what his motives were. When they got married, she had met none of Niraj's family or friends. Although she found it strange, she didn't question him about it because he went into a mood if she asked him, so she stopped asking. She knew Niraj sometimes went to meet his family, but she didn't know that he never mentioned her.

After being married for only six months, Janice fell pregnant. They had briefly discussed children, they decided that because their meeting, engagement and marriage happened so fast, they would wait for two or three years before having any children. After all, they were still young enough and could take their time. When Niraj found out about the pregnancy, he was not happy. He asked Janice to consider aborting the baby, but she said she couldn't and wouldn't do that. Janice pleaded with him by telling him the pregnancy was just an accident, and they could deal with it, after all they were in a loving relationship. But Niraj took ages to forgive her for not listening to him about getting rid of the baby and for getting pregnant in the first place. He didn't want to believe it was an accident. He stayed away from home a lot during that time. When Janice was four months pregnant and whilst he was away for work, she contacted Niraj's family and let them know about her and the baby. Janice went through Niraj's address book and found some numbers, they weren't his parents however she found a contact for one of his cousins who took her message. She said she wanted to meet Niraj's parents. Niraj's cousin then set up a meeting between them.

What a shock that meeting was for both Janice and Niraj's parents. They couldn't believe what Janice had told them and were speechless when she said they had a grandchild on the way. They were struggling to understand how Niraj could have married a 'white' woman! They couldn't even speak properly after Janice finished. Finally, Niraj's dad said, 'they would never be part of his family because their marriage was a complete mistake. Niraj could only be forgiven if he divorced her.'

Janice thought he was joking at first. When she realised that he meant what he said she wanted to know why they weren't happy for Niraj. He then said Niraj was already engaged to an Indian woman, and they were due to get married in a year's time. They had it all planned out, and then Niraj's Indian wife would come to live with them. It was Janice's turn to become speechless, 'Niraj had been engaged to someone else?' He never told her any of this, and it was now clear why he didn't want to introduce her to his family. She burst into tears, but they showed no mercy. They said she should do them all a favour and divorce him. Niraj's dad offered her enough money to look after the child on her own but never to speak about this marriage or the child to anyone in their family. That was the stipulation to getting the money. They offered her twenty-five thousand pounds to keep the wedding and baby quiet. Janice was defiant, she said she didn't give a shit about their money. If he wanted to divorce her, then he had to take that step. But she would never do it for them or the money.

Niraj's dad then accused her of being selfish and told her the money was a one-time offer. If she didn't take it now, they wouldn't give her anything later. Janice left their house disgusted, humiliated, upset and annoyed. She didn't know who she became more annoyed with, Niraj for not telling her the truth or his parents for being so nasty to her.

One week after that disastrous meeting with Niraj's parents, Niraj came back home, and he wasn't happy with Janice. His parents contacted him whilst he was abroad, and he found out about their ill-fated meeting. When he saw her, he had a face like thunder and spent over two hours shouting at Janice. He said he couldn't believe she did something so reckless; she was selfish, spoilt and unfeeling, she couldn't get a word in edgewise. She tried to explain her reasons for contacting his parents, but he was on the attack the whole time. She decided not to fight back, because she was afraid all that screaming would affect their unborn child. Niraj told her his family didn't want to talk to him anymore, and it was all her fault. He said that he was handling the situation his way, and in time they would have gotten used to the idea of Janice and himself being a couple. When they were ready, he would have then introduced Janice to them, but now, she had gone and spoiled everything.

She went to bed upset, Niraj didn't say much about his engagement to the other woman, and he was annoyed because his parents' wouldn't talk to him anymore. Janice would ask him about his engagement to that woman tomorrow when he calmed down.

But over the next few days, she didn't ask him about it, because he left the house and had not returned. He just left a note on the kitchen table saying, 'I can't deal with you right now, so I will stay at a friend's house for a while.' After reading that she felt more alone than ever before. Nothing seemed to be going to plan.

When Jonathan was finally born nothing much changed, Niraj was still aloof with Janice. He wasn't used to being segregated from his family, and he was still displeased about it, he blamed Janice for everything that went wrong. He decided being a dad was also wrong, so he stayed away a lot for his work, and when he came back home, he went out with friends, most of the time choosing to stay with them overnight.

Janice suspected he might have been having an extra-marital affair, and there was little she could do about it. For now, her hands were full with little Jonathan who was extremely cute and kept her very busy. Janice attended all the antenatal classes by herself, and she went to mother and toddler groups after Jonathan was born alone too. She organised everything that Jonathan ever needed in those early years. Sometimes Niraj was nice to Jonathan but not very often. Jonathan viewed him as if he was a strange uncle who he saw now and again. He never bonded with Jonathan, he felt his son was a hindrance he had to endure!

Niraj treated Janice the same way now as he did then, he didn't show much love for her. They didn't have a very active sex life, not just because he had been away most of the time, but because there was a distance between them after Janice's meeting with Niraj's parents. If they ever had sex, it was usually instigated by him, and she would just go through the motions. Niraj wasn't loving either before or after sex, so she didn't feel particularly loved. As far as she knew, she performed her wifely duties, and he expected nothing more.

After Jonathan's first birthday, life was settling down for Janice. Niraj seemed a bit happier, and he was kinder to both. They became more socially active, they went to parties and barbecues and even invited people over for dinners at their house. His wife, Niraj realised became an excellent hostess, something she learned from her mum. Their friends liked Janice, and they invited the Rice family to most of their functions. He liked the feeling of being socially acceptable, he used his charm on his friends, especially the females. They thought Niraj was a good catch, and Janice was lucky to get him. Although Janice was a great hostess, they thought her plain as a daisy. She had nothing special about her, unlike Niraj who could be the life and soul of the party. Janice knew this, but it didn't bother her, because for once in her marriage she felt accepted, not just socially. Niraj became more agreeable to them, and everything had been going well for her. They never brought up the subject of his parents, and Janice never asked Niraj about what had happened to that girl he had been engaged to in India.

Life had been going as well as it could get living with Niraj during Jonathan's early years. Niraj's mood swings were less frequent, and his verbal attacks became few and far between. Things then took a turn for the worse after they had that incident where Niraj and Janice had an almighty row when Jonathan was nine. If Jonathan hadn't arrived when he did, Janice was sure she would have been dead!

Janice worried about Jonathan's memory lapses and his bipolar disorder. Jonathan was her world, and she would do anything to protect him from anyone. She would endure walking on hot coals for him. Niraj knew this and resented her for her devotion to her son. She sometimes turned a blind eye to some of Niraj's 'low level' bullying towards Jonathan, because she didn't want to upset the status quo. She noted and monitored everyone's behaviour towards her son, and Niraj's little tactics weren't gone unnoticed by her. Every time he did something nasty to Jonathan, she wanted to retaliate, and on a few occasions she did, but he would just laugh it off saying he was 'only kidding.' It didn't matter what he said, she knew the truth, she thought, 'Niraj was a nasty bastard that dared to call himself a husband and father!'

TWO MONTHS AGO

13

After a few weeks of trying to speak to his mum alone, Jonathan succeeded. His dad went out on Friday night saying he was going to play poker with friends and wouldn't be back till the early hours of the morning. He told Janice not to wait up for him. Jonathan figured this was a perfect opportunity to confront his mum, and this time he wanted the whole truth. He promised himself he wouldn't accept half a story.

Jonathan told his mum he wanted to talk to her after dinner that evening. She knew Jonathan had become nervous about something, she could sense it during the meal. He was distant and very monosyllabic with his answers as opposed to being usually chatty if his dad wasn't around.

'What do you want to talk about son?'

'I know dad tried to choke you against the wall!' He blurted it out, not wanting to beat around the bush.

Janice missed a heartbeat, and she flushed, she didn't know how he found out and she felt ashamed for not telling him the truth. She was also feeling guilty for staying with Niraj after that incident. Now her son remembered and wanted an explanation! Jonathan read his mum like a book, he realised he had touched a nerve. He knew she didn't want to talk about it, but he wasn't that young boy anymore, he had grown into a person that could deal with anything she told him. If they were on the same side and his dad on the opposite. He didn't rush her, he let the fact sink in and gave her time to remember the story, so she could tell him everything.

After a few moments, she spoke, 'I am sorry you had to endure such a terrible thing. You were only nine when that happened. You forgot about it after a few days, and then I realised you probably suffered from psychological amnesia. I assumed if you had forgotten, that memory wouldn't haunt you anymore so I could get past it too.'

Jonathan became sad listening to her. 'So, tell me everything.'

She hesitated not wanting to tell him all her issues with Niraj.

'For god's sake mum, I am not small anymore. Please tell me, or I will forever wonder or be forced to ask dad about it instead. Trust me, he is the last person I want to confront!'

Janice still hesitant said, 'I accused your dad of having an affair with a woman who came to our house for lunch that day.'

'Why did you accuse him, did you see something?'

'In a way yes, he started excessively flirting with her. They were giggling and laughing at private jokes, and he didn't speak to anyone else at the lunch party. I suspected something had gone on between them, I can't describe what exactly, but I knew, sometimes you just know.'

'So, you confronted him when everyone had gone, and he denied it?'

'Well, not really. I became more annoyed that our

guests would notice his behaviour. Personally, I was not a happy wife, I didn't care for him—sorry son! I did care people could have talked about his behaviour and it worried me, they would have excluded you from their kids' parties, etc. So, I told him after the party, if he wanted to carry on with her, he should do it in private.'

'What happened next?' He asked.

'He went crazy and ranted on about how he was the king of this house, and as the king he could do whatever he wanted to whoever he wanted and said he didn't care if the universe saw his behaviour and he was proud if people thought he was with her. He said she was beautiful, and they would realise even beautiful women found him attractive. Knowing he was drunk I shouldn't have challenged him, but it annoyed me, and before long, I blurted out what I thought.'

'But that's no excuse for violence, couldn't you have left him after he tried to kill you?'

'I seriously considered it, but he became really nice after the incident. Despite that, I wanted to leave him, but when you lost your memory, I decided to stay. You were my main concern and if you had been unaffected by it, then who was I to deprive you of a father?'

'Deprive me of a father? Mum, he has been an absolute asshole to both of us. How can you think we would have been better off with him?'

'Jonathan stop swearing.'

'My swearing is the least of our worries mum. You knew there was something wrong, so we should have left him then. We didn't have to play perfect families. I would rather come from a broken happy home than this. Did you know after he tried to choke you to death he came into my bedroom several times to threaten me?'

'Nooooo, why did he do that, what did he say?'

'He said I could never tell anyone what happened or what he did, or he would tell the police it was all my fault!'

'Are you sure son?'

'I am one hundred per cent sure, he said he would tell the police I tried to kill him with that vase.'

'But that is ridiculous, I could have counterclaimed he tried to kill me first, and what you did was try to defend me!'

'I was a lot younger then, and he scared the life out of me, so I guess in fright I blocked out the memory!'

Janice wished she had left Niraj then. He caused Jonathan's problems, and if she knew this then she would have been long gone by now, that was despicable of Niraj. Her blood was boiling, but she was trying to remain calm and not show her feelings in front of Jonathan.

'So, couldn't we have left him?' He asked.

'I wasn't aware he threatened you, and if I had known, there would be no question, we would have gone so far away he would never be able to find us. Unfortunately, it isn't as easy as you think. Most people frown upon broken homes.' Janice said hoping he agreed with, her after all she didn't want to think she suffered under that tyrant of a husband for nothing. She wanted and needed her son's approval.

'Mum, we aren't in the 1950's, are you still going to think and behave like we are? There are plenty of kids in my school from a broken home, and all of them are nice.' Then as an afterthought, he said, 'I think they are, I am not sure, because I don't really have any close friends in school.'

'What about Peter, Misty and Nick? You are forever talking about them. I haven't met them.'

'They are my best friends, but they aren't in my school.'

'Oh, how did you meet them?'

'I met Peter in the park, I saw him often, so one day he came and started talking to me. He isn't really a shy guy. He talks a lot, sometimes we have a job shutting him up!' Jonathan said laughing. 'Then one day Peter introduced me to Misty and Nick.' He tried to say Misty's name quickly so that his mum wouldn't notice that he fancied her.

'Oh really?' Janice said raising her eyebrows.

'Yes really.' He said dismissively.

'Anyway, we digress, so what happened after that incident?' Jonathan noticed his mum's expression change, and she became more serious.

'What do you mean? Nothing happened.'

'I mean you said he was nice to you for a while, how long did that last?'

'I can't remember it was so long ago. He then went on one of his trips, so it was a great relief to me. I didn't have to look him in the eye, and I suspect he didn't want to look at the damage he had caused every time he looked at me.'

'You must have hated him.'

Janice hesitated answering this, she didn't want Jonathan to find out how much she hated him, but she knew she couldn't lie to him. He was a smart boy. 'Hate is a strong word. I despised him for quite a while, and when he was away from home, it became easy to forget what he did, and I blocked it out like you did. You don't realise how lucky you were to forget that. I wish I had forgotten just as easily.'

'Really mum, it wasn't as easy for me to forget. Now I know what happened I am amazed that you stayed. It was terrifying at the time. Can you imagine someone that was young having to watch the one thing in the world that they love going through that?'

'Oh my god, sorry love. It wasn't easy for you, but I am so glad you forgot. When did your memory come back?'

'A few days ago, I was going to ask you everything earlier, but dad was always around.'

'Your memory came back? Just like that? One morning you woke up, and you remembered?'

'Well, it wasn't that simple, my friends helped jog my memory.'

'You told them?' Janice looked shocked. The last thing she wanted was for outsiders to find out.

'They know, and everyone should know mum, he is a monster in disguise, he tried to kill you, and he is a bastard to both of us. I wish he stayed with that other woman, I saw them a few times during the other incidents.'

'What other incidents?' She looked alarmed. 'I caught them in bed one night when I was four or five years old. That was the first time I saw her. I am not sure where you were, I got out of bed scared because it was dark, and my night light wasn't on, so I ran to your bedroom and found them together in bed!'

Janice was too frightened to ask any more questions for fear of the answer. She didn't care that Niraj cheated on her, she suspected that already, but she was upset that Jonathan knew and found out the way he did.

'Anyway, he threatened to take you away and leave me in a cold dark place if I ever told anyone.'

'He didn't!' Janice said tears rolling down her face.

'Yes, he did, and I was terrified. I told no one about it, but I soon forgot it happened like the other times he threatened me. This could have been one of my first bouts of amnesia. I didn't remember this happened until a few months ago.'

'What were the other times he threatened you?'

'I never saw him with her the second time, but I heard him say he loved someone on the phone. When he caught me eavesdropping he locked me in our pantry in the dark for several hours. You were asleep, so you wouldn't have heard anything.' Ignoring the shocked look on her face, he continued. 'After a few hours, he came to let me out and again threatened me. This time he said he would leave me alone in the woods and take you away from me if I said anything to anyone. Obviously, I was scared. He continued his threats for a few nights as he did the last time, and I was too scared he would lock me up again, so I didn't say anything. After a few days, I completely blanked this memory. Then the third time was bad.'

'Oh god a third time! When did this happen, I mean how old were you?'

'About seven I think. And the third time I was nine years old.'

She couldn't believe what he was telling her or even imagine how Jonathan must have felt.

He continued regardless, 'the third time it happened when you went to hospital for your routine operation. He organised a sleepover at Anthony's house. I wasn't too pleased with that, because I didn't really like Anthony, but I couldn't say I didn't want to go.' Jonathan then recited everything that happened on that occasion in a matter of fact kind of way. He didn't want to stress his mum out. She was already starting to look at him with a pained expression.

When he finished, she asked, 'why didn't you say something then?'

'What would it change? I only found these memories out recently and regarding that woman, for all I knew he was no longer seeing her.'

Finding this out now made her upset, and she was glad they were having this conversation. So Niraj threatened Jonathan at least four times to get him to keep his mouth shut, and this frightening the life out of Jonathan which made him forget everything! It was crazy!

Now they had discussed Niraj's underhandedness

they knew what they were dealing with. After hearing from Jonathan, she hated her husband even more. She felt like they were just there so that he could take his frustrations out on them. If he had a bad day or life, then it was their fault.

Both the son and mum looked at each other with pity, each pitying the other for various reasons. Jonathan, however wasn't satisfied with her responses. He could tell that she told him the whole truth about the choking incident, but there was more that he was missing. He could get Misty to do another session with him, but it was too traumatic to deal with afterwards. This time he preferred to hear it directly from his mum. He would insist that not only would she tell him everything, but they should come up with a plan of action to leave his dad.

He took a deep breath then said, 'so what else aren't you telling me, mum?'

She looked thoughtful and said, 'nothing, I think that's all there is to say about him.' As nonchalantly as she could.

'But there is something?'

'Jonathan, I handled everything until now, and you have been none the wiser. So, what's the point of opening old wounds that are healing or have now healed?'

'Mum don't make me beg you.'

Janice looked frustrated, she knew he wouldn't take no for an answer so she said, 'okay, but I don't want you to get upset.'

'Anything you tell me about that fool would upset me if he hurt you!'

'This is going to be so hard' Janice thought. She took a deep breath and said, 'a few years ago your dad and I went out shopping for groceries. He would only drop me and wait in the car, it was around Christmas, and the supermarket was busy. He called me several times on my mobile to find out why I was taking so long. I picked up his calls and explained that the shop was busy, but he got increasingly annoyed at me for keeping him waiting. He then came into the supermarket and found me on one of the tills paying for the shopping. I had only bought half of the things I wanted on my list because he was harassing me to hurry up.

When he saw me, he came over and grabbed me by my scarf that was around my neck and shouted in my face, "When I call you, you answer bitch! You are slow and walk like a fucking snail, no wonder you can't do anything around the house. You're nothing but a lazy bitch." The whole shop heard him shouting, and everyone froze. I wanted the ground to open up and swallow me. I had never been humiliated or embarrassed like that before. His eyes were bulging, and he looked like he was filled with hate.

Obviously he hated me but I don't know what I did for him to hate me that much. Then from somewhere in the crowd a man yelled, "leave her alone mate". Well, that set him off again. He looked at me saying, "see what you have done? You made me look bad and like a fool! Just you wait, your time is coming…", and saying that he dragged me out of the shop by the scarf on my neck. The lady at the till said, "She is about to pay, hang on..." But he didn't care. Suddenly the man that shouted to leave me alone was in front of your dad looking twice as big and bellowed in his face, "I said, leave her alone!" I was so scared, I didn't know if he would hit me first before trying to kill that man or if that man would punch him first. If he had, Niraj would have flown across the room with one punch!' Janice gave a brief smile then continued.

'Niraj looked at me with a long hard look and threw me to the floor saying, "I'll wait in the car, this isn't over!" and stormed off. The man came over quickly and helped me up.

He told me he could take me home instead. He asked if I had somewhere to stay for the night, suggesting I better go there because that would be safer for me, even if it was for only one night. I couldn't just go with that man, your dad would have killed me for sure, eventually. So, I told him it was ok that my husband just found out his dad died and wasn't thinking straight. The man wasn't happy I went back home with your dad, whilst he was already annoyed, but I didn't think I had many choices, so I abandoned the shopping and went to the car empty-handed. There was no way I could go back to the till and face the checkout operator or all the people that had gathered around to see the show. When I got back in the car, he said nothing and drove home like the devil was chasing us.

Luckily for me, you were on the second day of your ten-day school trip. He was silent for the whole journey. When we got inside the house, he grabbed me by the scarf again and said in a low voice, "if you humiliate me like that ever again I will kill you!" I tried to speak but nothing came out of my mouth, I was terrified. Then he shouted about what an embarrassment I was, that I couldn't even do a simple shop without causing a scene. I wanted to defend myself and tell him I did nothing, and I just went to get groceries. If driving was an issue, then I could have driven myself, but I was too scared to say anything. I knew whatever I said would sound like I was being insubordinate to him. I don't know what drove him to such anger, but I knew whatever it was, I hadn't caused it. So, while I stood there trembling, he continued to rant on about how rubbish it was being married to me, my mind wandered. I tried to determine at what point in the day he got angry. Had he spoken to someone that day? Had he watched something on TV that could have upset him or had work issues that was worrying him? But I didn't understand.

After what seemed like ages, he told me to go to the spare room and stay there, because he couldn't tolerate seeing my face anymore. He practically dragged me up the stairs by my hair and threw me on the bed and slammed the door shut. I started crying and was so glad you weren't around to see or hear anything. He had hardly gone for long when he came back and said if I wanted to cry then I should do so silently. He didn't want to know I even existed, he said he would tell me when my punishment had ended and when I deserved to be let out the room. The funny thing was, none of our room doors have locks from the outside so I could have left at any time, but I was scared and needed this nightmare to end.

I don't know how long I stayed there for, and I might have dozed off for a while, but a slamming car door woke me up, I couldn't remember anything for a minute or so but when I remembered, I sat up in bed not knowing if I should go out or not. Your dad had come back inside the house, he must have gone to get some shopping because after fifteen minutes he came and put a microwave meal outside the door. He knocked once and said your dinner is outside. He left it there with water and a fork.

I wasn't hungry, but I forced myself to eat, otherwise that would be another reason he would be angry with me. Nothing made sense, I just didn't want to live like this. Part of me wished I had taken the plunge and left him that first time he tried to choke me.

I must have gone to sleep at some point, but late at night I heard your dad shouting at someone on the phone. I went to the door and put my ear against it, whilst trying not to make a sound. It was about two am and I think he was on the phone for quite a while before his raised voice woke me up. From what I could gather, he was talking to a woman. I suspected it was that lady he was having an affair with. Something annoyed him, and he was trying to keep his voice down, so I didn't overhear his conversation.

He said, "why can't you understand how hard this is? You know I can't leave her, she will tell everyone I am a bastard, and she will take my son away from me. My pride and joy. You know how much I love my son…., no I can't take him with us. She will fight for him and win, I know it. Haven't we already spoken about this, why are you bringing this up again?"

Then there was silence, whilst he listened. Then I heard, "What the fuck, you can't threaten me with that Saroj, please don't do this. I love you so much, you know this. It's only Jonathan and you I want to be with. Please don't say that."

Again, the silence as he continued to listen to her.

"Ok can't we talk about this when we meet up tomorrow?"

Another silent moment whilst he listened.

Then he said, "You have got to meet me, we have been together for so long, this will never be the end for us, and you know it. I have only loved you. She has meant nothing to me. I only married her because I felt sorry for her. Look at her, she is plain Jane. I didn't want to marry that village girl my parents planned for me and Janice was a stopgap. You should know this, it's been only you, please Saroj."

It devastated me hearing this conversation, I started crying by the door wishing I had never met your dad. I felt like such a fool. All this time they were laughing at me. Now it all made sense. He married me because he wanted an escape. He thought I was a nobody, someone to pity. I didn't want his pity, this pain or his rotten family anymore. I wanted to live a simple life with you. If I had you, I had the world. He could go to hell with Saroj as far as I cared. At that moment, I didn't cry tears of betrayal. I cried tears of despair and loneliness. Why didn't I leave him that first time? When he tried to choke me, that time it was Saroj that he was flirting with. It had been her all along. After dragging myself to bed, I wondered why he didn't leave me for her. Why did he lie to her like he was the world's best dad? Why did he continue to make my life miserable? I would have been pleased for them both, but I realised that he wanted to show he was a happily married man, a model husband and a father. That meant more to him, what other people thought of him.

I felt sorry for Saroj if he told her you were someone he couldn't live without, and how much of a lovely dad he was, he could have told her a hundred lies. She had been his mistress for years not knowing the truth.

Now I realised why he got so upset that day. Saroj wanted him to leave us and go to her or she would leave him. He preferred his game, 'to have his cake and eat it' but today she must have given him an ultimatum. He didn't like someone else to call the shots, especially a woman. I had always been the submissive in our relationship, and with her, she was in control.

Anyway, that day he got angry with me for being me, for being his wife, for impeding his relationship with Saroj. It all made perfect sense. It was a total mess.

I didn't know what he planned to do next. If he had left us, I think it would have done us both a favour. But he didn't.

Over the few days you were gone, he said I could come out of the room to clean and cook, but other than that he didn't want to see or hear me until you got back. He still pretended that he was angry with me over the grocery incident, and I didn't tell him I knew the real reason. What would have been the point?

At night I could hear him talking to her, and I gather she stopped seeing him but didn't stop taking his calls. He continued to beg her to reconsider her decision, but a few days before you got back things took a turn for the worse.

One morning I waited for him to go out, he wasn't due to go back to work yet, and he went out every morning to get grocery's, and I suspect to make phone calls to Saroj. As soon as he left, I went down to clean up after his breakfast and to make myself something to eat. After thirty minutes he came back, far sooner than usual. Usually by the time he got back I ate and ran back up to the room, but this time he caught me having toast in the kitchen. I hadn't heard him come back as it was unexpected. He saw me there and went mad, he said I could only eat when he said so, he stomped over, and before I knew what was happening, he slapped me hard in the face several times. I tried to defend myself, but he was too strong, and he overpowered me. He continued to hit me and told me I was a worthless shit and used many other swear words whilst he continued slapping me. I stopped fighting and just sank down to the floor. He grabbed my hair and told me to stand up saying, "My life is a mess because of you. You are a witch god sent me for disobeying my parents. I wish you were never born." He kept giving me little slaps as he told me how worthless I was. I stopped looking at him and stared at the floor, so he pulled my chin up and made me look at him. He looked me straight in the eye and then spat in my face, it was terrible, I stopped crying silently to sobbing loudly. He let me go, and I fell to the floor like a used doll not needed anymore. I hated him, I hated myself, and by now I realised this wasn't the way I wanted to live my life. He said harshly, "get up and get out. Go to your room, and never come out till I tell you, I hate the sight of you."

Because I didn't hear him the first time he screamed, "Get out of here you ugly bitch!"

I jumped up off the floor and ran upstairs. He chased after

me, when he caught up with me he grabbed hold of my hand and dragged me to our bedroom. He shoved me on the floor of our room beside the bed and then went into my wardrobe and pulled out all my clothes. After piling them on the floor, he said he would burn them. I had no need for clothes because I was never going out of the house again.

I sat and watched him whilst crying all the while, he looked over at me and said I was a pathetic waste of a life. Before he left the room, he walked over to me, crouched down to my level and whispered in my ear, "hope you die soon, then I can actually live a life I deserve to have. I hate you and don't you ever forget that." He grabbed a bunch of my hair as he said it so he could bring my ear close to his lips, it was said with malice. He left the room, and soon after that I heard him leave the house. I went over to the pile of clothes he put there, grabbing all of them, I took them to the spare room I had been sleeping in for the last few nights. I didn't want to go back into our bedroom for my clothes again. I must have cried for ages, later I decided I needed a shower, I wanted to wash his dirt off me, I wanted to see if I was worth something once I had showered.

Afterwards, I looked in the mirror, 'nope' I thought. I still looked pathetic, worthless, ugly and plain, I tried not to cry anymore. I must have thought of a hundred ways of killing myself, but I knew I would never ever go through with it because of you. Maybe that is what he wanted me to do. I then realised that would have been the perfect solution for him. My suicide would make him a poor grieving widow, and he and Saroj would have you for themselves. What a perfect solution it would be if I did that. Maybe that was his tactic all along. To make my life so unbearable, to make me think so little of myself, to make my very existence a nonentity, to make me believe all these things about myself would be the reason for me to kill myself, and for a whole day I considered it.

I didn't do it, of course, I couldn't let him win that easily, let him have you, or leave you with that lying, cheating monster that didn't love you like I did. I needed to live for you.

14

J onathan sat in complete silence. He listened to his mum without interrupting her even once; he was afraid to ask her anything in case she stopped telling him all the details that he wanted to know. He was literally stunned into silence, getting more than he bargained for and he couldn't fathom knowing what he knew now, or why they were still with his dad.

He then said, 'I am so shocked and sad to hear this, and I know why you didn't want to tell me anything. I had no idea about this mum, it sounds like torture. I don't understand why we are still with dad now?'

Janice looked with sympathy at Jonathan. She tried to spare him from the treatment she received from Niraj. She wanted to paint a picture that his dad had been kind, loving and a family man, but she had to tell him the truth. Now at sixteen, he could deal with it better than if he found out earlier. If she said nothing today, it would have upset him. He asked for the truth, and she didn't feel she could have kept it from him any longer.

With a deep sigh she continued her story, 'I later found

out that the day he slapped, spat and dragged me upstairs was the day Saroj told him she would marry some other guy, because she got fed up waiting for him. I only learned of that because I eavesdropped into his late-night conversations with her. He'd gone out that morning, and that is when she said she decided to marry a man she had been seeing on the side. That enraged him enough to think I was the reason for all his problems, so that is why he took it out on me that day.

I never saw him much for the next few days, because he only came back late in the evening. I was on the lookout for his car so I could run upstairs, because I was fearful of another beating. He knew I had been coming down for food, and he even left microwave meals, bread and fresh milk in the kitchen, but he didn't want to see or hear me.

After a few days, he left me a note in the kitchen saying he will go away for work, and he wouldn't be home for at least a week or more. He said he would let me know when he came back so we could discuss our situation. I didn't know what "discuss our situation" meant, but I was glad he had gone. You were due to come home from your school trip soon, and I wanted you to think all was fine at home. I put everything back into place like it was. When you got home you were so full of joy and energy, I hugged you so hard, I could have crushed you. It took all the willpower I had not to cry holding you. Everything in the world felt right knowing you were home. I missed you, and it felt as if those few days never happened. For a little while, I forgot all my troubles.

After your return from your school trip, I went to the florist and begged them to take me back full-time, they knew I was a hard worker and they liked me, so they gave me my old job back. I thought long and hard about leaving your dad, and I started getting ready to leave him. Now I had my job back, I got an income which I knew would help.

I gave away all your old clothes and toys and took any valuable jewellery, along with my passport and kept them locked in the shop safe. I even started looking for flats we could rent. It would only be one bedroom due to my income. but at least it would be a haven for the both of us to live in peace. But before I finally told him we were leaving, I wanted to know what was on his mind. What could he say in his defence? I needed to know. Especially now I knew his 'precious Saroj' had left him to marry someone else.

Your dad didn't come home for a month. I think when he got back in the country he stayed at some friend's place or a hotel. I even thought I saw him one day and dismissed that thought for fear I was going mad or started to see things. In hindsight, I suspect he began following and spying on me at times because he wanted to know if I was having an affair or out partying. There was no doubt about it, he was paranoid. He wanted me to put a toe out of line. So, he could use that as an excuse to humiliate me in public before divorcing me. He was looking for grounds for a divorce that made him look good in the eyes of his friends and family.

Unfortunately for him, I didn't have time for anybody else but you and my job. Life went back to normal, but I never forgot how much he hated me. With the venom in his voice that last time he talked to me, I'd be a fool to forget, and I knew this.

When he finally came home, he gave me fair warning and asked if I could arrange a sleepover for you at one of your friend's houses so we had a chance to 'discuss our situation'. So, I did as he asked, and he came back on a Friday. You had gone over to your friend Jimmy's house for the night.

I made a simple dinner of pasta and garlic bread. The

house was clean, and everything was in the order he liked. I only did that, so he wouldn't come home and shout at me. When he got in, he said, 'Hi' and he came over to give me a hug. I was so shocked I stood there rigid, not knowing if I should hug him back or not, so I didn't.

I asked him if he wanted a cup of tea which he gratefully accepted, and we went into the kitchen. Whilst the kettle was on he paced around the kitchen. I could see he was on edge, but I truly wasn't aware of what to expect from him. He then walked over to me, holding my shoulders he turned me, so I could look at him and said, 'Janice I really don't know what to say, I am so sorry I behaved so badly. I can't believe that was me. I had a lot of time to think about what happened that week, and I don't know what came over me. How could I throw the one thing good in my life in the bin, because I was stressed and angry?' Then he waited for a response.

I said, 'why did you do it Niraj, what excuse do you have? Was I that bad you had to beat me, spit on me, drag me around by my limbs and hair and threaten to burn my clothes?'

He looked shocked when I brought up everything. I think he realised he did wrong, but he either couldn't remember what he had done, or it triggered his memories when I said it out loud like that.

He left my shoulders, raked his fingers through his hair and said, 'I can't understand my behaviour. It was my dad, he has been sick and in hospital, but they won't allow me to see him because I am still married to you. So, I took out all my frustrations on you, and I am truly sorry. I don't want you to leave me, I would be a broken man if you did that.'

I was trying to think quickly. If his dad was sick, then why didn't he say that to Saroj on the phone? I didn't hear him mention his dad once. Surely he could have stalled her with that piece of information, but it didn't come up, or he was lying. I suspect his dad might have been slightly ill, but not so bad that he needed hospitalisation. He used his family as an excuse after a month of thinking about it, good one! I didn't believe him but said, 'how is your dad now?'

'Yeah, luckily he pulled through. My cousin was sending me information and texting me his progress.'

'Oh ok.' I said without feeling.

'So can you forgive me and forget this ever happened? Can we scrap that episode completely? I really am sorry Janice, I love you.'

'If you get stressed another time, could this happen again?'

'I will leave the house. Just tell me to go till I calm down and then come back. I need your help please Janice, you are my wife.'

He has pre-planned this whole conversation, I thought to myself.

'Ok, can I have a little while to think about what you said? I was totally traumatised by how you treated me. Nobody can live like that. For your sake and our sanity, I would have left but wanted to hear you out first. It seemed only fair. Now I have heard what your reasons were, I will let you know what I decide.'

'Ok, how long will you take to decide? I want us to be a family and sleep in the same bedroom again, and I want everything to go back to when we first dated.'

'I don't know Niraj, before Jonathan comes back tomorrow.'

'Can't you decide tonight, that way we can go for a cele-bratory dinner. I want to wine and dine you like when we first met. That is why I wanted you to send Jonathan for a sleepover.'

I realised he thought I was too weak to leave him, he had it all planned down to a T. But he got me all wrong. I wasn't weak, I could have left him at that time, but I didn't because I put you first. I didn't want you to live in a small flat when you could live in a house. If you were shielded from this madness, then there was no harm in continuing the way we were. I would have lived in a hut just, so I could get away from him, but I had to think about you. You were my only reason for staying.

After a few hours, I put him out of his misery and said I had forgiven him and would stay. He said we should go and celebrate and have a nice romantic meal, but I didn't want to go, so I told him I made dinner, and I didn't want to waste it. I also suggested we had to take baby steps going forward. There was too much water under the bridge. We couldn't behave like before, no matter how hard we tried, it would never be like that again. He seemed to understand my reasoning and accepted it. Plus knowing him, he would serenade me and put on a show like he does. He acts like the world's best husband in public. He likes all the waiting staff and other dinner guests think how lucky I am to have him. I didn't want that, because I hadn't forgotten his past behaviour, and I have never forgiven him for that, but I know I did something I was proud of… I became a great actress deciding the only way this would work was if I treated him like a king he wanted to be. I acted loving in private and public and generally became 'over the top' happy. And that became my plan, to act every time he was with me, so he didn't know I hated him like the devil I thought he was.

From your dad's perspective everything had gone back to the way he wanted it. A nice happy family life, he behaved like a loving husband and father to you for a while, and that lasted a good few years. I must admit I thought he had become a changed man, I even considered giving you another brother or sister, but he wasn't so keen on that idea, so I abandoned it.

I suspected Saroj got married and your dad focused on what he had with us instead. He never again talked about his family, and even now I am not sure if his parents are even alive or not. This isn't a subject he likes to talk about. I was always suspicious about the times that your dad was away, some of it felt questionable. I wasn't sure if after Saroj, he had ever started another relationship with another woman. I guessed he hadn't, and I wanted to be right, not because I would be jealous, I didn't want a repeat of what happened to me when he broke up with Saroj to happen again. I knew this time he would take it out on both of us, and I was scared that you might find out first-hand how he behaved when he got upset. Any actual love I had for him he took away that week he locked me up after beating me. There was nothing I could do to love him again, so I treated him like a husband, but I felt like I was living with a friend I could just about tolerate.

So whilst he tried to become a better person, I had worked hard within myself (the non-actress part) to forget that terrible time we had. That horrible week when I considered leaving him or leaving life altogether. I wanted to believe deep within me that he had changed. I acted like I thought him to be a changed man, but I built up such a massive wall around my inner soul, it was tough for me to take it down. Some part within me thought he would become that monster again.

I was right, and glad I trusted my instincts. His behaviour lasted a few years and recently, over the last two or three years his facade started wearing thin. He is reverting to the man he was then. Now you are older, we can both deal with him together, we were always a team. If he gets that bad, we will work something out, together won't we?' Janice finally ended her story.

Jonathan didn't answer her, he was deep in thought. They sat there in silence for a few minutes. Janice could hear the clock 'Tick-Tock, Tick-Tock' as the minutes went by. She patiently waited for Jonathan's response.

He was trying to make sense of it all, he wanted to see everything from his mum's perspective, but it wasn't easy. He thought he would have preferred to live in a tiny flat than here with his hateful father. Now with what his mum told him about his dad, he wanted to kill him. He wanted him to suffer just as much or more than what he put his mum through, wishing he could lock him up in a cold dark dungeon, and throw away the key. Now he became even more upset, so he decided that he couldn't stay here and 'chew the fat' with his mum over his dad's behaviour. He wanted to cry, and he wanted to protect his mum, but he couldn't protect her from something that happened in the past, and he knew couldn't cry here in front of her. His heart was truly broken hearing how she put up with his crazy dad all because of him. It was hard for him not to feel guilty for subjecting her to his father's abuse, he felt responsible. He decided that he needed to get out of the house and see Peter, Misty and Nick, they could help him to think clearly.

Standing up abruptly he said, 'I need to get some air mum. Will you excuse me?'

'But Jonathan, don't worry it was ages ago.'

Not listening to her, he grabbed his coat and said, 'see you later mum. We can discuss this tomorrow ok? Don't worry about me, I am fine.'

Saying that he shut the door behind him.

Janice felt deflated, telling Jonathan the whole story brought up memories she preferred to forget. It made it real again. It made her angry, depressed and now troubled that Jonathan didn't want to either speak about it or address the issue. She didn't want it to upset Jonathan, but now she felt she had unsettled him with that story. She decided that she would have to have another talk with Jonathan about it tomorrow, because they couldn't just sweep this conversation under the carpet. He was unnerved, and he needed to deal with the situation rather than just ignore it. She also didn't want him to bring the topic up with Niraj when he came back the next day. That would be a disaster waiting to happen. She had to persuade Jonathan to keep his cool.

15

'I will kill him, I swear it.' Shouted Jonathan in anger as soon as he entered Peter's house, he was in such a rage. Immediately after Peter opened the door, he rushed in and paced around the living room. Peter hurried over, 'oh my god JR, what happened? Did he hurt you?'

'Not physically but he hurt my mum.'

'When, just now?'

'No, it's a long story.'

'Ok wait let me call Misty and Nick to come over then you can explain everything. Plus, it will give you a chance to calm down.'

Jonathan continued to pace, and Peter left him to it. Jonathan's heart was racing, and his head swimming with his mother's words, and he couldn't relax or concentrate. Peter came in the room and shoved a joint of weed in his hand.

'Smoke it, it should calm you.'

He took the joint and had a long drag from it. Peter had been right. After a few minutes, he had become a lot less agitated. He sat down, his heart rate finally returned to normal. When Misty and Nick got in, Misty went quickly

153

over to Jonathan and gave him a hug. 'You look like you've seen a ghost.' Misty said worryingly.

'You should have seen him when he first got in. He looked like crap.' said Peter.

Misty glared at Peter for a second, then Nick said, 'You know what I suggest? I think we should all go over there and kill that bastard!'

'For fuck's sake Nick, do you have to be so stupid? As usual, you're never rational.' Said Misty.

'I'm not stupid, but let's face it, Jonathan has been through the wars. The least we could do is go there and do some serious damage. Peter, where is the weed?'

'This isn't some show, the poor boy is struggling. Can't you see? Peter don't give Nick anything. Let him clear his head. He is talking out of his arse!' Misty said in anger.

'Ooohhh someone's getting all defensive over poor Jonathan! If you really cared about him we should do as I suggested. In my opinion that dad of his needs a few broken bones. You guys are too soft!' Said Nick.

Misty ignored his comments, and she looked over at Jonathan and said, 'so what happened? Last I heard, you were going home to confront your mum and to glean more information from her, so we didn't have to do any more hypnotherapy sessions.'

Jonathan recounted the whole story to them. They all listened politely asking questions in between to clarify what he was saying. Even Nick started paying attention, throwing in the odd question or two. Peter was pacing the room slowly, but when he told them about the week of hell his mum had, his pacing got increasingly quicker. Misty told him to sit down or he would wear a hole in the floor, but he didn't hear her, he was still marching around the living room.

Jonathan continued his story till the end. He told them everything. After he finished, nobody spoke for a while.

'I'm going to fucking kill him if you don't!' Said Nick.

They looked at him, he was at breaking point. He had a violent streak in him they didn't often see, but when he spoke his mind it was obvious.

Misty, being the most level-headed amongst the group, said, 'Are you all fucking mad? We are talking about Jonathan's dad here. You can't kill someone just because he is a fucking asshole of a husband and father. Plus, he has done little wrong since that time. He may still try to change himself. If Jonathan was around nine at the time, then that makes it only five years ago. Didn't your mum say for two or three years he had been good to her?'

'Yes she did, but he has since reverted to being a jerk. I don't think he knows any better. From what I found out, nothing that bad has happened to her since, but I wouldn't put it past him. I won't stand for it now. If he so much as puts a toe out of line I will come down on him like "The Hulk" on steroids!'

Peter said, 'You know what, we need to have a plan. For now nothing can be done but keep an eye on him. We should plan what we can do to help JR if his dad has a mad moment or two.'

Misty looked at Peter in awe, 'wow, so you finally engaged your brain!'

'Don't be a sarcastic bitch, I'm trying to help too.' Peter said becoming defensive.

'Ok, ok I was trying to being funny, but you have a point. What do you think Jonathan?'

'Yes I agree. For all we know one day he might lock us both up! Then what? Or he might try to kill my mum when I am not in. He has started to lose his temper again, and with him not jet-setting around the globe, it's harder for me to be nice to him now I am aware of the full facts.'

'So what do we do, monitor the situation for now? Man, that's just lame. Why can't we go there and sort that bastard out?' Nick asked.

'Yes, we have no choice but to monitor the situation. We can't go around killing or hurting people Nick!' Said Misty.

'Even if he tried anything with JR's mum or JR, what can we do about it? Plus, if we don't do this right, Jonathan's mum may side his dad instead of Jonathan, then we all will be back to square one' Peter was frustrated.

Jonathan looked deflated. He decided that he could tell the police if anything happened this time around or make sure they left his dad. But he wanted to hurt his dad, he wanted to shout at him in public and humiliate him as he had done to his mum.

Misty then said, 'to be honest, for now at least we know about it, it's not like we are in the dark anymore, we will take it as it comes.' She said, trying to reassure Jonathan.

They sat in silence for a while thinking. Jonathan looked at them, he felt terrible about bringing their spirits down with his story, but he was glad he wasn't the only one dealing with his problems. He was pleased they had become united and were happy to decide as a group. What did Misty call them one day? "The Four Musketeers".

Jonathan left Peter's house after a few hours still not wanting to face his mum, he believed he let her down by not being there for her, he didn't tell his friends he felt responsible, because he didn't want to burden them with his concerns. Deciding his depression was coming on he thought he would start his depression tablets soon, he couldn't remember if he had any left over from the last time he took them.

When he got in, his mum was watching TV. She smiled and asked him if he was hungry, but he said he wasn't and wanted to relax in his room.

'If you want to talk over what I told you earlier, I am happy to discuss it at any time.'

'I don't think I can deal with talking about 'him' anymore mum. Dad has fried my brain, he caused my depression, my amnesia, and the headache I have. So, let's forget him for now. Maybe tomorrow, or maybe never!' He then dragged his feet upstairs and into his room.

His mum said nothing nor chased after him. She knew Jonathan could be suffering from 'information overload,' and she wanted to give him time to process it, he would come to her when he was ready.

He didn't know why he couldn't face his mum. He thought about what his friends said, and they were right; there was nothing he could do at present. Being a general jerk didn't qualify them to leave his dad. But yet, Jonathan had such an uneasy feeling of being near Niraj, like an outsider in his own home now knowing the truth, his dad was a volcano waiting to erupt, but he wasn't aware of how dormant or active that volcano had become. He hated keeping his guard up all the time, and for once he realised what his mum had gone through.

Walking on egg shells in your own home wasn't nice. The one good thing his mum had these past few years was the respite of his dad's work. Jonathan knew he didn't want to keep his mum on edge, worrying about him all the time so he would speak to her tonight. It may be difficult to talk about his dad, but it was something that needed to be done. First

Jonathan got clear in his mind what he and his friends thought about his dad.

He sat on his bed, put his head in his hands and decided what his next steps should be. He had to convince his mum to stand up for herself. He had to make her strong, and together they needed to show their joint power of strength to their dad, then he would have to back down. They had to make him walk on eggshells for a change. To make his life so miserable he left instead of them. Personally, he wanted to just smash that vase over his head again. That would be the icing on the cake!

After an hour of thinking, he decided he was ready to talk and went out of his room to find his mother. She was in the kitchen cleaning. She looked up at him and said, 'I knew you would find your way here when you got hungry. Do you want me to warm you up some dinner?'

'Mum, can we talk about dad?'

Janice stopped what she was doing. 'Yes, of course, do you want a cuppa? Then we can talk in peace.'

'Yeah that sounds good, and can I have painkillers, I feel a headache coming on.'

'You can't take a tablet because you think a headache is coming on!' She said alarmingly.

'I have a slight one now, but if I don't take it will get worse, I know it.'

'Fine, ok go and sit on the dining table and I will come over with both soon.'

He did as he was told and soon enough he had a steaming cup of tea in his hands. He knew at last that everything will be ok if they stuck together and solved their issues with a good cuppa!

Janice began, 'so what's on your mind now that you heard what I had to say?'

'Well for one, I wish I could smash that vase on his head again!' He said angrily.

She smiled, 'I expected you were angry but didn't expect that!'

'It's not funny mum.'

'I know, but I imagined it, and it made me smile. He would get a shock of his life if you did that and not to mention a concussion!'

'And secondly,' he continued, 'we have to stick together as a team. He should know I don't think he isn't an angel. I want to treat him like he treated us.'

'We can't just go around hitting him on the head. He has his moments, but I don't think making him suffer is the way to go. I agree we should stick together, when or if a suitable opportunity turns up, we can mention the fact you found out about his past behaviour, but we need to think how to approach the topic gently.'

He opened his mouth to respond, and his mum put up her hand to stop him.

'Before you say anything, and I know you want to say he doesn't deserve gentle treatment, I agree with you, but I have seen him go from behaving normally to going absolutely mad in a matter of seconds. I have seen him manipulate words I have used to explain things, he made them out to be something he could use as a weapon. When he is backed into a corner, it brings out the worst side of him. We need to leave at a drop of a hat if he goes mental, and we need to have ready money stashed somewhere because I know what he is like. Do you think he will open the door for us if I forget my purse? We have to be cleverer than him, as it is he thinks he is the most intelligent person in the world!'

'Ok, I understand we have to play it by ear. When my friends and I were discussing it…'

Janice looked shocked, 'you discussed what your dad did to me with your friends?'

She didn't look pleased, and her eyebrows knitted together thoughtfully. Then she said carefully, 'Can I meet them?'

'I will ask them and see what they say. Anyway, they suggested the same as you, take it one step at a time. I know that too, but I am fed up with dodging him, pretending I know nothing. He could lose it at any time, and god help him I won't just sit back and take it.'

'Maybe we are getting ahead of ourselves. So far, since he has been home, he has been nice most of the time. He is still moody I know that, but it's not unbearable.'

'Hmmm, fine.'

'Ok don't worry about anything for now. Just go to bed, tomorrow will be a good day, I can feel it. How is your headache?'

'Yes, it's gone, I will sleep like a baby.' He said smiling.

Niraj got back the next morning at around six am. Janice heard him come into the bedroom, she pretended to be asleep. He was drunk, she could tell because he was bumping into everything. He wasn't exactly trying to be quiet either. Janice waited until he got into bed and within minutes she heard him snoring. She got up to leave, she couldn't stand sleeping in the same bed as him.

She freshened up and went downstairs to make a brew. She remembered her conversations with Jonathan and got worried about him, because she didn't want him to become involved in her problems with Niraj, she was dealing with it in her own way. After an hour of pottering around the house drinking her tea leisurely on the dining table reading her emails, Janice watered the house plants, then she heard a strange buzzing sound. It came from the living room, when she got close she realised it was Niraj's phone, which he had left on the coffee table when he got home. She couldn't help herself by reading the text notification from someone called SH.

> *'So much fun tonight, so glad you could make it. Jason was not happy you kept winning you should...'*

> *'Anyway let's hook up for coffee. Text me when you're free'*

> *'Goodnight, I'm finally getting into bed, Zzzz. Lol.'*

> *G'night sexy'*

Janice put the phone as she found it and didn't clear the notifications, so she could pretend that she hadn't seen them. So either someone called SH was flirting with Niraj or he was flirting with her, or both. Until that last message saying 'G'night sexy', Janice thought it could have been a male that had texted, but no man would say that to Niraj!

It confused her, after Saroj, she didn't think Niraj would get himself into another affair. Janice thought maybe a huge part of Niraj must have loved Saroj, and she felt like she impeded the two lovers. So, she assumed when Saroj severed ties with Niraj it broke his heart, and he wouldn't have another affair. Now, she wasn't sure. She just had to wait and see.

She remembered when Niraj and Saroj were having an affair, he was always in a good mood with her. He was mainly mean only when he had an argument with Saroj. So, bearing that pattern in mind, maybe the same thing may happen with this 'SH' too. Janice considered confronting him with the messages to see what excuse he came up with. It would make him stop to think about the damage he might cause at home if he continued. But then again, Janice didn't care enough about Niraj to confront him. So, what if he did have an affair with SH, if that happened he would be out of the house more often and be happy to leave Jonathan and her alone. The short-term plan was good, but she wasn't sure about the long-term consequences. She shelved those thoughts for now. Let's see how he reacts when he saw those messages.

Jonathan got up before Niraj, he asked his mum if his dad came back home, and she said yes so, he went silent. The last thing he wanted to do was say something negative his dad would overhear. He had his breakfast speedily and made himself scarce. It was the weekend, so he decided he would go to Peter's house for the day.

After breakfast, he said, 'mum hope you don't mind, but I want to spend most of the day at Peter's house. If you need me, you can call me on my phone. I don't think I want to be around when dad wakes up. I need time to digest this new information and avoid him as much as possible.'

'You can't avoid him forever.'

'Yes, but knowing everything I know, I need time. Surely you can understand that?'

She looked troubled but nodded her head. 'Ok, I'll tell him that you went to the library with your friends.'

Jonathan got ready and went out an hour later. Janice paced the house not being able to concentrate on anything. She was just too worried. She thought if she shared her problems with Niraj to Jonathan it would make the burden less. It didn't, and she now had the added issues with those text messages to deal with. Sometimes she wanted an end to it all.

When Niraj woke up his head hurt. For a moment he thought he was coming down with flu, but then he remembered his night out. He smiled, it was a good night, and Sarah was nice, sexy, and why she came on to him so strongly was beyond him. She knew he was a married man. Despite that, she lavished attention on him, and 'like a fool' he loved every moment. He then felt downhearted when he realised he was stuck with a boring life, wife and inadequate son. 'What the hell did I do to deserve this' he thought.

He then switched his thinking to 'sexy Sarah', how good it would be if he spent a night with her. He smiled at the prospect, getting out of bed so that his head didn't throb anymore.

When he went downstairs Janice was pottering around in the kitchen, he could hear the radio on, noticing his mobile phone on the coffee table, he realised he had been too drunk to put it on the charger, so it was most likely dead. He picked it up, but it still had ten per cent battery remaining. He saw the messages from Sarah, 'SH' because he didn't want to put her name on his phone. He didn't know why he did that. It's not like they did anything wrong, but now seeing those messages, he was glad he had done that. If Janice heard his phone beep, she could have seen the notifications, but luckily for him his phone was still on silent. He read her messages and smiled, Sarah was naughty, and he liked it.

Niraj realised the probability of Janice noticing anything

whilst his phone was on silent was very slim. He walked in the kitchen with his phone in his dressing gown pocket, safely away from Janice. She smiled and said, 'Ah, so at last sleeping beauty awakes!'

'Yeah, my head hurts, so don't talk if you can help it will you love?'

Janice was shocked at his bluntness, but then again, she should accept it. This was his usual tone of voice whenever he wasn't in a mood. He looked at her like she was a servant in the house and said, 'can you make me breakfast and bring it to the couch? I need to relax on something soft. And please tell that son of yours not to make a sound. My head hurts!'

Janice turned away and started on his breakfast saying, 'Our son has left to go to the library. He has gone with his friend, so you don't have to worry about him, I will go out shopping, and you can relax without us.'

'Gone out? So early, Janice you let that boy get away with murder.'

'I don't understand what you're complaining about, you said you wanted peace, and that is ideal for you isn't it?'

'Darling, I think you're getting above your station, aren't you? Sarcasm from you? Really? Surely you don't want to go there with me!' Niraj said with venom in his voice.

She said nothing and continued to make him breakfast. He left banging the kitchen door behind him. He wished he hadn't done that, because his head suddenly felt like it was just punched! 'Damn her' he said under his breath.

Janice couldn't believe it, it was like living with the devil most of the time! She was glad that Jonathan went out, otherwise there could have been a fight between them today, she was sure. Jonathan had more sense than her, why couldn't she learn that Niraj would never change? What was keeping her here now that her son knew the truth? He wasn't a little boy anymore, if she continued to stay, it would cause more damage to Jonathan than if they left. At that moment she decided that leaving him was her best option.

'Wow,' she thought, 'I will leave him, and I am over the moon.' Jonathan would be happy. The instant she decided she would leave Niraj she felt free. Nothing he could ever say would hurt her, and she wanted to run around the house jumping for joy. But she reigned in her jubilation for now. She had tons to do, she needed to find a place to stay, speak to Maisy the owner of the florist to give her more shifts, and her mind was racing. She knew she wouldn't talk to Niraj until the plans were made, or he could make life difficult for them. Janice felt happier than she had ever felt in ages. She knew in her heart the time was now. Within a month or two they would be out of here, and she was so excited.

Wiping the expression off her face, she brought Niraj's breakfast to him. It took all her determination not to drop the hot tea onto him!

Jonathan came home later that day. The house was calm when he got in which was unusual. His mum wasn't in the kitchen or downstairs, and he was reluctant to go into their bedroom. He didn't want to bump into his dad. He went back into the kitchen and texted his mum, 'where are you? Are you ok?'

After a minute Janice replied, 'Yes, I am, are you at home now? Stay away from your dad, he is moody today because his head hurts from a hangover.'

'Great.' he typed with an eye to heaven emoji to show his sarcasm. 'Have you got any food stashed anywhere, I'm starving and when will you be back?'

'It's only five pm, I'm aiming to get dinner on for seven

pm so should be back in an hour. There is ham in the fridge, just make yourself a sandwich until then. I'm at the florist having a chat with Maisy.'

'Ok don't worry about me, where is he?' Jonathan couldn't bring himself to say 'dad' anymore. He hated to call him that after what he found out.

'When I left, he said he was going for an afternoon nap, so I assume he is either sleeping, in the bedroom or watching something on his iPad in bed.'

'Ok, I will see you when you get home. I still want to stay clear of him.'

'See you soon, I love you.'

'Me too.' Jonathan sent the last message and proceeded to make his sandwich. He wanted tea as well, so he filled up the kettle and put it to boil. Just then Niraj walked into the kitchen and looking surprised said, 'Oh Jonathan, I thought you were your mum making all this racket. My head is a lot better than it felt earlier, thank god. What are you doing?'

At first, Jonathan was surprised that his dad stood there, he assumed he could have avoided him today, but that didn't happen. He wanted more time to prepare for an encounter with him, but he now realised that would not be the case. Anyway, it had been better like this, like a plaster being ripped off quickly was best after finding out about his dad's past behaviour.

'I'm starving, so I made a ham sandwich.' Jonathan said.

'I can't eat a thing but are you making tea?'

'Yes.'

'Good lad make me a cuppa and bring it to the living room will you?' Saying that, he left the kitchen abruptly.

Jonathan stood there for a few minutes, not wanting to make anything for his dad but he couldn't say no either, so he grudgingly made it. When he took it to Niraj he didn't get thanked for it, Niraj just grunted an acceptance of the tea.

He went to the dining table, ate his sandwich and then took his tea up to his room. His dad said nothing more to him.

Dinner became a calm but strained affair. Janice tried to lighten the mood by saying she saw their neighbour, Mr Rawling, sneaking into the house at seven am hoping his wife wouldn't find out he had been out drinking, but he was making such a racket he fell over the bins and made a loud noise! Then his wife came out and shouted at him. She giggled about the incident because Mr and Mrs Rawling were a sensible, young couple that had only moved in a few years ago. That behaviour was so unlike Mr Rawling that she thought it was hilarious.

Jonathan smiled and said, 'They are nice from what I have seen.'

Niraj sneered, 'that's the trouble with you Janice, you make fun of everyone. He is a nice man, you made him out to be an alcoholic. Poor guy, I bet his wife is understanding, not like you! You can't help yourself, can you? Putting people down when they are just having a laugh and letting their hair down.'

Jonathan said with a huge grin, 'first, he has little or no hair and second of all, he put himself down when he fell!'

Both tried to stifle a laugh, because Niraj was glaring at them. He wasn't happy that they didn't take him seriously either. He then said, 'look at the pair of you, no better than a bunch of kids. I don't see what's funny!'

They tried to stop laughing, and Janice brought up the weather with a smile on her face that was still there from laughing at Mr Rawling falling over the bins. Niraj couldn't stand the fact that they didn't get intimidated by his rant earlier. He said he had enough, he would get an early night and didn't want to be disturbed. 'Janice could you please sleep in the spare bedroom tonight. I don't want you snoring like a stuck pig when I am trying to relax! Night, jokers.' He said sarcastically and left the table.

When Niraj had gone upstairs, Jonathan sensing his mum's embarrassment said, "like a stuck pig, night jokers" trying to mimic his dad's voice and looked at his mum with a grin on his face then they both giggled again.

Niraj went into his room and heard them laugh just as he closed the door. He was scowling but then he had bigger fish to fry. He wanted space from Janice, so he could text Sarah, and the last thing he wanted was for Janice to find him texting in bed. Niraj contacted Sarah who replied immediately. She suggested they talk on the phone, but he said he couldn't because he didn't want his family to hear him. They texted for ages after an hour the text messages got sexual. Sarah wanted to know what he did and didn't like in bed, and she told him what her fantasies were. She then asked if he had ever stepped out of his marriage with another woman, and he said he was always faithful to his wife. Sarah asked why he was being so open and flirtatious with her, was he considering doing something more?

Niraj thought for a while and said, yes, he was, he said his marriage had lost the spark it once had, and he wanted to have fun. Sarah agreed that she wanted to have fun too.

Niraj was getting excited at the prospect of sleeping with Sarah, she was young, beautiful and open to trying new things, and best of all she wasn't looking to have a long-term relationship unlike Saroj. 'Ideal' he thought.

ONE MONTH AGO

16

Over the next few days Janice and Jonathan kept a low profile. After the weekend Jonathan went back to school as usual, Janice got busy planning her exit from her marriage and from their home.

Jonathan also spent more time at school and Peter's house with his three friends than he did before. They didn't waste a lot of time talking about Jonathan's dad, which helped him forget what he was really like. When Jonathan got home, he ate his dinner with the family in silence answering only questions when required, then he went to his room. Sometimes Peter climbed into his bedroom from the window, and they smoked weed and just generally hung out. Peter was always trying to find out what Jonathan's feelings for Misty were. Jonathan said although he liked her he would be too shy to instigate anything. He also told Peter that he felt like something was not right with her, but he couldn't put his finger on it. Peter agreed that she was a bit blunt when she spoke, but he couldn't see anything wrong in that.

Peter said, 'so have you ever…. you know…?'

'Ever what?' Jonathan looked puzzled.

'You know… been with a girl?' Peter said with a grin on his face.

'Oh that, erm… not really.' he said shyly. 'Have you?'

'Oh yeah, tons.' Said Peter confidently.

'Like I can believe that!'

'Seriously, I have, but not with your precious Misty.'

'She isn't my precious Misty, and I don't believe you. Tons? Maybe in your dreams.'

'Believe what you like.' Peter said nonchalantly.

'Anyway, it's eleven pm, you better go in case someone finds you in here.'

'Ok fine, I know when I'm not wanted, He gave Jonathan a wink and opened the window to go out. 'See you tomorrow, you baby.'

'Yeah, whatever!' Jonathan said looking out the window watching Peter leave. He closed the window and got ready for bed.

A few weeks later Janice texted Jonathan to tell him to come home early that day, she wanted to talk to him about something. She said his dad was going out with some friends for drinks and wouldn't be back till late. This Friday evening Jonathan planned to spend time alone with Misty. He asked Peter and Nick to make themselves scarce for an hour that evening, he considered telling his mum to wait, but he felt bad doing that, because she rarely asked him for much.

He texted Peter and told him he had been summoned home after school and couldn't come over that evening and asked, 'can we still keep the original plan but change the day?'

Peter replied almost immediately as if he knew Jonathan what would text. 'Sure, no worries. I will tell Nick. Have a good chat with your mum. See you tomorrow.'

When Jonathan got home, he could hear his mum singing

to some music in the kitchen whilst she cooked. He felt glad that whatever she needed to discuss wasn't something worrying, because she sounded happy.

When they finished their dinner, he helped her tidy up the table and sort out the dishes. They sat on the couch, and she said, 'I got good news for you.'

'What?' he asked excitedly.

'That weekend when your dad went out to play poker a few weeks ago I decided we would leave your dad for sure this time.' She paused to see what impact that statement had on him.

'Oh my god, really?'

'Yes, and I was so happy about my decision. How do you feel?'

'Wow cool, but are you sure we can afford to?'

'Well I have spoken to Maisy at the florist, and she agreed to take me back full time. And I have been saving some money in one of my private bank accounts since you were a baby. So yes, I think we can. I will use some of that for a deposit on a flat, and we can move in, how about that?'

Jonathan and his mum hugged each other excitedly.

'Man, he will be so pissed! I assume you haven't told him anything yet?'

'I have told no one except Maisy and now you. With my job, I will have enough money for the flat deposit, and enough to cover any ad hoc expenses, so I think this pretty much seals the deal. All I needed was your go ahead, and now that I have it I will tell your dad.'

'When?'

'This weekend I think but not till Sunday. He will have a hangover for sure tomorrow so it won't be ideal. I have looked at a flat that I know you will like and have put a deposit on it, I can pick up the keys on Monday. However, if things get bad when I tell him, the estate agent told me they are open over the weekend, if I want to, I can come to their office and get the keys. They are doing a small paint job in the flat this weekend otherwise I could have had the key's already.'

'So I need to pack?'

'Well, yes you will need to, I kept some boxes for you in your room. Start as soon as you can but keep the boxes hidden for now. I don't want him to know before I get the chance to tell him myself.

'Great, I can't wait to tell Peter and the others.' He said excitedly.

Janice smiled at him, and he left her to go upstairs to pack. She got a text message from Niraj saying he might be drinking and would stay at Frank's place tonight. Frank had been a school friend that Niraj still saw regularly. They always held poker nights at his house. So, Janice decided to take some of Jonathan's packed boxes to Maisy's house tomorrow morning. 'Perfect' she thought. She texted Niraj back to say that was fine, and they would have a quiet night in.

Janice told Maisy almost everything about her marriage to Niraj. She asked Maisy for some storage space to remove things that were hers from the house and to keep it at the shop. Maisy was more understanding than Janice expected and told Janice that she had a spare bedroom in her house. Janice could keep things in there till she moved out. Janice was over the moon.

Maisy owned the florist for over twenty years, and she kept Janice on, giving her breaks whenever Niraj came back home or made a fuss of Janice working there. Maisy liked her and treated her like a daughter she never had. She loved how hard she worked, not to mention how good she was with the customers. Maisy also didn't want to lose Janice as an employee just because she had a bastard for a husband! Maisy became secretly glad that she decided to leave her husband, but she didn't say that to her directly. That is why she was happy to do anything she could for her.

Janice now looked around the room for things that she needed to take over to Maisy. She already removed her passport, jewellery, photo albums, especially of Jonathan when he was younger. She cherished them, they would be no good to Niraj she thought. He always claimed Jonathan wasn't his son, sometimes she wished that too!

Niraj didn't come back in the morning as expected. Jonathan continued to pack boxes, and Janice went in and out of the house taking Jonathan's things along with hers to Maisy's house. Janice's Fiat 500 was a great little run around for her, especially whilst she went back and forth to Maisy's house which was a fifteen minute drive.

They were both exhausted by the end of the morning. They took as much as they could without the house looking like it was missing things. Janice wanted none of the expensive gadgets or furniture. But she took most of her clothes and all of her heirloom jewellery that once belonged to her mother.

Niraj got back in the afternoon looking surprisingly rested and not grumpy or hung over at all. He said a cheery, 'Hey you two, hope you had a fun evening without me. I need a long shower. Janice, you don't need the bathroom, do you?'

'Hey back to you too, how was last night? Did you win anything, and no I don't need it.'

'I didn't really win, but it was a good night, not as much drinking as I did last time. I decided not to drink much. The last time I got excessively drunk, and it took too long for the hangover to clear. I can't get rid of a hangover like I used to in the past.' He had a wry smile climbing the stairs as he said the last sentence.

Jonathan was also sitting in the living room with his mum smiled and raised his hand as if to say 'hi' and continued looking at his phone. He was glad that it would only be a matter of time before he didn't have to see his dad anymore.

Jonathan then told his mum he would go over to Peter's house and be back for dinner. She warned him not to be late, and shortly after collecting his headphones and jacket, he left.

Niraj went to their bedroom and closed the door with a sigh of relief, 'got away with it' he thought. He spent the night with Sarah, and it was a brilliant night. Sarah was everything Janice and Saroj were not, adventurous, flirty, naughty and full of life. He wanted to be with her for the whole day today as well. He reluctantly left her in bed. They had a night of dinner, passion, laughs, wine, sleep, more passion, breakfast, a shower and then he left. Sarah looked so beautiful lying in bed he had to have her one more time before he left for home. She was too tempting, and the prospects of spending more time with her excited him.

Niraj thought back about how his night with Sarah came about. Frank had been the encouragement Niraj needed, because he was hesitant to start anything with Sarah. Frank reminded him how boring his life was with Janice, and that he hated to see his friend waste away his life like that.

Niraj agreed, 'yeah but look how things with Saroj turned out!'

'But Saroj wanted more than you could give her. Plus, she thought threatening to get married would get you to leave Janice. She had balls that one!'

Niraj froze, 'Threatened? What did you mean?'

'Oh nothing, forget her, so now what do you say about Sarah?'

'Hang on a minute, she didn't get married?'

'Niraj man, forget it.'

'Frank, for fuck's sake I have known you almost all my life, and if you can't tell me the truth then who the hell can? There is no point in having friends if they hide things from you.' Niraj became annoyed.

'Oh god' Frank said looking up to the ceiling not wanting to answer, he said, 'okay, she didn't get married from what I last heard.'

'But she told me all about this guy she met who was loaded, handsome and how he was so in love with her.'

'Yeah that, I think it was a big fat lie.'

'A lie? Then why didn't you tell me if you knew the truth?'

'Because by the time I found out six months passed since we had spoken. I asked you if you heard from Saroj and you said you hadn't spoken to her in months. So, I didn't want to rock the boat. I realised it took ages for you to get over her, and I didn't want you to associate yourself with her knowing she would go that far to lie to all of us.'

'But that was my decision to make not yours.' Niraj said with a burst of anger.

'I know you would have done the same if the tables were turned, so I said nothing.' Frank looked at Niraj, hoping their friendship hadn't been affected by this turn of event. Luckily for Frank, Niraj agreed with him.

'I guess if she couldn't be honest with me, what was the point in being with her? I don't appreciate that she tried to force my hand that was very unscrupulous. She will never realise how much strife she caused me. Those months were a nightmare. Janice and I had the worst time in our marriage after Saroj left.' Not revealing that because he was miserable, he made Janice's life difficult.

Niraj knew what he had done to Janice, it wasn't nice, but he didn't care then or now. If he pursued something with Sarah, Janice would just have to deal with it. In Niraj's eyes, Janice was living a comfortable life, hardly having to work. She had him as her husband! Every time he went out and women made a pass at him, he reminded himself how lucky she was. And at home, most times she blanked him. In bed sleeping with her was like sleeping with a silicone doll!

'Fuck it, I will go out with Sarah. You're right Frank.' Niraj said with a ton of enthusiasm. 'I have wasted time with that bitch Saroj, she broke my heart you know. Now I got a lifeless Janice. Fuck it, I need some excitement!' He said laughing.

'"Fuck it" is the right word to use! I am always right, and the sooner you learn that, the better!' Frank said laughing clapping Niraj on the back. 'Good lad now go call her. See what she says, and I will cover for you on the night she is free.'

Niraj didn't waste time dialling her number.

Now back in his room he recalled that conversation with Frank and was glad his friend had his back. Niraj then remembered he had to ring Frank who agreed to be his cover for last night. Frank picked up within two rings.

'What the hell Niraj, why did you take so long to call? I was about to ring Sarah to find out if everything was ok. I am worried Janice found out something.'

Niraj whispered, 'no everything went well. Thanks for covering for me but I'm home now and can't talk. I rang to say if anyone asks, I left yours at one thirty ok?'

'Yeah, ok call me later to tell me all the deets.'

'Fine, see ya. Oh, and Frank,' Niraj whispered, 'she was one hell of a lay. Man, it was good.' He said laughing.

'You dirty dog, don't forget to call me when the coast is clear.'

'Cool, speak to you either later or tomorrow.'

Niraj put down the phone still feeling amazing, he got in the shower a happy man.

Downstairs Janice paced the floor, she wondered how to bring up the subject of leaving him. She knew Niraj was in a good mood. He wasn't hung over like the last time, which was great, but she needed to sort out dinner, then maybe tell him first thing in the morning when Jonathan was still in his bedroom.

Dinner was simply spaghetti Bolognese with extra grated cheese for Niraj and Jonathan. Both of them liked a lot of cheese on top. She had made the sauce earlier, all she had to do when Jonathan came home, was make the spaghetti. Niraj had been downstairs watching TV waiting for Jonathan so he could eat.

Janice served dinner in her usual calm manner, she thought, this could be the last dinner we would have together as a family. She wasn't sad about it in fact, she was secretly happy. She wanted to smile but tried not to, she wanted dinner to be out of the way so she could get on with her life, without Niraj. Over the last month, the more she thought about leaving him, the more excited she got. She felt like she could breathe again. And it would be amazing, she just knew it.

Jonathan finished first and said he had homework to do, could they excuse him? His dad gave him a glare and nodded. Janice smiled, and taking this as a confirmation from his mum, he went upstairs.

When he got to his bedroom, he softly closed the door behind him and went to his window to check if Peter, Misty, and Nick were outside. They planned to have a few bottles of cider tonight. Jonathan went to the shop and bought some with his pocket money for them earlier. He wrapped them well with free newspaper he got at the newsagent, so they didn't clink together in his backpack. Jonathan warned Peter that they would have to keep it quiet, as his parents were at home, they promised they would. He put on some music, but not too loud, or his dad would come up and complain.

After ten minutes they still hadn't arrived, Jonathan wondered what was causing the delay, but just then, Peter gently opened the unlocked window and jumped in. Next in was Misty and then Nick.

'At bloody last, I would have sent out a search party.' Said Jonathan.

'Calm down JR we are here, and so is your precious Misty.' Peter said smiling.

'Fuck off!' Jonathan replied laughing.

Misty rolled her eyes and said to Nick, 'boys will be boys!'

'Come on then, don't keep us waiting. Where is the cider you promised?' Nick said scanning the room.

Jonathan fished the bottles from his bag and gave them all a bottle each, they passed the opener around and opened all the bottles.

'Cheers JR' said Peter. 'This is possibly the last time we get together in this bedroom. Next week you might be in your new place.'

'God hopefully.' Said Jonathan. 'Cheers everyone.'

They clinked their bottles and Jonathan said, 'Ssshhh not so loud!' They all giggled quietly.

17

Meanwhile, downstairs Janice cleared up the table and then cleaned the kitchen. Niraj watched TV and drank more than he usually did. He had gotten over the high he had felt being with Sarah; he thought about Saroj. 'That fucking dirty little bitch', she lied to him, then tried to force his hand. She made his life miserable. The more he thought about it, the angrier he got. He hated anyone lying to him. Especially women, they were all the same, 'fucking users'. He couldn't believe he fell for her. He wanted to leave Janice for her! Then his thoughts wandered off to Janice, his dutiful, foolish, snivelling wife. He wished he hadn't ever set eyes on Janice. Where would she be without him? He was feeling used, and he didn't like that at all.

The day he went to that florist to buy flowers for Natalie. He remembered how pretty Natalie was, if he could only have convinced her he was better than her pathetic boyfriend, things would have been different. But it wasn't to be, and Janice was the next thing he moved on to, so that he could get his mind off beautiful Natalie and that Indian village woman his parents wanted him to marry. Why didn't he sleep with Janice and leave her? Why did he have to marry her? His family would still have been talking to him if he had said no to that village girl and not married Janice! And look at her now, pottering around his house. She would be nothing without him he thought. He poured another large measure of whisky and downed that neat. It burned his throat, but he felt he needed it to calm his nerves. He then poured another, this time adding Coca-Cola.

Janice had finished clearing up and started shaking, the more she thought about telling Niraj they would leave him, the more scared she got. She knew if Niraj suggested a separation her she would have to deal with it, but he hated her taking control and deciding for them. He wouldn't be happy.

When she decided she couldn't hide in the kitchen anymore, she came into the living room and sat at the opposite end of the three-seater couch. Slyly looking at him from the corner of her eyes, he was drinking his favourite, 'whisky and coke'.

He then said, 'can you hear him upstairs?'

Janice couldn't because the TV was on so loud, but then she heard the music on and Jonathan laugh. She smiled and said, 'he is probably watching something on his phone.'

'Do you think that's all he is doing?'

'What else could he be doing?'

'No point discussing it, you will only take his side.' Niraj said becoming grumpy.

'What do you mean?'

'You know there is something wrong with him and you happily hide it.'

She got angry, she hated it when Niraj was mean to their son. She could deal with him being horrible to her but not to her precious Jonathan.

'Just be careful what you say Niraj.'

He looked sharply at her. 'And what? What will you do? Stomp around the room cleaning?' He said laughing at her.

She said nothing. Niraj was a jerk when he drank whisky. The silence between them got awkward. It was only eight pm and too early for her to go to bed, so she sat there not really watching what was on TV. Her mind had wandered off to what she would do when she was all alone in her new apartment. It wasn't large, but it would be well decorated and peaceful.

Niraj suddenly said, 'you really know how to ruin the mood don't you?'

Janice was gobsmacked, she couldn't understand what she had done wrong now.

'So, you're just going to sit there and say nothing?' He demanded.

'I don't know what you are talking about.'

'You are sighing and looking uncomfortable at being in my presence. Hell, if you want to go upstairs, or go out with your friends, go do that and stop sitting around like a mannequin.'

'Don't you want me here? If you don't, say so, you don't have to be rude.'

'Ooohh she has a voice!' Niraj said mocking her. 'But hang on a minute, you can't go out with your friends, because you haven't got any, have you?'

Janice didn't respond to that comment, but she was getting angry.

At the same time, Niraj was getting annoyed by Janice's presence. He wanted to either spend the evening with Sarah or alone. And here she was, sitting there like the grim reaper! He was fed up with her, and he decided to piss her off a bit tonight, till she went upstairs and left him alone.

'So, can't you defend yourself?' He said still trying to harass her.

'Niraj why do you have to behave this way?'

'What way? I am asking you a simple question.'

'I can tell you are trying to provoke me into an argument I don't want to have, particularly tonight.'

'Oh really? And what's so special about tonight?'

'Nothing.'

'You can tell your darling husband, can't you?' He said coming closer to her so he could whisper in her ear.

She turned her head to the other side.

'I knew it, you can't stand me, can you? My precious mute little Janice!'

'Don't talk rubbish, maybe you have had too much to drink.'

'You know what my problem is apart from you? I haven't had enough to drink!' He said laughing loudly.

She realised the evening would take a downward spiral if she didn't leave now, so she got up to go.

'Hey, where do you think you're going?' Niraj blurted restraining her arm. 'I didn't tell you to leave yet, did I?'

'Niraj let go of my arm for god's sake.'

He yanked her arm hard, so she fell onto the couch. Then he said menacingly in her ear, 'You go when I tell you to go.'

Janice could smell the whisky on his breath. She didn't understand what happened. He usually drank a lot more before he became this bad.

'Please, you're hurting my arm.'

He let go of her arm and with venom in his voice he said, 'you're a thick bitch, you will be a thick bitch forever! God knows what I did to deserve you.' Saying that he moved over to his side of the couch again.

Janice couldn't stop herself and said, 'you don't have to

worry about me anymore. Jonathan and I will leave you in peace soon.' As soon as she said that she regretted it. This was the worst time to say such a thing to him.

His head snapped over to her, 'what the fuck are you talking about?'

'Nothing.' Janice said hoping he hadn't heard her.

'You and Jonathan are leaving me? Is that what I heard?'

Janice said nothing.

Niraj was on her within seconds, he grabbed her by the collar of her top and said, 'Did you just say you were leaving me?'

With courage she didn't know she had she spat in his face, 'yes you fucking asshole, we are both going to leave you, and the sooner the better.'

He was so shocked he dropped his hands and stood up towering over her, he said nothing for a whole minute. His mind started racing. Janice couldn't leave him, it would disgrace him. His friends and family would think he was weak, and once his parents eventually found out his 'white' wife had left him, and they would have been right all along. Not to mention what Sarah would think.

'Over my dead body, you bitch. After all I have done for you, you think you can just pick up sticks and leave? I will lock you up in the room like I did before if you don't take that foolish idea out of your head. You remember what happened last time? Don't make me go there.' He shouted.

'Keep your voice down, Jonathan is upstairs.'

'I don't give a fuck if he hears me, he probably talked you into this didn't he?'

'Jonathan doesn't know about this, so don't bring him into our problems.'

'If you think you can leave me you got another think coming!'

Janice said defiantly, 'I will leave you. I have decided, and you will never make me change my mind, so you can go to hell.' With that she stood up to leave.

He came over in a flash, grabbed her by her hair and dragged her back on to the couch, 'you fucking bitch, you are fucking going nowhere, you hear me?'

He was still holding her hair tightly, she struggled to get out of his hold, but it hurt her head too much. 'Niraj stop.' She screamed.

'Not till you tell me you were a silly little girl, come on now say it. "You were just joking" weren't you?'

'No, I wasn't, I hate you and we are going to leave you, asshole!' she screamed at him. 'Now let me go!'

He stared at her with bulging eyes and slapped her hard on her face.

She cried. He slapped her again. He wanted to hurt her, to see her suffer. How dare she disrespect him in his own home he thought.

Still pinning her down he said, 'oh so now you're going to cry? Bit late isn't it?'

Through her tears, she said, 'Niraj, Jonathan is upstairs. Please let me go.'

'Go where bitch?'

'I just want to go upstairs to bed.'

'Oh, to our marital bed?'

'Niraj please, if Jonathan finds out what you are doing he will get angry.'

He laughed at her, 'Jonathan will get angry, and what can he do?'

'Please, let me go, this marriage isn't working for either of us. If you're worried about what your friends and family will think then just tell them, you threw me out of the house.'

'Oh, I will not tell them that, because you aren't leaving.'

'I don't love you.'

'I know that, and I don't give a fuck about you either, but you aren't going anywhere. Plus, you have nowhere to go.'

Janice wanted to tell him about the apartment, but she wasn't sure if she should. She couldn't think straight. He still held on to her hair and sat on top of her on the couch staring at her face. She was completely pinned down.

'Ok fine I won't leave, but you have to get off me, I want to go to bed.'

Niraj released her hair and still sitting on her, staring at her said with a smile, 'now that's a good decision, who will help me with my cooking, cleaning, and laundry if you left, eh? You are good for some things, I should let you know how useful you are now and again. Hopefully, that will stop these silly little ideas you get in your head won't it?'

Janice nodded. He got off her and stood over her. She was terrified he would hit her again, so she got up quickly and went to the dining room to look at herself in the mirror over the fireplace. The last thing she wanted was for Jonathan to find out what happened tonight. Looking at her reflection she wanted to cry. Her hair looked a mess, and both her cheeks were red. She hastily wiped her tears from her cheeks and smoothed over her hair. She thought her best option was to run to the spare bedroom and stay there. She knew he wouldn't bother her in that room.

Suddenly, from the reflection in the mirror, she saw Niraj behind her, he came right next to her back and stared at her in the mirror with an odd smile on his face. 'There now, you look decent again. Remember never to think such thoughts again, do you understand me?'

She nodded.

'If anyone has reason to leave this marriage I do, but

where you get these silly little ideas about leaving is beyond me.' He said snarling at her.

She said nothing, not wanting to provoke him again.

'So you don't love me eh? This is all a charade?'

'Niraj please.'

'So why don't you love me? You have everything a woman can have, a beautiful house, a child, a handsome husband that all the girls still want a piece of. So many things, yet you pretended to love me! So when did you stop, my love?'

Janice stood there stock still. He whispered everything right in her ear, hovering so close behind her. She could feel his breath at the back of her neck and could smell the whisky.

'When did you stop, bitch?' He screamed.

Janice jumped at the sound of his voice so close to her ear and cried automatically.

'Niraj please don't.'

He whispered again, 'so when?'

Fearing he would shout again, she said, 'just recently.'

'How recently? Last week, last month, last six months? How long?'

'A few months I guess.'

'A few months?' Niraj said raising his eyebrows. 'And you played the good, dutiful, loving wife since then? Oh, I see.'

Janice stepped aside and walked around the dining table to get away from him but sensing her movements Niraj grabbed her shoulders, keeping her still, then he said, 'not so fast mon chéri.' He repeated her words back to her in a whisper, 'a few months, eh? You are quite the crafty woman, aren't you? I think you would make a good actress. Forget about the florist and go on stage. Who knows, you could win an Oscar someday with those acting skills.' He said smiling at her.

He was scaring her, she wanted to escape but, he continued, 'My foolish little Janice, having wild thoughts about leaving. What fantasies, why you could even go on to write a book with an imagination like yours!'

He turned her around to face him and with one hand grabbed her jaw and squeezing it tight, so her lips were puckered. He whispered, 'look at that face, pretending to be all innocent but we know you aren't, are you? You are just like the rest of them, crafty little bitches, the lot of you!'

Janice tried to pull his hands off from her face, but he didn't like that. With the other hand he grabbed her hair and smashed her head hard on the mirror behind her. She tried to scream in pain, but he held on to her jaw. Tears were streaming down her face.

'Now now, don't wriggle away from me when I am talking. When will you learn this is my domain? What I say goes, you got it? I am the king of this house, and you will do as I say, bitch.' Then nearly touching her lips with his, he continued whispering to her, 'I hate you, you whore. You have ruined my life.'

Janice turned away from his breath, but he was still holding on to her jaw, he turned her face towards him. 'You will never leave me because if you do, I will hunt you down like an animal and kill you, you're a worthless piece of shit!'

Janice was now terrified of him, he was angry enough to kill her. She could see from his eyes he meant it. She didn't know what to do now. How could she and Jonathan get away from him, could they go somewhere that he would never find them? Her mind was racing, time had stopped, and every moment she took a breath in, she felt like an age had passed. Her mind wandered to Jonathan and hoped that he wouldn't come downstairs to see his dad like this. There would be an almighty fight between them.

Niraj then released her jaw and slapped her face again. 'Filthy bitch' he said and left her there as he walked to the living room to take a sip of his drink. Janice ran to the kitchen, when she got there her legs couldn't hold her up anymore, they felt like jelly, so she sank onto the floor and sobbed silently. She didn't want Jonathan to know anything. She couldn't understand what made Niraj change, one minute he was ok, and suddenly he switched. She picked herself up and tried to get to the bedroom without antagonising him any-more. Just as she got up from the floor and wiped her face with a kitchen towel, he came into the kitchen and looked at her with a grin. She looked away quickly and tried to walk past him, but he blocked the exit from the kitchen.

She said, 'I'm going up to bed.'

'Did I say you can go up to bed?'

Janice didn't answer.

'I'm talking to you bitch.'

'No, you didn't say I could go.' She said under her breath.

'What was that? I heard nothing.'

She said it once again a bit louder this time. He smiled as if he liked this cat-and-mouse game he was playing with her. He then stood there looking her up and down for a few seconds then said, 'plain Jane aren't you my pathetic little wife? Poor thing, you should try to make an effort now and again. Then maybe I could take you out a bit more. For now, I will continue to make excuses for you and go out with my friends by myself. Who wants to show someone like you off?'

'And meet girls like SH? Don't think I don't' know about that!' Janice said, gathering every ounce of spite and courage that she didn't think she had. But she regretted saying it almost immediately. She wanted to kick herself, she forgot about Jonathan for a second and just wanted him to stop harassing her. She wanted him to know she knew about the skeletons he had in his closet.

'What the fuck are you talking about bitch?' He was on her like a shot. He grabbed her by her hair again and stared at her thinking, 'how the fuck did she find out about Sarah? She couldn't know much because she would have said Sarah and not SH. Then all the pieces fell into place. Janice must have read the text messages from Sarah that day he came back drunk from his poker night at Frank's house. She must have been planning her get away since then, she was going nowhere, he would make sure of that.

'What the fuck did you say?' He screamed at her.

She found some courage to yank herself away from him and run to the other corner of the kitchen, but he raced behind her yelling, 'Come back here you whore!'

'I hate you, and I am going to fucking leave you. Do you think I wouldn't find out about your extramarital affairs? You are a dirty bastard, you will never find us or see Jonathan or me ever again after tonight you vile monster.'

Hearing that he saw red, he grabbed a pan from the draining board and threw it at her. She ducked, and it bounced off the wall landing on the floor with a loud crash. He took another item, this time a glass and threw it at her again missing her, it crashed and broke apart as it hit the floor. Glass went everywhere, Janice tried to run away again, but he caught up with her.

Upstairs, Jonathan hearing a noise switched his music off and told everyone, 'ssshhh listen did you hear that?'

They all quieted down whilst they all listened. Jonathan heard his dad's raised voice and knew his parents were arguing. He said, 'Oh my god he is fighting with her, I need to stop him.'

'We are coming too.' said Peter.

'Whatever.' Jonathan said not caring if they came or not. Right now, he needed to get to his mum.

Jonathan ran into the living room with the rest of his friends following him. He then heard the noise coming from the kitchen. He ran into the kitchen, and to his horror he saw his dad on the floor on top of his mum strangling her. His mum wasn't really fighting back.

Peter, Misty and Nick were right behind him. Misty screamed, 'oh my god, he is killing her.'

Jonathan ran over to his dad and tried to pull him off, but Niraj was much stronger. Jonathan's efforts did not stop him. Jonathan looked at his friends. Peter shouted, 'get the frying pan from the floor JR and hit him over the head with it. Hurry JR hit him. Hit him quickly. He is killing her.'

Jonathan picked up the pan and swung it at his dad's head. His dad saw him from the corner of his eye and moved. The pan came down on his shoulder hitting him hard enough for him to stop strangling Janice. The pan flew off and went clanging to the other side.

Niraj left Janice and stood up quickly, stopping Jonathan from grabbing the pan again. Misty was screaming, 'he has killed her. Oh god, your mum is dead!'

Jonathan didn't hear her clearly, his dad pushed him, so he flew onto a cabinet. Jonathan said crying and screaming at the same time, 'have killed her! You killed my mum! I will kill you!'

Niraj just laughed at him, 'you and whose army? You are a joker just like your fucking mum! I am glad I killed her, she was nothing but a bitch and a whore. The sooner you realise that, the better!'

Jonathan couldn't believe his dad had just killed his mum and was laughing. Jonathan was crying and trying to get past his dad to see if they could revive his mum, but he was pushed by Niraj who said, 'let her be, she deserved everything she got.'

Nick was shouting at Jonathan, 'Kill him, Jonathan! We should have killed him a long time ago!'

Misty was sobbing next to his mum.

Peter standing next to Misty, then said, 'Finish him off JR, get a knife from the knife block. A life for a life.'

Niraj was laughing at Jonathan who was confused by the whole scene, it felt surreal. His mum was just lying there, lifeless!

Niraj said, 'you're a coward just like your mum.'

'Kill him, kill him, kill him.' Is all Jonathan could hear his friends yelling at him. He was getting increasingly upset, he wanted to die and be with his mum, but not before he took care of his dad first. His dad couldn't get away with this, not again!

'We will kill you!' Jonathan screamed defiantly.

'We?'

'Yeah, my friends and I, you bastard.'

'What, are you going to ring them? Hang on let me get my phone for you. You can use mine, don't worry!' Niraj said laughing at Jonathan.

Jonathan was confused, he could hear Peter shouting, 'Come here, get the knife.'

Jonathan moved at lightning speed to the knife block near Peter and pulled off the biggest knife then turned around to face his dad.

Niraj laughed at him, 'you think you can kill me? You pathetic, stupid boy!'

The others were shouting at Jonathan, 'kill him, finish him off. He killed your mum.'

Jonathan ran over to his dad with the knife, but his dad didn't move. He was still laughing at Jonathan, like he knew Jonathan couldn't go ahead with his threat. Jonathan got close and with the despair of his mum, the shouting in his ear from all his friends saying, 'kill him, kill him, kill him' he stabbed his dad shouting at the top of his voice I hate you!'

At that moment Niraj was stunned, Jonathan actually did it. Niraj's next thought was a mixture of confusion and disbelief. It wiped his smile off his face, Jonathan felt a sigh of relief. He did it, he avenged his mother. He hated his dad, he pulled out the knife and stabbed his dad again and again. His dad fell to the floor staring at Jonathan in the eye, and Jonathan had a huge smirk on his face as he let his dad fall.

After a few seconds, all Jonathan could hear was a tremendous silence, his friends were quiet. There was peace at last. Then he cried for his mum, he was weeping for his losses, and the mess this had all turned out to be. He was devastated she had gone. His life would never be the same again. Without her he didn't want to live anymore.

PRESENT DAY

18

Jonathan entered the interview room led by Barry, he looked nervous when he saw it was not just Dr Rao in the room. He did not expect to be interviewed by someone else too.

Dr Rao smiled at him saying, 'Good Morning Jonathan. I trust you slept well. Please take a seat.' Then addressing Barry, he said, 'Thank you, Barry, I will call you when Jonathan is ready to be escorted back to his room.'

Barry nodded and then winked at Jonathan who stared at Barry wishing he didn't have to leave. Barry said, 'Ok doctor, call me if you need me.'

When Barry left the room Jonathan looked at both men and wondered who the other man was. Dr Rao noticing Jonathan's confusion said, 'Jonathan I want to introduce you to Detective Superintendent Brown who knows about your case and would also like to interview you today. Is that ok with you?'

'I don't have a choice, do I?'

'It will be easier if you get interviewed by both of us because we can get to the answers we need much quicker.'

'Fine, but bringing in a detective, what did I do to deserve that?' Jonathan said with sarcasm in his voice.

The detective got fed up with this purposeless banter and intervened. 'Hi Jonathan, I am Detective Superintendent Brown, and I'm in charge of your case. After speaking to Dr Rao yesterday, he has informed me that you are suffering from a temporary loss of memory. This could be due to the trauma you have recently been through. Since meeting the doctor yesterday, do you remember anything of what led you to this hospital?

'Not really.'

Dr Rao took over. 'Jonathan, can you remember if you have ever suffered a loss of memory growing up?'

Jonathan looked uneasy and shuffled in his chair. He knew he had but wasn't sure if he should tell these two anything till his mum got here. He decided that Dr Rao was nice, and if anyone could help him tap into his memory, it was him.

'Yes, I suffered from several growing up.'

Dr Rao continued his questioning, 'and these bouts of amnesia, did they occur in times of stress or occasionally?'

'All I know is, every time I got amnesia my dad was involved!'

'On how many occasions did that happen?'

'I can't remember. At least four.'

'Can you describe one of those occasions?'

'Doctor, do I have to go into it? I find this very stressful.'

'I am sorry Jonathan, and I realise this can be upsetting, to make it easier can you recall one occasion.'

Jonathan didn't really want to say anything. His mum was a private person, opining up to them about his dad being a dick was the last thing he wanted to do. He felt comfortable talking to Dr Rao, though, so he told them about the first incident that Misty helped him recall. How his dad threatened him when he saw his dad in bed with that woman.

They listened intently without interrupting him. When he finished the detective said, 'so your friend Misty helped you remember this through hypnotherapy? Before that, you did not recall this had ever happened?'

'Until then I had no idea, I suffered from amnesia. My mum knew it, but she didn't want to stress me out, so she said nothing to me. Why don't you ask her? She can verify my story.'

Dr Rao said, 'It's not about verifying your story. We believe you, but we want to find out your viewpoint and determine if you had ongoing issues with amnesia. I suspect I know the answer to my next question, but I need to ask it anyway.'

Jonathan looked uneasy.

'Since you've been in this hospital, have you had any dreams that were lucid or something that may be troubling, that you can't put your finger on?'

'No doctor, I feel completely rested and relaxed, I am sleeping like a baby, I have had no such 'lucid' dreams and have been generally untroubled. I can't understand why I would have done such a thing to myself. Slitting my wrists! That is the only thing troubling me. Why did I do it? Can you tell me why I did that if you know, please? I need to find out.' Jonathan looked pleadingly at the doctor.

The doctor said with pity in his voice, 'of course if you don't remember we can fill you in, but I have a few more questions to ask you. Please answer as truthfully as you can, we won't judge you I promise.'

Jonathan nodded a yes to the doctor.

'Have you taken any drugs recently or do you regularly take drugs?'

Jonathan took a moment to think, and then said, 'yes I have smoked a few joints of weed with my friends, but I wouldn't say I was a regular user.'

'How did you get the drugs?'

'Sometimes I bought it from a friend who sells that stuff in school and share it with my three friends, and sometimes I got it at Peter's house. But I only smoked it a few times.'

'Do you smoke cigarettes?'

'Nope.'

'Weed now and again?'

'Yes.'

'Have you suffered from depression?'

'I sometimes took medication for it.'

'Light drug use can bring on depression, cannabis will interfere with the way your brain processes information. If you take too much, you will feel anxious and paranoid. It can affect parts of your brain that processes what you see, leading to hallucinations. I think there is another more serious issue we need to address.' Said Dr Rao.

'What's that?'

'Because you are a light drug user and suffer from depression, you may have a condition called schizoaffective disorder. Have you ever heard of that?'

'Are you crazy, doctor? I haven't, but I assure you I am as normal as you are.'

'Don't get worried Jonathan, we are merely trying to determine your condition. Schizoaffective disorder is like bipolar disorder. It's just a chemical imbalance in your system. If that is what we are dealing with, then we have to prescribe you the right medication to help your body correct that imbalance.'

'Please doctor, I am fine, and you need not wow me with your big words.' Jonathan smiled at him.

Dr Rao suspected Jonathan wouldn't believe him, because he couldn't remember the real reason he was in the hospital.

Then the doctor looked at the detective and said to Jonathan, 'I will need to confer with the detective before we go any further. Why don't we have a little tea break and talk after that?'

'Whatever you say.' Jonathan said shrugging his shoulders.

The doctor summoned Barry to get Jonathan tea and refreshments and said they should reconvene in thirty minutes. When they were alone, the doctor turned to the detective and said, 'what did you make of that?'

'He really can't remember, can he?'

Dr Rao shook his head, 'no he can't'.

'Poor bastard! He will get an almighty shock when he finds out.'

'He will for sure. Are you ok to inform him about what happened at his house detective?'

'Yeah of course, as long as you think he can handle it?'

'It will be hard, but he will need to be told at some point, and the longer we keep it from him the harder it will be.'

'Yes, I agree, and he will be seventeen soon. Old enough to understand.'

'Hmmmm, I guess.'

'Ok doctor, let's bring him in.' Said the detective.

The doctor started worrying about Jonathan, he was alone with no family support. In a strange hospital with no close friends or family around him. This would be hard enough for a normal adult to deal with, but Jonathan was only sixteen years old. The doctor wished they didn't have to tell Jonathan anything for longer. He sounded happy and relaxed, and the doctor knew his world would be turned upside down soon.

But finally, the doctor concluded that telling Jonathan

about what happened was inevitable. Sooner was probably better than later. Dr Rao also wanted to keep his good relationship with Jonathan, he wanted his trust, so he preferred if the Detective would tell him what happened that night.

After both men decided what their roles were, they went back to the interview room and asked Barry to bring Jonathan in. When Jonathan came into the room, he looked nervous. They asked Barry to stay and monitor Jonathan for his reactions, and to give him support if he needed it.

When they had all settled into their seats, Detective Superintendent Brown spoke to Jonathan. Addressing him he said, 'The doctor and I are going to tell you what we know so far and why you were admitted to this hospital.'

Jonathan was too nervous to speak and nodded his head. He realised it was something serious, because both the men looked more formal. Especially Dr Rao who was caring and supportive previously.

The detective then said, 'On the night of Saturday 24th March at 10.34 pm, the police were called to your house, 44 Longwood Road, by your next-door neighbours Mr and Mrs Rawling. In their statements, they said they first heard raised voices coming from your house at 10 pm. They realised it was your parents arguing about something. They could predominantly hear your dad more than your mum.

Approximately 20 to 30 minutes later they heard a loud crash, and some screaming coming from the back of the house. They thought the screaming sounded like a woman's voice. They came to check out if anyone needed any help and they heard a male voice screaming, and I quote: "We are going to kill you".

Mr Rawling said his wife asked him to go back inside and call the police. He heard shouting coming from inside your house, a male voice yelling, "I hate you!"'

During the detective's recital of the statement from Mr and Mrs Rawling, he was reading the exact wording in the statement and looking for a reaction from Jonathan. Jonathan just sat there looking stunned. When the detective paused, Jonathan asked, 'what happened next?'

The detective briefly glanced at Dr Rao and continued.

'Mr Rawling called the police at 10.30 pm saying they heard a massive argument coming from your house, and that he heard you or maybe your dad saying they would kill someone. The Rawlings did not enter the house, as they weren't sure what to expect, so after calling the police they waited outside to see if they could hear anything more, but all they heard after that was just someone crying.

When the police got there at 11:25 pm, they knocked on your front door and heard a something alarming coming from inside. They broke open your door, and they said they heard crying coming from the kitchen.'

The detective paused and took a deep breath whilst Jonathan waited patiently, the detective then took a sip of water and resumed.

'When they got into the kitchen, they found a teenage boy, they identified as yourself, lying in a pool of blood with both your wrists slashed, and a knife on the floor beside you. At first, they thought you had stabbed the female you were lying next to, because there was so much blood, she was covered in it.

On the other side of the kitchen they saw a middle-aged Asian male who was stabbed to death.'

The detective paused looking at both Jonathan and the doctor for signs he should continue. Then the detective said, 'would you like a break Jonathan, you look pale?'

Jonathan didn't answer, he had zoned out and stared into space. His eyes were focused on the wall behind the doctor and detective. Dr Rao looked concerned but still said nothing, because he wanted to see how Jonathan reacted to this information.

Jonathan felt faint, the room seemed to be spinning around, and he tried hard to focus on what the detective was saying. After he heard the detective say he was lying next to his mum, he couldn't hear or comprehend anything else. There was this loud noise in his head, and he wanted to cover his ears and curl up in a ball. Jonathan cried, at first it was just a tear or two rolling down his face. Dr Rao suggested that they end this interview for now for the sake of Jonathan's sanity.

The detective agreed and left the topic. Jonathan's tears were flowing faster, he held his head saying it hurt. He was now crying hard. He wailed, 'oh noooo, I killed my mum.'

The doctor got up quickly, but Barry got there in a flash. He tried to coax Jonathan by talking to him. 'Jonathan it's me, Barry. Are you ok, you look so weak? Please stop crying.'

Jonathan sobbed loudly saying, 'I love my mum, how could I have killed her? You should have let me die there on the floor. No wonder I didn't want to live.' He got up from the chair and shrugged Barry's hands off his shoulders and went to the corner of the room. He sank onto the floor still crying and rocking himself.

Barry became upset for him, he felt helpless, he went over to Jonathan, sat down beside him and hugged Jonathan's shoulders. He turned to Dr Rao and gave him a hard look. He wanted the doctor or detective to tell Jonathan the whole story, but the doctor just shook his head vigorously mouthing a 'not now' to Barry.

Dr Rao went out of the room to get Jonathan a sedative. He too wanted Jonathan's pain to end, even if it was just for the night. The detective looked on, unsure of what to do next. He knew they had to take baby steps with Jonathan because he was so fragile. The detective thought Jonathan came across strong and sure of himself but watching him there now, in that corner, wishing he could have died too, it was disturbing. He felt powerless and realised this whole case was more sensitive and complicated than he thought.

The doctor came in with a nurse that looked like she meant business. She was nearly six feet tall and walked into the room like she oversaw Dr Rao. She had a masculine bone structure and looked constantly irritated.

'Right,' she said hurrying towards Jonathan. 'It's time for some relaxation Jonathan.' Her voice was kind, and she tried to get as close to him as possible without him turning away. She knew that if she approached him in a gentle and kind manner, he would reciprocate and make her job easier. Jonathan was in his own world, he acknowledged no one. He was too upset to talk, she administered the injection with little fuss. After a minute Jonathan got drowsy, so Barry took him back to his room once he had organised for a wheelchair to be brought in. After he tucked Jonathan into bed, he went to speak to Dr Rao to see if there was anything more the doctor required of him. Barry hoped that Dr Rao didn't need him, so he could go back and supervise Jonathan.

Dr Rao and the Detective Superintendent Brown were still in the interview room when Barry got there. The doctor was happy to dismiss Barry, but before Barry could leave, Dr Rao said, 'Barry just before you go can I ask you a few questions?'

'Sure, doctor.'

'The detective and I was wondering if we should give Jonathan a rest day tomorrow from interviewing, so he could process the information we gave him today. It will give him a chance to calm down. What do you think?'

Barry thought for an instant then said, 'I think that is noble of you doctor, but if I were Jonathan, I would want to find out everything. Jonathan wasn't in any state to hear any more today, but he might be tomorrow. Don't you think we should ask him this question instead? Despite everything that has happened he has been very polite and a model patient. Something crazy went on in that house that night I understand that, but we need to get Jonathan's perspective on what happened. All we have are the police reports from the neighbours, and what the police saw when they got there. As Jonathan is the only person we can ask for now, shouldn't we try to do everything we can to find out what he knows? Surely there must be an explanation?'

'Yes, you are right' Dr Rao said sighing heavily. 'He is old enough to deal with the situation. We can tell him what we found out, but we do need to know everything from his point of view too. What do you think detective?'

'I agree, the sooner we sort this out, the better for all of us. It's been nearly a month since the murder, and we aren't any further forward in finding out exactly what went on that night. Jonathan needs to tell us what happened, from his perspective. If he finds it difficult, which I am sure he will, then he is in the right place for it already.' Ended the detective.

All the men agreed. Barry was pleased that they got closer to the truth. Dr Rao had no more questions for Barry, so he went back to look after Jonathan, he was getting fond of his teenage patient and wanted to help and support him as much as he could.

Dr Rao told the detective he would visit Jonathan in his room tomorrow and ask him how he wanted to proceed or even if he wanted to find out what had happened that night. The detective decided that he would await further instructions from the doctor the next day, going 'all guns blazing' in this case wouldn't be required or necessary. After today even he was softening towards Jonathan, and he wanted to find out the truth. At first, he wanted to punish Jonathan for what he had done, but now he wasn't so sure Jonathan was in the right frame of mind, hence the murder. He wasn't condoning it, but he realised there were other aspects of the case that had come to light that he hadn't expected. Jonathan's mental state of health for example. But for now, they would have to wait till tomorrow to determine their next steps.

The next day Jonathan woke up and was still tired. He remembered having lots of dreams, but he could not actually remember what they were. He sat up in bed, and suddenly he was starving. When he scanned the room, he saw Barry sitting on the chair staring at him with a newspaper in his hand, rubbing his eyes Johnathan said, 'oh hi Barry, what are you doing here?'

'Morning, how are you?'

'Good, but I am starving. Fancy getting me a full English breakfast?' He said smiling cheekily.

'This is a hospital not a hotel' Barry said with a smile on his face, but as soon as it came out of his mouth he wished he hadn't said it.

Jonathan's features clouded over, and he remembered the events of the previous day. He then said in the saddest voice, 'I guess what the detective said yesterday was real and not a dream? Please tell me it wasn't real. I don't know if I can go on like this!'

Barry felt as if he had been punched in the stomach. He wanted to help Jonathan, but he felt powerless. He could see how much Jonathan's love for his mum and the thought that he had been responsible for her death was not something he could handle. And this was just the beginning. Barry decided that they had to tell Jonathan the truth, he didn't kill his mum!

With a heavy heart Barry said, 'I am sorry Jonathan but yesterday happened, and today will be another difficult day for you. Dr Rao wants to come and see you as soon as you have had breakfast.'

Jonathan flopped back in bed and put the covers over his head, then from under the covers he said, 'I don't want to see anyone, tell them to leave me alone.'

Barry looked on helplessly. 'Ok just relax, I will get you something nice to eat. How about a hot sausage sandwich?'

'I'm not hungry.' He said from under his blanket.

'Yes, you are, I will be back in fifteen minutes, can you go and freshen up?'

'No.'

'Yes.'

'No.'

'Yes, you will, and if you do, I promise you at least one piece of great news today. Trust me you will love it.'

Barry was determined to make sure that Dr Rao told Jonathan that he didn't kill his mum. They couldn't let him keep thinking he was responsible for his mum's death, it could make him try to commit suicide again. And Barry had been devoted enough to him to see that Jonathan was close to the edge. Luckily for Jonathan Dr Rao had already prescribed him medication for his schizophrenia and bipolar depression, and the effects of that were helping him. Barry, however, made a mental note to suggest Dr Rao increase the dosage of the bipolar depression pills.

'I don't want to hear any more.' he yelled.

'Ok, I will be back shortly. Get into the bathroom once I am gone please.'

Before he could answer Barry left the room. He realised that Jonathan was just being immature, and although like a child Barry wanted to soothe him, he also needed to be firm. Leaving him for a little while would calm him down. Once he had eaten and taken his medication he would be ready to see Dr Rao.

After Barry ordered Jonathan's breakfast from the kitchen, he went over to see the doctor.

'Morning Barry' the doctor said cheerily. 'How is he today?'

'Hi doctor, well he woke up happy and hungry, but when he realised what happened yesterday was real and no dream he got upset. He said he didn't want to see anyone today.'

'Oh, I see.'

'And another thing, doctor. Please tell him he didn't kill his mother today. He is struggling.' Barry said pleadingly.

'I know, and we will tell him, I hoped he would get a shock, and that could have made him remember, I guess he has said nothing about remembering what happened that night, has he?'

'Not really. I will let you know if he does, in the meantime I better go. His breakfast might get cold.'

'Yes, of course, tell me when he is ready, and I will come over.'

Barry nodded and left the doctor. He went over to the kitchen, collected Jonathan's breakfast and took it to him. When he went into the room Jonathan wasn't in his bed. Barry set the tray down on the table. Thinking he was in the en-suite bathroom Barry went over to let him know the break-fast was ready, but when he knocked on the door, it pushed open. He looked inside calling out Jonathan's name, but he wasn't in there.

Barry panicked, 'Jonathan?' He shouted out, he was trying to think clearly. The door to his room had been locked so he couldn't go out that way. Barry looked over to the window and ran over but as he got there, by the side of the bed, on the floor was Jonathan calmly lying there facing upwards with his hands behind his head.

Jonathan said calmly, 'stop panicking Barry, I'm here. From down here you can see the whole sky, and it's so blue today. Come and have a look.'

Barry was so relieved to see him there, 'Oh I never realised, budge over and make room for me. I'm much larger than you.

Jonathan shuffled over, and Barry lay on the cold floor next to Jonathan and looked up at the sky through the window. Jonathan was right it was blue, lying there staring at the sky, it was strangely relaxing. They stayed like that, not speaking for a few minutes then Jonathan said, 'Hope you brought breakfast because I could eat a horse!'

Barry stood up chuckling, 'yeah mate, it's over here. Have you had your shower already?'

'No but I will after breakfast.'

After Jonathan had eaten and showered Barry called Dr Rao over. The doctor gave a brief knock on the door then came inside without waiting for an answer.

'Good morning Jonathan how are you feeling?' He said beaming a smile at him.

'Hi, doctor, fine I guess considering I found out yesterday that both my parents are dead, and the police found me beside my dead bloodied mother with a knife in my hand! Oh, and the other thing, that small little fact I can't remember a damn thing. So yeah, other than that I am perfectly fine!'

The doctor looked at Barry and said, 'Sorry Jonathan, I can see you are distressed, but the sooner we sort this out the better. What do you say?'

'Yeah, I guess.' He said with little enthusiasm.

'So, I was thinking about putting you in a hypnotic trance, so we can get your side of the story. Is that something you will agree to?'

Jonathan looked up at the doctor sharply, 'That's how I discovered the other memory lapses. Misty and I tried hypnotism, and it helped me remember.'

'Oh, your friend.' The doctor said with raised eyebrows. 'Yes, we should try that. Do you think you can do it today?'

'Like you said doctor, the sooner the better.'

'Great, I will get myself prepared and come back in an hour, I prefer this room as you are most comfortable here.'

'Ok, fine doctor. See you soon.'

The doctor left. Barry, listening to the conversation, was getting increasingly worried for Jonathan. He wondered how Jonathan could deal with such grave issues so calmly. He knew the medication was helping him, but it would still be hard for him. Barry vowed to be there every step of the way after Jonathan finally told them what he knew. Today would be one of the hardest days of his career and probably of Jonathan's life.

The doctor came back with a notepad and pen, some of his briefing notes and a portable speaker which he connected via Bluetooth to his iPad. He also brought in a smartphone, so he could record the session and play it back later for Superintendent Brown, who he had briefed earlier. The detective was adamant he wanted to be in the room, but Dr Rao had put his foot down saying that his presence would only distract Jonathan. The detective wasn't happy, but he said he would have to make do with just the recording.

He found Jonathan pacing around his room and Barry sitting on the chair trying to read the newspaper. He knew that they were both were anxious about this session, he was a bit concerned himself, but he was here to do a job; to get the truth out of Jonathan. He said, 'Ok let's begin. Jonathan are you ready?'

Jonathan just nodded a 'yes'.

'Great, Barry will you please draw the curtains and take this phone, so you can be in charge of recording the session?'

'Sure, doctor. Do you want me any were in particular?'

'Yes, Firstly I want Jonathan to lie on the bed and stay as relaxed as possible. Barry, I want you on a chair between the window and the bed, and I will sit on the chair on the opposite side. And Barry, I know I need not say this, but I will anyway. Try not to respond to Jonathan even if he sounds distressed, please don't come to his aid whilst he is in a trance.'

'Okay, doctor.' He said feeling even more anxious but not outwardly showing it. Barry then looked at Jonathan and smiled reassuringly, 'Don't worry you're in good hands. Dr Rao is the best, and when this is all over, I will be right next to you.'

Jonathan gave him a feeble smile, it was the all he could muster. Dr Rao looked at the exchange between them and felt a tad relieved that Barry was there for Jonathan. As a professional, he too would do his best but was mindful not to get too attached.

When everything and everyone got into position, the doctor started the session. The sounds the doctor chose was relaxation music akin to the ones the massage therapists played in the expensive spas. It was relaxing and incredibly soothing.

Barry was thinking, 'at this rate, I will be asleep too!'

The doctor said, 'Ok Jonathan I want you to keep your eyes closed and clear your mind of everything. Just let it go blank. Think that you are as light and as free as a bird gliding through giant white clouds. Don't think about anything else but flying through those clouds. You are free and happy there. Are you doing that Jonathan?'

'Yes doctor, it feels nice.' Jonathan was thinking, 'this is better than when Misty took him into a trance.' He relaxed.

The doctor smiled glad that Jonathan was getting into the mode he needed to be in. Then he continued, 'Now hear my voice as I count down from a hundred is that ok?'

'Yes.'

'As I count you will feel lighter and lighter and sink into the bed. Your body will be completely relaxed, and all you will hear is the sound of my voice. …………….. When I get to fifty, you will be in a trance. Listen to the numbers, and as I count down, you will go deeper and deeper into a hypnotic trance. Now just breathe, one hundred… ninety-nine… ninety-eight… ninety-seven…'

The doctor continued to count patiently, pausing gently with each number. His voice also went increasing lower as he counted down to fifty. After every ten numbers he said, 'you are now deeper into your trance,' and this continued till he got to fifty. The music was still playing in the background, but the main sound came from the doctor's voice.

Dr Rao said, 'Jonathan, can you hear my voice?'

'Yes.' Jonathan replied.

'Ok Jonathan, can you tell me your mum's full name?'

'Janice Rice.'

'And what date were you brought into this hospital?'

'I can't remember.'

'How many brothers and sisters do you have?'

'I have none.'

'I want you to go back to the last time you were at your house, can you tell me what happened that morning?'

'I can't remember.'

'Do you recall if you went out in the morning, it was a Saturday.'

'Yes, I did.'

'Where did you go?'

'To Peter's house.'

'What did you do there?'

'Hung around, smoked weed then I went home.'

'Did you go straight home or to another person's house?'

'I stopped at the corner shop near Peter's house to buy cider for our party later.'

'You were going for a party later?'

'No.'

'Then what party?'

'My friends snuck into my bedroom, so we could have a few drinks in my room.'

'Why didn't you have a party at Peter's house, why did they have to sneak into your room?'

'Mum and I planned to leave my dad on Sunday, and that was the last time we could all be together in my – soon to be old bedroom.'

'How was the party?'

'Fun, Misty sat on one of my boxes and fell in. It was funny.' He said smiling.

'Were your parents in the house at this time, during your party?'

'Yes, they were, so we had to be discreet.'

'Why didn't you tell your parents that your friends were coming over to see you?'

'Because my dad wouldn't have liked them.'

'Did you tell your mum about them?'

'Yes.'

'Did she like them?'

'She never met them.'

'What time did the party finish?'

'We stopped it when we heard a noise coming from downstairs.'

'What was the noise you heard?'

'I don't know so I turned the music off to listen.'

'Then what did you hear?'

'My parents arguing.'

'Can you tell me what happened next?'

Barry was gently rocking on his chair from side to side feeling very eager for what Jonathan would say next.

'I heard the noise coming from the kitchen. My friends followed me. When I got there, I saw my dad was on top of my mum strangling her.' Jonathan was getting upset and breathed harder. 'Stop it, you're hurting her.'

The doctor tried to calm him, 'Stay with me Jonathan, it will all be ok. Stay calm, and just tell me what happened next?'

'My mum wasn't moving, she wasn't trying to stop him! Misty screamed that my dad killed my mum. I ran over to pull him off her, but he wouldn't stop, so I found a frying pan and hit him with it. But he dodged me, and I only hit his shoulder. I tried to hit him again with the pan, but it flew out of my hands, so I went to get it from the floor, but my dad pushed me away from it.'

'Your dad stopped strangling your mum and fought with you?'

'Yes there was so much noise, Misty yelled he had killed my mum, and Peter and Nick were shouting, "kill him". My dad came over and started saying bad things to me.'

'What things Jonathan?'

'That I was a loser and a coward like my mum and that she was a bitch and a whore. Then Peter suggested I take a knife from the knife block to avenge my mum's death. But I couldn't do it. I didn't want to do it. But then my dad stood there laughing at me, and the more he laughed, the angrier I got. So, I went over to the knife block and pulled the largest knife from the block.'

'Why was he laughing?'

'I think because he thought I wouldn't do anything.'

'What happened next?'

'I could hear Peter and Nick saying, "kill him," they were also upset and crying. I wanted the noise to stop, everyone was shouting, but I knew my friends were behind me, I knew that they were right, and I had to kill him, so I got the courage from them and ran over to my dad and stabbed him as hard as I could. I wanted to wipe the smile off his face,' Jonathan cried. 'He killed my mum, I didn't want to live with him. I hate him, I hate him…'

Barry stopped rocking and stared at the doctor. The doctor waited for Jonathan to stop saying he hated his dad. Then he said gently.

'What did you do next Jonathan?'

'I couldn't believe I had done that, there was so much blood everywhere. My dad looked shocked when I stabbed him, and I was happy that I avenged my mum's death. But the more I thought of my dead mum lying there, the more upset I was. When my dad fell to the floor, I crawled over to my mum to hug her. She was so beautiful just sleeping there calmly. But then I remembered she was dead, so I cried more.'

'The police found you next to your mum when they got in. Do you remember seeing the police?'

'No.'

'What did your friends do when this had all happened?'

'I don't know.'

'The police said nobody else was in the kitchen when they found the three of you there. Do you think your friends left?'

'I don't know what happened to them. My dad said I could call them on his phone when I threatened to kill him with the help of my friends.'

'Why did he say that?'

'I don't know, he looked at them but didn't seem to care, I don't know why he wanted me to ring them when they were right there with me. They were all upset too.'

'Did he say anything to them knowing they were upset and crying?'

'No, he just turned back to me!'

The doctor and Barry looked at each other.

'Do you remember anything else about that night?'

'Yes, when I saw my mum lying there so peacefully, I wanted to die too.' He began crying hard now. 'I used the knife in my hand to slash my wrists. Oh my god, it hurt! I couldn't breathe for the pain. I couldn't move. I wanted to die next to my mum.'

The doctor took in a deep breath. 'Do you remember what happened next Jonathan?'

'Yes, I woke up in the hospital.'

The doctor decided that he didn't want to stress him any more. He got the information he needed from the missing hours of his memory. He had more questions for Jonathan, but they weren't about that night, so he brought him out of his hypnosis.

'Ok Jonathan, I will count from fifty to one hundred, and as I do, you will slowly come out of your trance. Do you understand?'

'Yes.'

The doctor started his count from fifty to one hundred. He responded nicely and was fully awake and aware when the doctor got to one hundred.

Both Barry and the doctor looked at Jonathan. Dr Rao spoke, 'Are you ok?'

Jonathan thought for a while, nobody spoke. Then he said, 'I guess.'

They let him be alone with his thoughts for a few minutes.

Then Jonathan said, 'I now know my dad strangled my mum and in my anger at him for that, I stabbed my dad. I am glad I didn't hurt my mum. But...' he sobbed, '... but I don't know how I can live without her.' He said looking at his healing wrists and continued crying.

Barry went over to Jonathan hastily. 'Hey, stop this. It's not that bad I promise you.' He rubbed Jonathan's back trying to pacify him.

But Jonathan couldn't hear him, he was still crying sitting up on his bed. Barry was holding his shoulders tighter to support him. The doctor said to Barry, 'please stay with him for as long as it takes. I don't think I can add much value here, he is closer to you. You can support him better than I can. I will tell the nurse to bring him something, so he can sleep.'

'Normally I would agree with you, doctor, but I think Jonathan needs to get this out of his system by crying it out so don't worry I won't be going anywhere as long as

Jonathan needs me. If he gets worse, I will tell the nurse to give him something to get him to sleep. Can you please tell her that I will call in that injection if I need it?'

'Of course. I will go and email this recording to Detective Superintendent Brown. I should be back in an hour or two.'

The doctor left, Jonathan was still crying, and Barry continued to support him. A million thoughts were going through Barry's head about the night Jonathan's dad was murdered. He wanted Jonathan to get back on the road. In all the time Barry was with Jonathan he was the model teenager. He previously wondered what would lead a lovely young boy like him to commit such a crime, killing his dad so brutally with a knife and strangling his mum. Now he knew he was trying to protect himself and his mum and lash out at his dad due to the grief of losing his mum. 'So, his dad was a bastard, really!' thought Barry. Why else would he want to kill Jonathan's mum?

20

Dr Rao had a short phone call from Detective Superintendent Brown after he sent the recording over. 'Morning, Doctor.'

'Good morning, have you heard it?'

'Yes, doctor, I'm coming over now, so see you soon. Bye.'

With that the detective put the phone down, he was at the hospital thirty minutes after that phone call, he briefly knocked the doctor's office door and without waiting for a reply walked in. The doctor was sitting on his couch and staring into space. He hadn't even heard the detective knock, but he saw the door open, looking at the detective he said, 'Hi, you got here quick.'

'I can't believe what you sent me, I had to come over to discuss it.'

'I realise, it's completely unexpected?'

'So, doctor, let me get this straight. When he saw his dad strangling his mum, he tried to stop him and then stabbed and killed his dad in grief?'

'Correct, he didn't strangle his mum like we guessed, we were suggesting it was a double attack on his parents.'

'So now we are we are looking at a murder committed, arguably in defence! That's amazing. So, we still need to speak to him to find out the background on his family life. He didn't say why they were arguing. We need to find out if this was a common thing in the family and if it ever resulted in violence in the past. We also need to touch upon the topic of his friends, the ones he talked about being in his room. I know he mentioned them in the interview the other day, but we have no reports of anyone else there, and we have not been able to locate them. The neighbours, Mr and Mrs Rawling, didn't mention seeing anyone else coming out of the house, and they are the ones that called the police.'

The doctor said in a very 'Poirot' like manner, lifting a finger in the air as he did so, 'unless.'

'Unless?' Asked the detective.

'Unless they weren't real.'

'What do you mean?'

'I have suspected they were characters made up by him.'

'Seriously, you think Jonathan's psyche made them up?'

'Unfortunately, I strongly think so. As a trial, I have put him on antipsychotic medication to see if his friends return. So far reports from Barry have indicated he is behaving well and hasn't mentioned seeing his friends at all.'

'But they were his friends for months from what I gather.'

'He must have imagined it all. He said his dad didn't see them in the kitchen that night or even acknowledge they were there. His dad offered to ring them at one point! Why would he do that if they were around?'

The detective gave a big sigh, rubbing his forehead whilst in thought. Then he said, 'well, I understand, but we need to interview him again and get the whole picture.'

'We do, but I will take the lead. I don't think Jonathan realises those friends are imaginary. We need to tread carefully, so I am best placed to speak to him.'

'No worries, I am happy to observe, but if I have a question during the interview I will ask, you may have missed something.'

'Okay.'

'So when can we interview him?'

'Not today I am afraid. I left Barry to keep an eye on him. Jonathan was glad he hadn't hurt his mum. Barry, bless him has taken quite a shine to the boy and is supportive of him. That works out well for me because it would have caused a conflict when I interviewed him and asked him the hard questions.'

'Yeah, you're right. Good for Barry. He is an asset to this hospital.'

'I didn't know how much till now, I must admit. He has excelled looking after that boy.'

'Just to get this straight, we will ask Jonathan about his family history of arguments, violence and what he knows about it, his "imaginary" friends and tell him about his mum?'

'But not till we get everything out of him first. I want to find out more about the story and see if it fits in with what we think. We better tell him about his mum soon, Barry is giving me dangerous looks.' The doctor said smiling.

'I realise he is protective of the boy. I must leave, doctor. If I think of anything else, we need to clarify with Jonathan before the interview I will call you.'

'Ok, see you tomorrow, and if I find out later that Jonathan may not interview well because he is still upset, then we might have to leave it one more day. I will see him to assess him and speak to Barry privately on how Jonathan is coping after the hypnotherapy session.'

After the detective left, Dr Rao kept thinking of Jonathan's predicament. He was relieved that Jonathan wasn't the monster that everyone thought he was.

After looking in on some of his other patients and doing necessary paperwork, the doctor popped in to see Jonathan. He wanted to go as soon as the detective left but he needed to give him time and rest. When he got to Jonathan's room, Barry was sitting on the chair looking like he was working out a crossword puzzle on a newspaper. Barry looked up when he saw the doctor and placed his finger on his lips signalling the doctor not to make a noise. After noticing Jonathan fast asleep, Dr Rao motioned for Barry to come out of the room, so he could talk to him.

Both men stepped out of Jonathan's room, when the door was closed the doctor whispered, 'so how is he?'

Barry whispered back, 'as can be expected in these circumstances, doctor. He is going through the wars!'

'What has he done since I left?'

'Cried, slept, he doesn't feel like eating anything, and it's worrying me.'

'It is something that he does need to go through. He will eat when he calms down, it will take time. He has you which is such a good thing, I must thank you for that.'

'That's fine doctor, I am doing my job.'

'But we both know how fond of the boy you have become. He needs you right now, so I am glad you are there for him, I appreciate it.'

Barry was getting embarrassed. It was true he was becoming fond of Jonathan, something he didn't do with other patients he looked after. He nodded at the doctor shyly.

Then Dr Rao whispered, 'the detective, and I decided today isn't the best day to continue our interview with Jonathan, so we will try tomorrow depending on how he is. I want you to stay with him, try to keep his spirits up and observe him closely. He is in danger of trying to kill himself again with this new information. It's a hard pill to swallow.'

'I understand doctor, of course I will monitor him.'

The hospital had rooms for staff that stayed over, and Dr Rao knew Barry hadn't been home in a few days, so he asked, 'When did you last go home?'

'Don't worry about me doctor, I am happy to stay here.'

'How long?'

'Over a week.' He said reluctantly.

The doctor raised his eyebrows, 'Those rooms aren't equipped for long-term stays, are you comfortable?'

'I am, I don't have a family to worry about, so I don't mind. Really, I don't.'

'But I mind, so I will speak to management and get them to give you one of the doctor's quarters. They are much larger and more comfortable.'

Barry began feeling embarrassed again.

'That's unnecessary, doctor.'

'It will make me feel better. Now go back to Jonathan, and I will arrange for the rooms to be made available to you. I will send in Nurse Flowers to keep an eye on him whilst you change rooms. Jonathan knows her, she gives him all his pills and injections when he needs it. So, if he wakes up he will see a familiar face.'

'But doctor, I want to be there when he wakes up.'

The doctor smiled, 'Then I suggest you better change rooms quickly!'

'Ok, doctor, thanks a lot.'

'And another thing Barry, I want to meet up with you later to get a rundown of Jonathan's day. I will also stay overnight, and I will try to speak to you after Jonathan goes to sleep for the night. For now, try to keep him awake till the evening, or he won't get any sleep at night.'

'Yes, doctor.'

'Oh and Barry, work your magic, and get him to eat.'

'I will try my best doctor.'

'I know you will.' Dr Rao said smiling and left.

Barry felt special to be getting rooms in the doctor's quarters, they were much larger and had en-suite bathrooms. Not that it mattered much as he was spending a lot of time with Jonathan, anyway. Still, it was the thought that counted, and he was happy Dr Rao was kind to him.

Nurse Flowers stayed with Jonathan for the hour it took Barry to move, and when he got back, he found him still asleep. The nurse said, 'not a peep out of him. Sleeping like a log he is.'

'Good, you want to stay longer?'

'No, he is all yours. Let me know if you need anything. Dr Rao said whilst you are looking after Jonathan, I am supposed to look after you. Have you eaten yet?'

He smiled, 'Lord! You don't have to nurse me too. I am fine.'

'None the less, I will do what the doctor said, and you better not mess with me!' She laughed.

'Alright, I won't.' He said smiling.

Whilst the two of them were talking Jonathan woke up and started watching the banter between them. He spoke breaking up their chat, 'get a room you two! Don't flirt in my room!'

Barry and the nurse both looked over in shock at

Jonathan. Barry spoke first, 'Sorry mate we didn't mean to wake you.'

'It's ok, it was like watching TV!' He said smiling.

Nurse Flowers adopted a more formal approach, 'So you're up at last, good lad. If you need anything just ask for me, and if Barry or anyone else gives you grief, let me know. Trust me, nobody will mess with me!'

Jonathan gave Barry a cheesy grin, 'I sure will Nurse.'

'Ok boys, I will leave you to it. Barry don't mess with my charge you hear?'

Barry gave the nurse a smile and a military salute, 'Yes mam.'

She smiled and left the room.

Jonathan said, 'is there something going on between you two? You can tell me, don't worry, man to man!'

'Please, there is nothing to dig there so don't bother.'

'So why are you all red and blushing?'

'I am not.'

'Yes, you are.'

'Ok, she is nice, but we have to behave professionally.'

'If you say so, anyway I'm starving. What does a guy need to do to get food around here?'

'Good, you got your appetite back.'

'Yes, and it's four in the afternoon!'

'It's not my fault you slept like a baby!'

Jonathan rolled his eyes heavenwards and flopped back in bed saying, 'Barry after my lunch do you suppose we could get out of this room? It is beginning to feel like a prison.'

'Sure. Hang tight, freshen up and I will be back in ten minutes.'

Whilst Barry was away Jonathan paced the room lost in thought. He didn't know what to do now that his mum was gone. He suspected they would lock him up and throw away the key, and to be fair, what else could he do about it? Strangely he was glad his dad was gone. He felt no remorse for what he did. The hate he had inside him for his dad was still so strong. Then remembering his friends Peter, Misty and Nick, and he realised he missed them, especially Misty. She was so much fun, he smiled when he reminisced about what they got up to in Peter's house. Then Barry came back in the room with his lunch, and within seconds he could smell the food. He was hungrier than ever!

After lunch Barry said he had spoken to the doctor about going for a walk, he suggested they take a tour of the gardens, but Jonathan had to get appropriately dressed in a jacket and his boots because it was cold outside. Jonathan was glad, he could do with a walk.

When Jonathan was dressed, Barry escorted him out of the hospital. Jonathan said, 'wow this hospital is huge and like a maze! I would never find my way around here.'

'It's big but not that big, after a while you get used to it. I was wandering around here for a few weeks still looking at the map directions and signs before I found my way around naturally. From your perspective, you have only seen a small part of the hospital when you went to see the doctor, so I guess you didn't get the whole picture.'

'It looks like a nice hospital and a good place to work. Do you like working here?'

'Yes, I do, I am lucky that I found my calling in life. I get to work with lovely lads like you.'

Jonathan wanted to ask him more questions, but he got distracted when they reached one exit of the building. It was a beautiful but cold day. There was no wind at all and Jonathan could hear the birds and the swish of the trees. It was very peaceful.

'It's pretty. Bet the gardener is kept busy!' Jonathan said.

'There are many gardeners for a place like this, I don't think one gardener could cope.'

'Oh.'

They walked on for a few minutes, neither of them spoke. Then Jonathan said, 'Do you think I am a bad person for killing my dad?'

Barry was relieved that Jonathan started talking about his actions, so he said, 'I don't think you are a bad person at all. From what I have seen about you, you are a lovely lad. Considering what you have been through, you have been well mannered and behaved most of the time. I can only conclude that your family life was not as calm as you wanted it to be. And I can't judge you mate. Nobody knows what you have been through, so they shouldn't judge if they don't know the circumstances of your case.'

Jonathan said nothing, he was glad that Barry didn't think the worst of him. They continued their walk whilst Barry told him about the history of the hospital, how it has been on this land for over one hundred years, and that it was a mental asylum that had a bad reputation. The new hospital has only been in its present state for twenty years. Jonathan was listening to him with some interest, then his mind wandered over to his mum. He was missing her. He tried to focus on Barry's words, but he found it difficult. Then he said, 'Barry I miss my mum, I don't know how I can live my life without her!'

Barry stopped walking, and he felt sorry for Jonathan. He said, 'Aaaww mate, I know it's difficult, but I will be there for you, whatever happens, hope you realise that. I know I am not family, but I will always be by your side.'

Jonathan's tears fell, he nodded looking down at his shoes. 'I'm tired, Barry can we go back please?'

'Sure, hang in there. I know it will be ok. I feel it.'

'They will probably lock me up for killing my dad, and I don't care. I hated him anyway, and I am glad I am the one that got rid of him. I wish we had left him ages ago!'

'We don't know what they will do with you, let's wait and see, and not think about it eh?'

Jonathan nodded. Nobody spoke till they got back to his room. Barry asked him if he wanted to play a board game or read books or watch TV. Jonathan said he didn't want to do anything, but Barry was insistent, so Jonathan suggested Ludo.

Barry said laughing, 'Ludo, you're not five years old!'

'Yeah but I guess that was a good easy time in my life, so I want to be five again.'

'Ok get into your track suit bottoms and slippers, and I will find a Ludo game and be back shortly.'

Barry came back fifteen minutes later with the game and said to Jonathan, 'guess what, we will be playing in my room in the hospital do you want to do that?'

Jonathan's eyes lit up, 'really?'

'For sure, it will get you out of your room, and you can see what I do when I am not on duty. What do you say?'

'I say let's go.'

'Good, shall we stop at the coffee shop and grab some coffee, tea or hot chocolate?'

'Great idea.' Jonathan said excitedly. 'I want a hot chocolate, and you're paying for it!' He laughed.

'Nurse Flowers said I could have anything I wanted so technically, she is paying!'

They both laughed.

When they got to the canteen, it was clear to Jonathan all the staff were fond of Barry and were very respectful to Jonathan. They grabbed their drinks and walked to Barry's new rooms. When Jonathan went in, he said it was nice and clean. Barry confessed that he had just moved into the doctor's quarters due to his long-term stay in the hospital.

'Long-term? Something happened to your house?'

'Not really.'

'Then?'

'Well, I haven't been home since I began looking after you, so they gave me bigger rooms to get more comfortable.' Barry said reluctantly.

'Oh because of me? You don't have to do that Barry, go home to your family at night, I will be fine, I am not a baby!'

'I know, but I don't live with anyone, so I have no one to go back to. Plus, I enjoy looking after you.'

'If you say so. Now, where are we going to play? No cheating! You look like the type!' Jonathan said laughing.

The evening went well. They played several games of Ludo, after a few hours they watched a re-run documentary of 'Planet Earth' by David Attenborough, the episode on mountains, it fascinated Jonathan. He loved the programme and told Barry he wanted to see all the chapters in the series. Barry promised that he would get them for Jonathan and suggested they see them all together. Jonathan liked that idea.

They had a late dinner in Barry's room at ten pm and discussed the making of 'Planet Earth' and the volcanoes featured in the programme. Jonathan said he thought the part on volcanoes was the best bit.

Later Barry walked Jonathan back to his room. He was exhausted, Barry could see he had an exciting day, he was living with the facts of what had happened to his family. Barry wished him a good night and said he would make sure he got a nice breakfast in the morning. Jonathan said he was too full to think about breakfast.

When Barry had gone Jonathan got into bed still thinking about the documentary they had watched and discussed. In his sleep, he dreamt about volcanoes, mountains, and snow leopards featured on the programme.

Barry went to see Dr Rao in his quarters, which wasn't far from his room. The doctor was awaiting Barry's visit.

'So, how is he?'

'Actually, he is doing well. He even ate!'

Barry went through the day he had with Jonathan since the hypnotherapy session with the doctor. Dr Rao was pleased with Jonathan's progress. He knew the Detective Superintendent Brown and he could continue their interview with Jonathan the next day. He then thanked Barry for his dedication.

Then Barry asked, 'I don't mean to impose but do you think I could also be there when you interview Jonathan tomorrow? I feel like he trusts me and is comfortable with me so if I am there he might be more relaxed and open up more.' Barry felt bad asking for this chance, he didn't want the doctor to think he was nosey. He felt that Jonathan had nobody on his side and he wanted to be there for him.

'I wouldn't want it any other way. If you hadn't asked me, I would have suggested you be there too.'

'Oh, good doctor, I felt bad asking.'

'You don't need to, now get some rest, you have definitely earned it.'

'Goodnight doctor, see you tomorrow.'

'Goodnight Barry.'

21

The next day Jonathan, Dr Rao, Detective Superintendent Brown and Barry all sat in the interview room. Jonathan was glad Barry could attend as well, it made him feel more relaxed.

Dr Rao started the questioning, 'Barry tells me you had a nice evening yesterday. Are you ready for today?'

'Yup it was fun. We watched 'Planet Earth', I love that programme. Have you seen it, doctor?'

'I have, a long time back, but maybe I need to see it again. What episode did you watch? There may have been six or seven in the series.'

'The episode on mountains, it was fantastic. Barry told me he will try to get me the whole series so I can watch it in order.'

'That's kind of him. Yes, watch them all, they are great.'

Changing gears and wanting to get today over and done with Jonathan said, 'Ok doctor, I am ready for today, so ask me whatever you want but I need to ask you some questions too.'

'Ok you can ask me later, now can you give me a brief background on your family life?'

Jonathan began by telling the doctor about his dad's behaviour, how he hated his dad all his life but didn't know why until a few months ago when Misty helped him remember. He told them about how he found out about his dad's affair with Saroj and its effects on his parents' relationship. He recalled his dad's mood swings which were always erratic, then he started feeling particularly sad recounting the episodes of his memory lapses, starting with when he found his dad in bed with Saroj till when his dad tried to strangle his mum against the wall.

After over an hour the doctor suggested they take a break. The doctor saw that Jonathan needed one. Barry took Jonathan to the coffee shop to get away from the interview room. They didn't talk much, he didn't want Jonathan's momentum to slow down, so he didn't distract Jonathan with idle chit-chat. He wanted it all out in the open' so Jonathan could deal with the situation and move on.

After twenty minutes they went back into the room, and Jonathan continued where he had left off. He told them how he had to coax his mum into finding out what happened to him from her perspective. He mentioned his dad's family disowning them and how his dad blamed his mum for it. He also said his dad was like a Dr Jekyll and Mr Hyde, to the outside world he was the best dad, husband, family man and friend. But at home he was a controlling, mean-spirited person, always picking fault and talking down to the two of them. He touched upon how his dad insisted that he was not Jonathan's father. He said he didn't realise until recently how much his mum shielded him from his dad's moods, and he found out how much psychological and sometimes physical abuse his mum had taken from his dad to protect him.

The doctor asked Jonathan about other friends, apart from Peter, Misty and Nick, did he have other school or childhood friends? Jonathan admitted that some students in his school had always considered him odd, and they never wanted him to join in any of their circle of friends. That is why he was so glad when he hung out with Peter and the gang.

The doctor asked him how and when he met his friends and Jonathan explained that it was in the park after school on a day when he was feeling low. He said Peter was the strongest one in the group, he also introduced him to the others later.

After exchanging looks with the detective, Dr Rao asked if Jonathan had seen Peter since he was in the hospital and Jonathan looked confused saying, 'of course not, he doesn't know where I am!'

The doctor began to tell Jonathan what he suspected, 'Jonathan, I realise this may come as a shock to you, but I want you to trust in my judgement ok?'

'Yeah ok.' Jonathan said narrowing his eyes whilst still staring at the doctor.

The doctor took a deep breath, then said, 'Jonathan I suspect the friends you refer to as Peter, Misty and Nick aren't real!'

Jonathan looked at him in amazement, he turned to Barry questioningly, Barry said nothing, but he nodded in agreement with Dr Rao.

Jonathan looked back at the doctor and laughed, 'Don't be silly, doctor. What makes you think that?'

He thought the doctor was joking for a few seconds, but when he looked at all three of them in turn, they were all looking stone-faced at him, he realised they were serious.

He raised his voice without realising it, 'have you all gone mad? Why would I make up such lies? Do you think my whole story about my mum and dad in the kitchen was a lie?' Jonathan turned to Barry saying pleadingly, 'Barry, you believe me, don't you?'

Barry was shifting in his chair uncomfortably but said, 'I do Jonathan, I know you aren't a liar. Calm down and let the doctor explain.'

Jonathan looked at the doctor for an explanation, he said, 'I don't think you lied, you believe your friends are real!'

Jonathan said sarcastically, 'oh so now I am the mad one! I get it.'

The doctor continued, 'Jonathan I must tell you I have officially diagnosed your disorder.'

'DISORDER?' He said a little loudly, it shocked him.

'Unfortunately, apart from depression, you are suffering from both bipolar disorder and schizophrenia.'

Jonathan was astounded at what Dr Rao told him. But the doctor continued, 'Bipolar disorder causes mood swings characterised by extreme high and low moods. Schizophrenia is a mental disorder that causes abnormal thoughts and deregulated emotions. When you show signs of having both schizophrenia and a mood disorder like bipolar, we call it schizoaffective disorder.

Jonathan raked his fingers through his hair, 'you are saying they aren't real? That I had been talking to myself then? Surely, doctor, you can't be right.'

'I am pretty sure I am correct.'

'So I am some fucking loner with imaginary friends and a fucked up family that are now dead?'

It upset Barry to see Jonathan like this. He suggested they take a lunch break, but Jonathan didn't want to stop.

The doctor said, 'Jonathan can you tell me more about Peter?'

'Why, if he isn't real then what does it matter?' Just

saying it out like that made Jonathan feel like crying. He didn't want to acknowledge he would lose his friends forever. A million things ran through his brain, including the loss of his family, and now the loss of his friends too, 'would this nightmare ever end? He couldn't understand it, he talked to them, laughed and cried with them. He thought, "how can that all be in his imagination?" How could he do that? Of course, they were wrong. Maybe they are trying to trick me into believing my friends don't exist. I will take them to Peter's house. Did they imagine I fancied Misty? They are talking rubbish!'

'Please I need you to understand, I think if I ask you specific questions about Peter you might realise there wasn't any real detail to his life, just what you made up in your mind. Like for example, have you met his parents or family when you went to his house?'

'No, I didn't.'

'Where is his house?'

'He lived in a dark green house about twenty minutes' walk from my house.'

'Do you have an address?'

'No but I could take you there.'

The doctor looked at the detective saying, 'maybe one of these days you should, it will help you make sense of it. What was Peter's surname, can you remember? We can check him out on the system.'

'I can't remember, I didn't ask.'

'Any of your other friends second names?'

Jonathan shook his head and asked, 'if you don't believe they exist why are you asking me these questions?'

'I am trying to find detail to what you know about them. I don't believe you will have anything concrete and once we establish that you will start to believe they aren't real too.

That's the best explanation I can give you for now. So, did you go to Misty or Nick's house?'

'Never.' Jonathan was deep in thought as the doctor asked those questions then he suddenly said, 'oh yeah…. I remember Nick called him Sparker.'

'Nick called who Sparker?'

'Peter, his surname is Parker, but sometimes Nick called him Sparker because he was the active one in the group. You know, like a spark plug' Jonathan said smiling.

'Peter Parker?'

'Yes,' Jonathan said confidently 'Misty told me Nick used to call him that as a short form, like Peter used to call me JR instead of Jonathan.

Barry sat there stock still.

The doctor whispered, 'you used to read a lot of Marvel comics, didn't you?'

Jonathan sat there frozen, all the pieces of the puzzle started falling into place now, Peter Parker.'Oh my god, I made it up' he thought. He couldn't believe he could have done that, even now they were all vocalising it, it sounded so foolish. He felt like a fool, he made it all up like a small kid playing with toys! He was wrong, they weren't trying to trick him, but they looked and felt so real to him!

'Yes…. oh my god!' Said Jonathan as he realised what the doctor tried to tell him. 'You think I made that name up because I loved reading the comics?' He felt like the wind was knocked from his sails!

'Yes, I'm afraid so Jonathan.' Said the doctor.

'So if Peter is Peter Parker, Spiderman. Nick is… oh my god! You are right.' Jonathan said covering his face with his hands.

Barry said, 'We should break for lunch now doctor, what do you think? This is getting stressful for Jonathan.'

'Good idea' said the doctor. 'Let's meet up after lunch, say in an hour or an hour and a half?'

Barry suggested the latter, he wanted time to speak to Jonathan alone. Jonathan didn't move at first. He sat there with his hands on his face not believing what had just happened. Barry had to coax him out of the room, Jonathan didn't want to eat anything at first, but Barry was insistent and suggested they lunch in Jonathan's room, because he knew Jonathan needed space from everyone. When they had finished Barry said to Jonathan, 'I am sorry mate. This will be so hard for you.'

Jonathan said, 'I can't believe it. They seemed so real, I can't believe they aren't.'

'That's what happens to people suffering from schizophrenia, what they create in their head seems real to them. I am not that familiar with Marvel comics, but I know Peter Parker is Spiderman, but who are Misty and Nick?'

'There is a Marvel character called Nick Fury, and Misty is also a character called Mercedes "Misty" Knight. She was mixed race just like my Misty! God, they seemed so real. Why did I create these people Barry?'

'Schizophrenia is a complicated condition, and there are different types of schizophrenia. I don't know everything about it, these are the questions you will need to ask Dr Rao. We have patients in the hospital with the condition, and you aren't as bad as they are. With regular medication, you can control the condition.'

Jonathan said nothing, he listened and stared out into space. Barry concluded that he was trying to fit the pieces in his head about his meetings with his imaginary friends.

Jonathan finally said, 'I smoked weed with Peter, where did I get that from? It makes little sense.'

'Nothing will when you think about it rationally. You

may have bought it from someone in the park, or someone could have sold it to you in school. You could have just created the fact that Peter gave it to you even though you had it with you all along.'

'Wow, I made him up! Peter who I met in the park, Peter Parker, how fucked up must I have been! Then I made his surname up too, the one that Nick used to call him, Sparker!' He shook his head thinking about it all, then he said, 'What about the green painted house, was that all in my head too?'

'You were specific about that house, and one day we should find it. I think that house exists, and it's empty, you used to go there and hang out with your 'friends'! But nobody was inside apart from you!'

'And when they were in my room? They weren't there, were they? That is why Peter climbed up the wall so easily into my bedroom, he was fucking Spiderman for god's sake! When I tried to do that I couldn't! God that makes sense.'

'When did that happen?'

'Every time Peter came to my room he came from my window. I assumed he climbed up, or my mind told me he had!'

'Oh, I see. It's so strange how the mind plays tricks on us. Anything else that happened that you think was odd?'

After a few seconds of thinking, Jonathan said, well there was this weird time for about two months they disappeared from my mind.'

'Really? Did you do something different?'

'I can't remember what I did, but I must have.'

'We can ask Dr Rao when we get back. It sounds strange and a good question for him.

'And when I was hypnotised by Misty, or technically by myself, I remember meeting Peter in the woods. I guess in my distress which was brought upon by my dad, my mind created those characters, or at least Peter, at the time I was left in the woods alone for that night. You don't know how surreal this is Barry!'

Barry decided Jonathan will take a long time to piece together this mess. He then said, 'On that note, we better get back, or they will send a search party for us.'

'I don't want to go back!'

'You have to, once it's all over that's it, you can relax, you're on the right medication now.'

'But when will it be over? I'm tired of this shit Barry, it's one thing after another. One day I find out I have no family left and the next day no friends! They were all part of my fucked-up brain! I feel like such a fool, I don't want to go back and face the two of them knowing that.'

'Just hang in there, ok? Please?'

After sitting there in silence for five minutes, Jonathan said under his breath, 'Ok, let's face the music!'

Barry took Jonathan back, and the detective was the only one in the room. He told Barry to get Dr Rao now Jonathan was here. When he got to the doctor's office, Dr Rao quizzed Barry about how Jonathan coped after finding out about his schizophrenia and his imaginary friends. Barry told him everything that Jonathan had said.

'Oh there is another odd thing doctor, Jonathan said for about two months his friends disappeared from his life, well technically his head. I thought it was rather strange, and I asked him if he did something different for them to just disappear like that.'

'What did he say?'

'He doesn't know, but he will ask you about it.'

'Hmmm that sounds interesting, I think I know why that happened. Overall I think he is taking it well, although it's hard, it looks like the medication is working. Let's go back into the interview room.'

When they got back, Jonathan started first. 'Doctor, Barry said you would tell me more about my type of schizophrenia. And whilst Barry and I were talking I remembered that my… friends,' Jonathan, embarrassed to call them friends now he realised they weren't real, 'had disappeared for two months. Would you know why?'

The doctor looked thoughtfully like he was pondering something serious, he then said, 'You know our mind is a complex thing, if you had a chemical imbalance in the first place then you must have righted that imbalance during that time for the imaginations to go away. Were you taking any pills that were out of the ordinary at the time?'

'I can't remember. 'Jonathan said thinking by looking out into space for a few seconds then he said, 'I remember finishing my depression pills a few months ago, and that sounds like it was around the same timeline as when they disappeared. Do you think it was that? It was the only medication my doctor prescribed for me.'

'It's a strong possibility, although those pills wouldn't have removed your delusions completely, it affected you in such a way as to remove them temporarily. I must ask when your friends came back, did they appear suddenly, or was it gradually?'

Jonathan felt embarrassed to talk about it, but he knew he had to, 'Peter turned up first giving me a story about what happened to them, and I believed him like a mug!'

'Don't be so hard on yourself, it was your mind not you.'

'But it's difficult to accept that side of me now.'

'I am sure, but it's in the past, and you were a different person to who you are now. Jonathan it will take you time and counselling to get over this. You had friends that you knew and loved and now you don't. Of course, it will be difficult. On top of that, you have just realised you are suffering from schizophrenia. It's a big deal, but I am confident that with the right support and medication you will come out alright.

Jonathan looked thoughtfully at the doctor, and then Barry said, 'see, we all have faith in you mate.'

'Have you seen a doctor about these symptoms before?' asked Dr Rao.

'I have, I'm not sure if he knew I had schizophrenia though, and if he had, then he didn't tell me. Maybe he told my mum, but then he gave me the depression pills I said about earlier, nothing more.'

'Did he say anything else?'

'Not to me at least.'

'Well, he must have discussed it with your parents because in the notes I got from your doctor he diagnosed you with having a bipolar disorder as well as the earliest stages of psychosis. He was close because he had prescribed Haloperidol which is an antipsychotic medication, but he hadn't diagnosed you with schizophrenia. Giving you Haloperidol should have helped remove your hallucinations.'

'So, he gave me those a while back, but I didn't regularly take them until after my first hypnotherapy session with Misty. I was worried I was going to get depressed after that session, so I took those pills. I guess that is why they disappeared! At least now I know. Will I have schizophrenia for the rest of my life?'

'It is a serious disorder, and we can't take this lightly. It affects how you think, feel and act. In typical schizophrenic fashion, you had difficulty distinguishing between what was real and what was imaginary. Maybe you were withdrawn from your friends at school, and that is why they didn't take a shine to you. You probably had trouble in social situations.

You will be on medication for the rest of your life, but you will also need to go through counselling and later in life be supported to find and keep a job etc., if you need it. With your schizoaffective disorder, combining therapy and medical treatments will increase the chances of your recovery. Luckily for you, you are young and will be able to eventually cope with the disorder so you can lead a normal life. However, you must do the hard work of taking your medication regularly and go to counselling. Once you manage that you can lead as normal a life as anyone.'

Then Jonathan asked apprehensively, 'How can I lead a normal life if I might go to prison now I killed my dad?'

The detective answered, 'Jonathan, your case is not as straightforward as we thought. In the beginning, we assumed you attacked your mum and dad. I don't think you know, but I feel I must tell you that your dad had been found not just with stab wounds to his abdomen, of which there were a few but his mouth was also gashed with a knife like you were trying to stop him from ever talking again. He was nearly unrecognisable. Your mum had both your dad's and your blood all over her, but none of the blood was hers.'

Jonathan swallowed and covered his mouth looking disgusted, then he said, 'I did that to my dad? I don't remember.'

The doctor said, 'You may have acted out of anger, didn't you say your friends egged you on?'

'They did, and I listened to them. They were real to me!' He cried. It was overwhelming, in the cold light of day he felt disgusted with himself.

Barry got near Jonathan and rubbed his back soothingly as a show of support.

Jonathan suddenly exploded in frustration, 'I am fed up with all this crap doctor, I find out I tried to kill myself but didn't know why. You said earlier that I killed both my parents which devastated me, because I can't believe I did that to my mum! I loved her so much!' He paused for breath and to calm himself from crying further.

The detective interjected, 'We only suggested that because when the police got there, you were the one with the knife in your hand lying next to your mum. We assumed you stabbed your dad, strangled your mum, and then tried to kill yourself. Until you told us about what really happened in your hypnotherapy session, we didn't have any other option but to come to that conclusion.'

Jonathan continued barely acknowledging what the detective said, 'Then after the hypnotherapy session we find out I didn't kill my mum which was an enormous relief for me, but that bastard did. Now today I find out I'm fucking mad, I got schizophrenia, and I don't really have any friends. The friends I cared about were characters in my head I made up from my Marvel comics. I may go to prison for killing my dad who I hated with a vengeance and oh, I'm locked up in a psycho hospital. I miss my mum, I can't live without her. How do you expect me to cope? I don't feel like living and if I top myself knowing all this crap, don't be surprised...' The tears rolled down from his eyes, 'doctor I don't want to live anymore, please. I can't deal with this. I really have nothing to live for!' He looked at Barry who then hugged him as Jonathan sobbed his heart out.

Barry continued to hug Jonathan tightly. Barry said, 'Jonathan, please, it's ok. You know I am here for you.' Then Barry looked at the detective defiantly and said, 'Jonathan your mum is still alive, don't cry. You will see her again.'

Jonathan didn't hear Barry and was still crying, but the doctor didn't stop Barry from telling Jonathan.

Barry said again, 'Jonathan your mum isn't dead mate.'

'What?' Jonathan said looking up through his tears.

'She isn't dead.'

Then Jonathan looked at Dr Rao who nodded at him, 'Barry is right. She is still alive, she has been in a coma since the murder of your dad.'

22

Jonathan couldn't believe what he heard. He felt like he had won the lottery. But then he couldn't understand why they didn't tell him this information before. Since finding out about that dreadful night he thought his mum was dead, and they didn't correct him. He was angry with them, especially with Barry.

Addressing Barry, he said, 'You lied to me, you said you were my friend!'

'I am your friend, please don't say that. I was ordered not to tell you by the detective. It was so hard for me seeing you like this. I wanted them to tell you the first day you found out about the murders when nurse Flowers came to sedate you, but I wasn't allowed to tell you then.'

The detective said, 'Jonathan we needed to find out your side of the story first. If you knew your mum was alive, you might not have given us any of the information we required. We also needed you to think you are the only one alive in the kitchen that can tell us what happened that night. I am sorry, but I was doing my job. I had ordered both Dr Rao and Barry to keep silent on the matter. So, don't be angry with them.'

'Fuck you and your sorry explanations!' Jonathan said angrily to the detective.

Barry looked at Jonathan saying, 'come on mate, that's not like you.'

'Barry, I wanted to kill myself, without my mum I have nobody in this world, you knew that. Of course, I am angry.'

'You are angry mate, but the good news is that she is in the hospital, and you can visit her whenever you want.'

Jonathan's face lit up. 'I can't believe it, so she was alive then, when the police found her?'

Dr Rao answered, 'Yes, the police got there just in time for both of you. In your mum's case, she had suffered a head injury before the strangulation. When they got her to the hospital, they found swelling in her brain, called a concussion, caused by the head trauma and a lack of oxygen from when she was strangled. As you know, oxygen is essential for brain function, but I don't think she was deprived of it for long enough to cause lasting damage. The trauma put her into a coma. She was unconscious but not dead. I suspect if you hadn't interrupted your dad when you had she would have died.'

Jonathan couldn't believe it but was relieved he got there in time to save his mum, he hated his dad even more knowing he was so close to killing her. Now he felt relieved and justified for killing his dad. Then he asked, 'so now what does that mean for her? How long will she remain like this?'

The doctor answered, 'When she first got to hospital, she was in the intensive care unit to stabilise her condition and body functions. They X-rayed her and sent her for an MRI scan to determine the extent of the damage she received. They also had to monitor the concussion and ensure that her brain healed naturally. She was unresponsive when they found her, and she still hasn't responded to stimuli.'

'How long will she stay like that doctor?' He repeated his earlier question.

'In time she may gain consciousness but to be honest, we are glad she is still in a coma, her body needed healing. Now we are hoping with stimulation from your visits she can come out of it gradually. She has been in a coma for about five weeks, so I think she is about ready to wake up.'

'Do you think she may get amnesia like I did due to my trauma?'

'Everyone is different, you suffered from amnesia from an early age, but there is no reason to think she will have the same issues you had. We won't know anything till she wakes up. She may suffer from short-term amnesia. By that I mean, she may not remember the incident at all, but she might remember who she is, who you are, where she lives and works, etc. But all this is guesswork till she wakes up. Due to her brain injury, it's something we fear she could suffer with but all that is speculation. Alternatively, due to her coma, her body is healing itself gradually which is the best way, we are hoping for no lasting damage.'

'Me too, I am just glad she is alive. Actually I really can't believe it.' He said excitedly. 'Whatever happens now, I have her, and she has me. When can I see her?'

Barry replied, 'Once she was out of the intensive care unit we brought her closer to you, so you can help each other out. She is in this hospital, and I can take you to visit her later.'

Jonathan smiled, 'Can't I go now?'

Barry looked at the detective who said, 'yes you can, it's the least I could do since I kept the information from you. I will have to speak to my superiors about this case and find out what the best way forward will be for you. I know it may seem your schizophrenia is unlucky, but it can really help you. They may classify your defence as "murder due to diminished responsibility".'

'What does that mean? I will go to prison but not for long due to my schizophrenia?'

'I don't know yet. But I need to speak to our lawyers and the judge and see how we will proceed. I will ensure you get adequate legal representation, but for now you are confined to this hospital.'

'I don't care, my mum is alive, and I want to see her.' He said happily.

'Ok let's go.' Said Barry.

When Jonathan and Barry had gone, Dr Rao turned to Detective Superintendent Brown and said, 'detective, surely he can't go to prison for this. Can't you do something? You know all the facts in this case, and you know he didn't set out to murder anyone that night. Won't it be classed as self-defence?'

'I don't make the rules as much as I would like to. The rule of law is what I follow, and I know that might seem harsh to you. You have gotten close to that boy just as much as Barry has, and to be honest with you, I don't want him to suffer any more than he has already.'

'His dad was unscrupulous from all accounts, that must mean something?'

'There are many dads like him, doctor, it doesn't mean we can condone murder.'

'I am not condoning murder, I want you to press the point to the 'powers that be' that he was suffering from schizophrenia, dealing with a stressful home life because of his emotionally abusive dad. And don't forget his dad nearly killed his mum.'

'Doctor you worry too much. I will do my best for him. I have been here from the beginning. Firstly, wanting him to be locked up forever for the brutality of the murder, and now secondly, finding out the real facts of the case. I will press upon whoever I have to, to get justice for Jonathan and his mum too. The whole thing is a mess for that family.'

'Have you heard from Niraj's family?'

'Yes, they said they wanted the boy to be prosecuted and for him to receive the maximum sentence for killing their son. They are speaking through their solicitors. When they found out Janice was alive, they said she deserved whatever she got. They think Jonathan tried to strangle her like we did.'

'They won't like the turn of events.'

'I don't really care what they like or not, from what Jonathan was saying, they washed their hands of their son. No point playing the grieving family when they gave up communication with him and his family in the first place. I hate this hypocrisy.'

The doctor sighed, 'Ok detective, I wish you luck on getting the best for Jonathan and his mum.'

'I will do what I can for all concerned. I will call you in a day or two once I find out what Jonathan's legal status is. For now, keep him occupied. I might have to assign him legal representation who will have to meet up with him shortly.'

'Ok detective, I will await your direction.'

When Detective Superintendent Brown left the hospital, he went to the office to make a few phone calls regarding the Rice family. He spoke to the prosecutor of the case and agreed with her to make available Jonathan's and Janice's statement, he said he hoped to get Janice's statement once she was out of her coma. He would also gather statements from Dr Rao and Barry on the case. His subordinates had already collected the statements from the night of the murder from Mr and Mrs Rawling, along with character statements on the Rice family, from Janice's boss Maisy, and friends of the family.

Because Jonathan was under eighteen, they classified him as a youth offender, and the prosecutor said she would take into consideration all aggravating and mitigating factors. The prosecutor said the court looked favourably on the fact that Jonathan didn't have any previous convictions, and if his behaviour in the hospital was good, then that could go in his favour too.

Detective Superintendent Brown planned for a criminal defence lawyer to visit Jonathan and to get a statement that would look favourably to the judge in this case. Due to his age, he wouldn't have to attend court.

The next day the detective called Dr Rao. 'Afternoon, doctor how are you?'

'At last, I was getting worried. Is everything ok?'

'Yeah, all good, how has Jonathan been? Has he been to see his mum yet?'

'Yes, he has, and he seems a lot happier since then, bless him. And before you ask, she hasn't come out of the coma yet.'

There was a moment of silence then the detective said, 'oh I see. Ok well, I have some good news for Jonathan which I will tell him when I come over tomorrow. I must finalise details with the prosecutor today. Can I come over at eleven or twelve tomorrow to see Jonathan?'

'That's fine, see you tomorrow, and if they need more

than the statement I have given or have questions about it, please let me know.'

'Great thanks doctor.'

The day that Jonathan found out his mum was alive he had left the interview room with Barry and was getting very excited to visit his mother. He was nervous about seeing her, but he put his feelings to one side and calmly followed Barry. A million thoughts ran through his head. He hoped that as soon as she heard his voice, she would wake up, but he knew it was wishful thinking, and he wanted her to come out unscathed, he promised himself that he would be there to look after her. He felt all grown up and decided whatever the consequences, from now on, he will be the one to look after his mum. He wasn't a small boy anymore, he had grown up quickly.

He knew some of his problems stemmed from his schizo-phrenia, but some of them were because of his dad's emotional abuse. Now that his dad was gone, and he was under medication for his condition he knew he would be ok. All he needed was for his mum to come out of her coma with little or no damage. He would face anything that the police gave him because of what he had done to his dad.

When they got to Janice's room, Barry let him in whilst he hung back and stayed behind Jonathan. The room was moderately lit, but with the blinds partially open the daylight streamed in from the window. The privacy curtains around the side of the bed that faced the door was also drawn so Jonathan couldn't see his mum till he walked into the room and around the curtain.

When he got to the foot of the bed, she was sleeping

soundly, like she was in her bedroom without a care in the world. Jonathan came closer to her, afraid to make a sound in case he woke her up. But then he realised how ridiculous that was, he needed to wake her up. He looked at her neck where she was strangled by his dad but saw no bruising. She seemed fine, just in a coma. An image came into his head briefly of when he last saw her, when his dad was trying to strangle her, and she was motionless, she wasn't even trying to get his hands off her. He got upset, tears flowed down his cheeks, and he didn't even realise it. So much had happened since he last saw her.

Jonathan looked over at Barry hoping he was still there for support. Barry was looking at Jonathan feeling slightly choked up himself. He decided he had to be strong for Jonathan's sake and looked over at Jonathan nodding his head in a 'go ahead' gesture. Jonathan got closer to his mum and said in a whisper, 'mum it's me, Jonathan, it's time to get up.'

There was no sound or movement from his mum, he then said, 'don't worry mum, take your time and rest up as much as you want. I will be here waiting for you when you get up, and you will see, all will be OK. The dark days are over, we have a new beginning, and I can't wait.' He finished excitedly.

Barry was smiling at him and then whispered, 'I will get you a chair so you can stay longer. Wait here one minute.'

When Barry came back with the chair, he told Jonathan he would be back in half an hour and to keep talking to his mum.

Jonathan said, 'but I don't know what else to tell her.'

'Just tell her what you have been up to, tell her about the 'Planet Earth' episode you watched. Lots of things you have been doing since you were admitted here.'

He looked pleased, 'Ok good idea. You go, I will be fine here.'

When Barry left, Jonathan talked to his mum about everything that had happened over the few days he was out of his coma. He didn't even realise the time, Barry came back in what felt like five minutes.

Jonathan said, 'That was quick.'

'It's been forty-five minutes! I gave you a few extra, you want me to come back?'

'No, it's fine. Let's go, we can come back later. I need to eat, I am starving again!'

'You are always starving!'

'I'm a growing boy, bet you don't remember, it's been a long time since you were young!' Jonathan said laughing at Barry.

'You're a cheeky little crud, aren't you? I am only forty-one!'

'Well, still ages since you were sixteen though.' Barry ruffled his hair laughing at his cheekiness.

During lunch, Jonathan asked, 'Is there anything I can do to get my mum out of the coma?'

'In my experience, I have seen a few people in a coma from time to time. Because this hospital mainly deals with people who suffer from serious mental trauma, it's something we see now and again. Every case is different, so there is not one thing that will work for all. Some people remember things around them whilst they were in a coma but some remember nothing at all.

The best thing you can do is sound cheerful and happy when you are with her and just talk to her like she was awake. You could massage her feet or hands as there are pressure points that can stimulate her nerves, that might help. If you are having a coffee or tea, make assurances like "mmm this tastes so good, if you wake up you could have some too" etc. Reading to her will also help, if you like reading or play music she is familiar with. So, there are lots of things you could do.'

'In your estimation how much longer do you think she will need? She looks healed there were no bruises on her neck.'

'Don't forget that the doctor said she had suffered a concussion. To be honest, we are all glad she went into a coma. The body has a much better chance of healing itself then. Don't worry too much. You do what you have to do, and it will work out fine. Trust me.'

'You say that a lot, "trust me".'

'Yes, I do, because you have no-one to trust right now, and I want you to trust me because you had a difficult time growing up. You haven't had it easy mate, have you?'

'But I am fine, once we sort out what they want to do with me, I will be ok. I will take the counselling seriously.'

'You better do, or I will knock on your door and will take you there personally, even if you are kicking and screaming!'

'I wouldn't want to mess with you!' He said smiling.

After they had eaten Jonathan spent a lot of time with his mum talking to her, reading, and then he invited Barry over, so they could play Ludo in her room. Jonathan kept asking his mum to keep an eye on Barry because he felt he was cheating in the game. Barry, of course, pretended like the suggestion offended him. At some point, they forgot that Janice was lying there in a coma. They laughed and joked as they usually would. Barry ordered dinner to be served in Janice's room so they could stay with her longer. He hoped the smell of the food might stimulate her senses enough to help her wake up.

At night Jonathan reluctantly left his mum. He asked if he

could have a bed put in her room so he could stay the night with her, but he was told they didn't allow that. He would have to make do with all day visits instead. He didn't complain much, he suspected they would refuse, but he thought he would try his luck.

Barry told him that the detective wanted to see him and Dr Rao the next day and that he had news on the case. Jonathan had a happy day with his mum and didn't want to worry about what the detective might tell them. He took it as it came, when he got into bed, he went to sleep as soon as his head hit the pillow.

23

The next morning Jonathan woke up early, had breakfast and went to visit his mum. Barry accompanied him again. When they got there, Barry asked the attending nurse if there was any change in her status overnight but found out there wasn't. Jonathan looked a tad disappointed with the news, but he reminded himself that until yesterday he thought she was dead, so her being in a coma was better than not having her at all.

At eleven a.m. Barry and Jonathan went over to the interview room to meet up with Dr Rao and Detective Superintendent Brown. This time there was a woman with them too. The detective introduced her as Miss Mansfield who was the junior counsel for the prosecution.

Jonathan was feeling nervous to see someone official he hadn't met before. He sat there pleasantly acknowledging everyone. Barry could sit in too, which made him feel a bit better.

The detective said, 'Thanks for agreeing to meet us. Miss Mansfield is here to explain the status of your case, Miss Mansfield?'

'Hello Jonathan, I work for the prosecutor's office as a junior counsel. I have looked into your legal standing, and we are confident that we can take this case to the judge without your presence due to your age. After looking at all the facts, witness statements and character references for all of you, the only thing missing is your mum's statement. Until we get it, we thought it would be fair to tell you what your legal status will be going forward.

You as the defendant would typically face a murder charge, but due to the unique circumstances, we will proceed with the alternative count of 'Voluntary Manslaughter due to diminished responsibility, with the abnormality of mental functioning.' It means that you were in a state of mind that differed greatly from that of an ordinary human being, something a reasonable person would term 'abnormal'.

Another factor we took into consideration is aggravating and mitigating factors. There were no real aggravating factors that indicated that you either planned the murder or you took advantage of a situation when your dad was in a vulnerable position. The mitigating factors we considered were that your initial intention when you entered the kitchen wasn't to harm anyone, and because of the voices in your head, suffering from a mental disorder should go in your favour too. You also tried to protect yourself and your mum from your dad, and to stop any further deaths you acted in the way that you did. The other things that are big mitigating factors are your age, and you have no previous convictions.

Another point considered is the reasonableness of the force used in the murder of your dad. We know that you said you hit him with a pan on his shoulder in the first instance, there was evidence of bruising to his body to confirm your statement. We will support your need of using extreme force to remove a threat of further violence, bearing in mind the period in which you had to act was very short, and the state of your mental wellbeing was in question. To further save your mum and yourself you acted as you did against your dad. You also said you can't remember exactly what happened after you first stabbed your dad. He had suffered five fatal abdomen stabbings and one to his face, his mouth. We believe your mental health was to blame for that.

Dr Rao gave us your medical history which, including the amnesia you suffered regularly since childhood, you have schizoaffective disorder. We have also included statements from a few witnesses that affirm that your mum complained that your dad was emotionally and physically abusive which will be used to inform the judge presiding over this case.'

Nobody spoke when Miss Mansfield had finished speaking, so she continued, 'something else we were given was your mum's diary. Did you know your mum kept a diary?'

Jonathan shook his head 'I didn't.'

'We didn't think you knew about it because you hadn't mentioned it. But when we went to get a statement from Miss Maisy, she gave us your mum's diary. In that, your mum confirms that your dad abused both of you and was physically abusive to her in the past. She also mentioned the incident when your father tried to strangle her the first time which corroborates your story as well. Her account mirrors a lot of what you have already said in the statement you gave to the doctor and the detective, and we will use that in court. Once your mum wakes up, we will need a statement from her about the circumstances of the night of the murder, but for now, we can use her diary as evidence in court.

We will proceed to hear your case using what I have already mentioned. I will not take anything you say forward until you have a meeting with your counsel. We will be asking the judge to show mercy due to the circumstances of this case. We will request no incarceration because that wouldn't benefit you in any way.'

She stopped speaking and took a sip of water. Barry asked on Jonathan's behalf, 'does that mean that there is a strong possibility that Jonathan won't be put in a youth offender's prison?'

'Yes, it does, we will recommend regular counselling and a probation order for a set time.'

Barry said, 'Jonathan, do you want to ask Miss Mansfield anything?'

'When will all this all be over? I am tired of it!' He mumbled.

Miss Mansfield answered, 'About four to six weeks or thereabout.'

Nobody spoke for a few minutes. Jonathan wanted to get this over with and see his mum. The doctor then said, 'that's great news and a lot better than I had expected. Thank you, detective, for your compassion on this case.'

The detective said, 'well it wouldn't be fair any other way. Jonathan saved his mum's life when he came into the kitchen. Any later and there would have been another body to contend with.'

Jonathan looked at his healing wrists and realised if Mr and Mrs Rawling hadn't appeared when they did he would have been found dead along with his mum too. The more he thought about it, the more tired his brain became. Without realising it, he said out loud, 'what a mess this has become!'

They all looked at Jonathan, 'sorry I didn't mean to blurt it out loud. If my dad wasn't such a jerk in the first place, we wouldn't all be sitting here!'

The detective concluded the meeting saying he would get in touch with what the next steps would be and asked

Jonathan to pass any questions he had for them through his counsel.

After they left, Barry took Jonathan to his room to freshen up, and he seemed more excited about the news than Jonathan, who was quieter than usual for a while.

'I thought you would be happy about what Miss Mansfield had to say.' Barry said apprehensively.

'I am.'

'Then why the long face?'

'I was just wondering when my mum comes out of the coma where would we stay. I don't want to go back to that house.'

'Didn't you say your mum secured a flat somewhere before the whole ordeal?'

'She had, but it's been over a month. I don't think any landlord will keep a place vacant until we sort our lives out. I know my mum wouldn't want to go back home either.'

'Listen, mate, where you will live is the least of your worries. Just concentrate on what the judge comes back with once he has heard your case. For now, you can get busy helping your mum get better. It's that simple.'

'If you say so.'

'I do, now stop feeling sorry for yourself and let's go cheer up your mum. Who knows maybe today is the day she wakes up from her coma.'

'Hmmm hopefully.'

Barry took Jonathan over to his mum, then he left him to go to Dr Rao who wanted an update on Jonathan's demeanour. When he got there, the doctor asked, 'so how did he take it? Bet he was overjoyed.'

'Not really, doctor.'

'Oh, why not?'

'He is happy, but he is now worrying about minor things

like where they will live after they leave the hospital. He said he doesn't want to stay in that house, his mum wouldn't either. To be fair neither would I, so I told him to stop worrying about such things as they aren't as important now.'

'That's true.'

'So now what, doctor?'

'Now we wait and see, I guess. We must keep monitoring him, he isn't out of the woods yet. His medication will need reviewing now and again, and he might suffer bouts of mania or depression some days. Jonathan thinks that by speaking to his mum regularly, she will magically come out of the coma. She may, but she may not. And if she doesn't then he will get increasingly depressed, I am hoping that doesn't happen, so your work with him is vital. Hope you're still up for it.'

'I am here for him whatever the case may be, I won't abandon him.'

'That's good to hear. Has he said anything to you about his 'friends', the imaginary ones?'

'Not really, it looks like his medication is working well. Have you booked him into counselling sessions?'

'Not yet. I wanted to make sure his medication was working and give him time to deal with it all. Every day there is some drama or the other for that poor boy to deal with, but you're right the sooner we start, the better. For now, I want to counsel him myself and then gradually hand him over to someone who is closer to where he might be living.'

Barry looked disappointed, and the doctor was astute enough to understand quickly.

'Now don't look like that Barry, it's the nature of our jobs. He has to leave when he gets better, you can't have him stay here forever!'

'I know but…I have become so close to him.'

'You have, and you will get another patient to look after once Jonathan goes, and so the cycle will continue.' Dr Rao said in a 'matter of fact' kind of way.

'You make it sound so easy doctor, but Jonathan is special. We haven't had a case like his before.'

'He may be special, but life will go on, both for you and for him. Don't tell me I will have to counsel you too after Jonathan goes!' The doctor said smiling.

'Hilarious doctor, you can keep your specialist service for the ones that need it most. Ok, I better go and check up on him. He is with his mum.'

'Don't forget to tell me if anything out of the ordinary happens with him.'

'Everything that has happened to him has been out of the ordinary, doctor!'

When Barry got to Janice's room, Jonathan was reading a comic to her in an animated fashion. Barry stood at the door looking at him in admiration, thinking they must have had a special relationship before this mess. Barry was glad he could buy and give him some comic books that he was now reading animatedly to his mum. But he didn't want Jonathan to have access to the ones he had at home in case they brought back bad memories or worse still, his friends back in his life. Barry was confident in Dr Rao's medical assessment and medication he gave Jonathan. He should really have been diagnosed a long time ago, and if he had, maybe none of this would have happened. Barry sighed loudly, and that made Jonathan stop and look over.

'Oh, how long have you been standing there? I feel like a fool.'

'Don't be silly, you have a gift for voices. Maybe you have found your calling in life.' Barry said encouragingly, coming further into the room.

'You think so? Imagine what people will think, "that guy with voices in his head now expresses them out loud", I don't think so.'

'Don't sell yourself short, your imagination might be what makes you the man you could become. With your gifts you could write stories, movies, become an actor, voice-over artist... so many things. Do you realise Jonathan, to develop your creative abilities we need to recognise how rich our creative capacities are and the conditions under which they will emerge.'

Jonathan then thoughtfully said, 'I am so glad you are my friend. I wish my dad was like you.'

Barry was so touched he was lost for words for once, he wanted to hug Jonathan but didn't think it would be appropriate, so he refrained. He said, 'that's the nicest thing anyone has said to me in a long time. Thank you mate. You know I will do whatever I can to help you out.'

Barry didn't want to bring up Jonathan leaving, but he felt this was a good time to mention it.

'... once you leave here, you will find new friends and a new place to live and you can settle in nicely with your mum.'

'Won't I be allowed to see you after I leave?' Jonathan looked shocked.

'Not that you won't be allowed, just that you will be busy, plus you won't want to come back here, I can guarantee you that. It's been a hard time for you here at the hospital.'

'But we can meet as friends, can't we? Outside the hospital'? Then Jonathan said quietly and nearly under his breath, 'or don't you want to? Once I am not your patient?'

Barry heard him despite how silently it was said, 'Oh my god Jonathan I want to see you, but I don't want to be a constant reminder of your hospital days. You mean so much to me, and if I had a son, I would love it if he was just like you.'

Jonathan cried and went over to hug Barry. They stood there hugging for a while. Then suddenly Jonathan pushed Barry off gently and quickly wiped his tears. He said, 'we need to man up Barry! We can't be hugging like a bunch of girls!' Jonathan said it so seriously that Barry burst out laughing.

'We are men, and we need to behave like men! You know what Jonathan?'

'What?'

'How about if we make new, better memories outside the hospital?'

Jonathan's eyes lit up, 'really? You promise?'

'One hundred per cent.'

Jonathan said excitedly, 'this may be an odd thing to say, but I read or heard somewhere that "'everything happens for a reason", me being here is not ideal, but I got to meet you, and I know that I will have you in my life forever.'

'I am glad too but remember, we can't hug like girls. We can't have that girly relationship!'

'Yeah, we can't.'

They both ended up laughing after that comment.

Over the next two weeks, Barry kept Jonathan's spirits up whilst he was visiting his mum. They played Ludo, watched some more episodes of 'Planet Earth,' discussed why Jonathan found the comics so engaging, and Barry spoke to him about interesting patients he worked with in the past. He also made sure that Jonathan regularly attended his counselling sessions with Dr Rao. That helped him because Dr Rao could assess how Jonathan was coping first hand, and the doctor didn't need to rely on Barry's assessment of Jonathan's recovery.

Barry also watched movies with Jonathan that he would find stimulating. They both liked adventure movies. Jonathan wanted Barry to watch the Marvel movies, but he kept putting it off. Barry explained that it was still too early to watch those type of movies considering his 'imaginary friend' issues. Jonathan kept insisting he was fine, and that Dr Rao's medication was doing wonders, but still, Barry didn't want to take any chances.

Sometimes Jonathan would be in a mood and wouldn't talk much, only to his mum when he visited her, and stayed solemn for the day. Barry never knew when he would get like that or why. He supposed that Jonathan was still coming to terms with his new living conditions, and when that happened, Barry gave him a wide birth. He tried to be neutral on those days and only providing a basic service. The change in mood from his solemn days to the ones where he was in a good mood was stark. On Jonathan's normal days he would be overly bubbly, and Barry loved it when he was like that.

Jonathan said to Barry one day, 'Barry I haven't ever seen this version of myself.'

'What do you mean mate?'

'Well, I am definitely happier than I was in my old life. I am thinking about doing things I haven't ever thought of before, I want to learn more about nature, history, the arts, and maybe even try writing. I am not sure what, but I think about it a lot. Something I have never done before.'

'Wow that's great, do you think it's because you're on 'proper' medication for your condition?'

'Well... I guess that's part of the reason, but I suspect due to our many talks and things we have watched together, I have questioned the rationale for everything. I feel like I have been asleep for so long and haven't looked at the world around me.'

'God that's deep, you sure Dr Rao isn't overdosing you on your meds?' Barry said smiling.

'No Barry, I am serious.'

'Oh I am just teasing you, I think it's a great thing. Personally, I will never stop learning, and I encourage you to do that too. Just because you get to a certain age doesn't mean you should stop. Do something interesting, something new or learn a new skill, like a new language.'

'Yeah, great advice. So any idea when my mum might come out of her coma?'

'You ask me this everyday Jonathan.'

'But it's now becoming a habit. If I don't ask, then it's not a normal day for me.' He said smiling.

'Okay, I will tell you what I tell you every day, soon I hope!'

That night when Barry saw Jonathan to his bed, he went to Janice's room. The small night light was on, and the nurse attending to Janice was just leaving.

She said, 'Oh hey Barry, Jonathan forgot something here?'

Barry felt embarrassed, because he had no reason to be in Janice's room, he lied and said, 'Yes, Jonathan wanted a certain comic he left here, and I said I would find it and bring it to him.'

'Oh ok, I am just leaving. You want me to help you look for it?'

'No it's fine, I will find it. You off now?'

'Just going to attend to another patient, if you need anything come and find me in the nurse's station. I should be back there in ten to fifteen minutes.'

'Great thanks.'

When the nurse left Barry pretended to go to the pile of books, magazines, and newspapers that Jonathan had as a stash to occupy his time or read to his mum. After a minute of pretending to look through them, he glanced at the entrance to the room. Everything seemed calm outside, so he went over to the door nearly shut it but made sure it wasn't closed. He wanted no one to find him alone with Janice and the door shut.

He then went over to Janice and pulled up the chair to sit beside her, he looked at her sleeping peacefully and thought she looked very pretty and too young to be Jonathan's mum. Clearing his throat, he said, 'Hey Janice it's me, Barry. Hm-mmm… anyway, I came to tell you that you would do me a huge favour if you woke up soon. Jonathan misses you, and whilst you are sleeping there so beautifully, it is taking Jonathan longer to recover from his problems. I am sorry for putting pressure on you, but I care about him, and so do you. So how about we make a pact, and both help him together? What do you say?'

Janice didn't move or say anything, he wasn't expecting much of her, anyway. After sitting there in silence for a few minutes, he said, 'It was a rough ride for you too I hear. Don't worry it will all be ok. Jonathan is on the mend, and once you see that, you will be too. I will make sure. Ok, I better go in case someone finds me here. They might think it's odd, me coming to talk to you. Don't forget our pact ok? We help him together. You promised so I will hold you to it.' He said smiling. 'Goodnight Janice.' For a strange moment he felt like he should bend over and kiss her forehead, but then realised that would be foolish of him. So, he quickly left her room hoping that nobody would see him.

When he got to his room, he felt strangely at peace for talking to Janice. He wanted to talk to her again tomorrow night but didn't know how he would engineer it. Anyway, he didn't want to think any more about it, so he went to bed.

Barry went to see Janice every night for the next two weeks. At first, he would to talk to her for five or ten minutes but that soon increased to thirty minutes. He spoke about his day with Jonathan and how funny or amusing Jonathan was, and every night he reminded her about the pact that they made to help Jonathan. He felt lucky he wasn't found out, and he continued his visits. He couldn't understand how someone in a coma could make him feel comfortable, and he wanted more than ever for Janice to wake up. He wanted to look into her eyes, see that beautiful smile, watch her move so her hair bounced around her shoulders. He didn't like it being just combed and left on her pillow like that, he got annoyed with himself, 'what is wrong with you, you freak!' He said to himself. The woman was in a coma, for all he knew she had a bad temper and was an alcoholic! But deep down he couldn't stop himself. He wanted to see her to say goodnight, every night.

After four weeks of Jonathan finding out his mum was alive, she woke up from her coma.

24

Aphone call by the attending nurse woke Barry. The doctor had been called but hadn't arrived yet, and the nurse knew Barry would have to be the one to take Jonathan over to see his mum.

'Jonathan, wake up, wake up!' Barry shouted excitedly. He was trying to shake him out from his sleep.

'It's still dark outside Barry, what the fuck?'

'Your mum is awake, get the hell up.'

He sat upright in bed rubbing his eyes, 'what? She woke up? When? Why didn't you tell me earlier?'

'She only woke up about twenty minutes ago. The nurse is the only person who has seen her, the doctor has been called but hasn't arrived yet!'

'Hurry up, brush your teeth and come in your jammies.'

'Ok, ok I am coming.'

Barry was excited for Jonathan, but he also wanted to meet Jonathan's mum. He didn't know what he would say to her now she was awake. First, he had to let Jonathan and his mum connect again. They had a lot to talk about.

Jonathan got ready quicker than ever, he didn't even

change out of his bedroom slippers. He was out the door as soon as he was done, leaving Barry to walk quickly to keep up with him.

'Slow down mate, she isn't going anywhere.'

'What time is it Barry?'

'Four am.'

'That early? Well, she has had all the sleep she wanted, so time isn't a factor to her I guess.'

'You guess right.' Barry said breathlessly still trying to keep up with a nearly running teen.

When they got to the room, one nurse was outside with the door shut. She told them that the doctor had just got there and was giving Janice a quick physical check before anyone could see her. Jonathan looked disappointed. Barry said, 'only a few more minutes, and you can go in.'

After fifteen minutes of frantic pacing from both the door opened. Jonathan said, 'can I go in now, doctor?'

'Yes, son. She will be pleased to see you.'

Jonathan gave Barry a huge grin. Barry gave him a wink and a nod and followed the doctor whilst Jonathan went into the room.

Barry asked, 'So doctor, how is she?'

'Like nothing ever happened. She looked normal, knew what year it was, her name, address, her job, birthdate, everything.'

'Did she ask for her son?'

'Yes, the first thing she said. I told her she can see him in a few minutes once she answered my questions.'

'Anything else?'

'You mean about what happened to her?'

Barry nodded.

'Not really.'

'Oh.'

'Actually, it's a good thing. Let her focus on the fact she is well, her son is well too, and maybe later they can discuss it. I am only a stand-in doctor whilst Dr Rao comes back in later today. He will do all the assessments required. For my examination she did great.'

'Thank you, doctor.'

'You're welcome.'

With that Barry let the doctor walk off, and he turned back toward Janice's room. As he got there, he was feeling increasingly nervous. He felt a fool, what was he worried about? She was Jonathan's mum! But then again if he was honest with himself, he wanted Janice to like him. He had become a friend of her son, and her impression meant a lot to him.

He put those thoughts out of his mind, he paced outside her room like an expectant father waiting near the labour suite for his baby to be born!

Meanwhile inside the room: Jonathan walked in quietly. As soon as he saw his mum, he ran the last steps over to her shouting, 'mum. Oh my god, I missed you!'

His mum smiled at him, tears rolling down her cheeks as she stretched her arms out wide to receive him. 'Jonathan, my boy. Are you ok my darling?'

Jonathan muffled his answer through the hug, 'I'm fine mum. How are you feeling?'

She released him wiping the tears from her eyes. 'I am fine too, I feel rested and relaxed. Like I have been for a long nap.'

'Long nap? Didn't they tell you?'

'Why I'm here?'

'Yes.'

'No, they didn't, why?'

'What do you remember last?'

Her face gave him a small frown, her smile faded, and her eyes narrowed. She said, 'your dad and I arguing in the dining room! Where is he anyway? Now I am in hospital, I bet he will come with flowers and chocolates like the best husband in the world!'

It was Jonathan's turn to frown, she sensed his hesitation. 'What? Has he done something bad to you?'

Jonathan shook his head 'not really.'

'Then what?'

He whispered, 'mum do you remember what happened in the kitchen?'

Janice turned to the only window in her room to think, then she looked shocked and looking back at Jonathan she said, 'God, he was trying to strangle me again!' She put her hands on her neck saying, 'I couldn't breathe, I tried to get him off me.'

She was crying, Jonathan cried too. 'Yes, mum he tried to strangle you again. I got there just in time. You were unconscious when I got to the kitchen. You weren't resisting him, and I thought you had died!'

'Oh nooooo'

'I got so angry mum, I wasn't thinking straight.'

'You hit him?'

'Well yes at first with the frying pan that was lying around which made him let go of you and come after me.'

She couldn't breathe and stared at him.

'Then… then….' Jonathan stammered.

'Then what?'

'Mum I took a knife from the knife block.'

She put her hands to half cover her face terrified of what Jonathan would say next.

'He laughed at me for my feeble attempt at protecting you and looking over at you thinking you were dead I became possessed with rage.'

'You stabbed him? Oh god please tell me you didn't.'

'Yes, I did, and I am glad!' He said defiantly with a touch of anger.

'Where is he? In the hospital too? He will be so mad!'

'No, he isn't.'

'You talked to him?'

'No…'

She finally realised what he tried to tell her, she sank back on to her pillows and now covered her face. She was in total shock.

'I killed him for trying to kill you.'

Slowly she removed her hands from her face, and she stared at Jonathan, and said, 'It's all my fault! If I had left that bastard a long time ago, it wouldn't have come to this! And the police?'

'I am taking care of it, mum.'

Janice saw a new side to her son, a side she hadn't seen before. He looked all grown up and mature. He was more confident and even looked taller. Jonathan started by telling her everything that had happened since he was in the hospital. He told her that he was in a coma too and how Barry had been a rock of support for him during those dark days. Janice was crying when he told her how he wanted to die when he thought she had died, how he tried to kill himself by slitting his wrists. He also apprehensively told her about his 'friends,' his diagnosis of bipolar disorder, schizophrenia and schizoaffective disorder. He told her how Mr and Mrs Rawling saved their lives by calling the police, what Miss Mansfield said about his case and about the diary they had from Maisy that supported his story.

She listened patiently, going through a few emotions over the course of Jonathan's story. She was shocked, sad, and then happy when he mentioned the things he did with Barry. He tried to finish on a happy note.

Janice said, 'I know it's my fault, Jonathan. I am your mum, I was supposed to protect you from that monster, not the other way around. You have grown from a boy to a man in such a short space of time. I promise never to let you down again.' She said sadly.

'Aaaaawww mum, don't say that, you have been the best mum in the world. Now we have each other, just you wait it will be the best. Only you, me, and the wide-open world.' He said laughing.

'Easy, let's not run. We got to sort out what happens to your case, you need to continue with your medication and counselling. I will need counselling too after this. We need to find a new place to live, because I don't want to take you back there! There are so many bad memories for us there.'

'Yeah it's true, I don't want to go back there either. Anyway, aren't you starving? When I woke up from my coma, I wanted to eat everything!'

Janice laughed, 'Yes now you mention it I am starving, but I won't eat everything! Look it's getting lighter outside.'

'And you will want to have a nap after the breakfast. Barry is outside, I will ask him to get both of us some breakfast. You ok here?'

'Of course.'

Jonathan went out of the room after over an hour of being with his mum. Barry sat on a chair outside the room with his hands on his face, elbows resting on his knees. He looked like he was praying.

'Hey, Barry.'

Barry looked up, then stood up when he saw Jonathan.

'How is she, mate?'

'Unfazed! It's amazing. I told her everything. She was shocked about you know…' he trailed off.

'Your dad.'

'Yup.'

'And is she ok now?'

'Yes, she is blaming herself. She said if she had removed me from that situation in the first place none of this would have happened.'

'She can't blame herself. Hindsight is a great thing, but we live and learn from what we have experienced, I told you this already.'

'Yes, you have. She will need counselling too Barry. Like me!' He said smiling. He was glad he wasn't the only one going to counselling. 'Anyway, she is starving and so am I. Why don't you get us all some breakfast?'

'Of course, I'm on it.'

'Oh and Barry, I mean you too. We can eat together in her room. I want you to meet her.'

'Hmmm… I'm not so sure.' Barry said raking his hands through his hair.

'Don't be shy, it will be great.'

'If you say so, I will meet you there shortly. You want anything in particular?'

'No, whatever you can find at this hour!'

'Be back soon.' Barry said turning around to make his way to the kitchen.

Barry was nervous as hell. He couldn't think straight and wasn't sure now was the best time to meet Janice. Once he got breakfast ordered, he asked them to bring it over to

Janice's room. He walked back, knocked on the door briefly before letting himself in.

Janice was sitting up in bed holding Jonathan's hand. She looked over at Barry. Jonathan stood up and went over to Barry. 'Mum, this is Barry. Barry, my mum, Janice.'

Barry smiled and said, 'Hi Jonathan's mum.'

'Hi Barry, call me Janice. So, you are responsible for my son's maturity during his dark days?'

'Yes I am, and the pleasure was all mine.' He rubbed Jonathan's hair whilst he said so.

Jonathan interrupted, 'Yes he is mum, he literally saved me from going mad in here.' Realising his choice of words, he said, 'well, I was mad, but now he has made me sane again!' He said laughing.

'Don't be silly Jonathan, Dr Rao was the one giving you the right medication. I was there to support and look after you.'

Janice said, 'and what a great job you did. I feel like I know you. Have we met before?'

Barry looked embarrassed.

'Barry, you met my mum before, and you never mentioned it?'

'I don't think so, Mrs Rice.' He said sheepishly.

'Call me Janice, please. Are you sure? I feel like we've met.'

Jonathan said excitedly, 'mum you remember him from when we spent time in your room. When you were in a coma, we came here to read to you, play Ludo and hang out. You remember! Wow, that's amazing, right Barry, don't you think so too?'

'Yes, it is.' Barry said with relief, fearing his night trips to talk to Janice may have been revealed. 'I told you she could have heard us. Now we know she did.'

'Yeah mum we played Ludo, we need to have a game with all three of us, but be careful. Barry cheats!'

'I do not!' Barry said laughing.

Breakfast arrived, and Janice felt hungrier than ever. Jonathan had been right, she wanted to eat everything! Whilst they ate their breakfast Jonathan did all the talking, and Barry and Janice listened to him. She was so happy that Jonathan was in a good mood. She had never seen that side of him, and she loved it. The medication he was on was perfect for him.

Barry was lost in his own thoughts, he nodded and smiled and made the right noises when Jonathan addressed him, but his opinion of Janice preoccupied him. Firstly, she looked even more beautiful awake than asleep. Secondly, she had a gentle speaking manner, and Barry could tell that she thought the world of Jonathan. Thirdly, she would do anything to protect him. He was glad for Jonathan.

'... Don't you think so Barry? Jonathan asked Barry breaking his chain of thought.

'Yeah, I do.' Barry responded not knowing what Jonathan had been saying. He looked over at Janice who was looking a little tired. He said, 'after I clear the dishes Jonathan let's give your mum time to rest for a while.'

'Awww really? Mum, are you tired?'

Janice wanted to spend more time with her son, she could see he had missed her. Ten weeks in a coma was a long time, and she was sad when she found out that for two of those weeks he believed she had died! She decided when she saw that detective she would give him a piece of her mind!

'Yes, I am I guess. It's a lot to take in.'

Jonathan sadly remembered when he woke from the coma all confused. 'Yeah it is, just get the nurse to call us when you wake, and we will be back won't we Barry?'

'For sure.'

When they left, Janice snuggled into bed and immediately fell asleep.

As they walked back to Jonathan's room, he said, 'Isn't she great Barry? She looks like nothing has ever happened, and she didn't lose her memory like I did.'

'Yeah she looks beautiful...' Jonathan turned to look at him.

'Beautiful?'

'... I mean, rested and happy.'

'But you said beautiful! Barry... come on spill the beans!' He said laughing at him.

'It was a slip of the tongue! Don't be silly. She is your mum.'

'But you think she is also beautiful! Wait till I tell her. She will like that.'

'Are you crazy, don't say that. She will think I fancy her.'

'And you don't?'

'For god's sake Jonathan, she has just woken up from a coma, found out her husband is dead under difficult circumstances. People fancying her is the last thing on her mind.' Barry said scolding Jonathan. But Jonathan was unfazed by that.

'Ok, ok, keep your pants on. I am teasing you.'

'Good.'

'But you fancy her and don't want her to know it?' He said pushing his luck.

'JONATHAN,' He yelled, 'I swear if you breathe another word about it I'm going to...'

'You will what?' Jonathan said running to his room laughing.

Barry smiled thinking 'god that boy, he is too clever!'

Later, when Dr Rao came on shift, he went straight over to see Janice. He came to the same conclusion the night doctor had. Janice asked Dr Rao lots of questions about Jonathan which he willingly answered. She seemed pleased that Dr Rao was happy with the way he coped and how religiously he was taking his medication.

The next few days were a blur to Janice, she was out of her room a lot with the aid of her nurse. She needed to use the wheelchair for the first few days, as her body was getting used to being out of bed. She had to attend physical rehabilitation, and she soon walked with a cane. A few days after that she was ready to walk short distances without aid.

When Janice and Jonathan were alone Janice tried to understand the relationships Jonathan had with his imaginary friends, she wanted to get Jonathan to talk about them like they had been real, she found out each of their personalities and how they interacted with Jonathan's mind. She assumed Peter was the strong one that Jonathan looked up to because he wanted to be like Peter: self-assured and easy going. She realised Misty was Jonathan's idea of a girl he would be interested in romantically. Nick was the strong silent type, he had a violent streak that Jonathan wished he had. He wanted to lash out at his dad, and Nick brought out these violent tendencies.

Jonathan was not very comfortable talking about them to begin with because he was now on a steady dose of antipsychotic drugs, and he realised they had all been in his mind. Janice told Jonathan how she suspected he was talking to himself in the past when she took him to his psychiatrist who had prescribed him a very mild dose of an anti-psychotic drug. But as he grew up the dosage needed to be corrected but hadn't. She also told him how she confided in his dad about his imaginary friends and as usual, Niraj blamed it all on her and said it was 'unacceptable.' Janice felt she let her son down because when she suspected that he had those issues, she should have sought help.

In her alone time, she wished she had done more to help Jonathan but realised that Niraj was a drain on her time and energy. He sucked everything out of her, and she now got angry with herself for letting him control her like that. The cleaning was over the top, would it matter that there was a little dust in some nook and cranny that nobody looked at? She should have spent that time helping Jonathan, she wished she was stronger and stood her ground from the start instead of being timid and controlled by Niraj.

She realised it was all a mess and wished she had never met Niraj. When she thought about her beautiful son, she felt happy again. That was her destiny. The one thing she knew for sure was that there was no time for 'what ifs,' she had to finally take control and be strong for Jonathan's sake. She would never again put the need of any other person before her son ever again. 'Lesson learned,' she thought.

Over the next few days, the three of them spent an evening or two in Barry's room having dinner and talking on various subjects. Janice was getting fond of him. She was glad that Barry would still make time to visit Jonathan after he left the hospital. When Jonathan had gone to bed, they often went for coffee in the canteen to discuss the whole situation. Sometimes Barry would come out with funny things that made her laugh. She couldn't remember a time when she was genuinely relaxed. How ironic to be relaxed in a hospital she thought.

Janice had been interviewed by Detective Superintendent Brown so she could give her version of the story. Janice gave the detective a scolding because he let Jonathan think she was dead. The detective wasn't used to an interviewee giving him a hard time, and she was right to be concerned about her son.

He explained the circumstances at the time, saying Jonathan was the only witness that could state what had happened in that house that night. She relented, but she seemed in a mood with the detective for a while after that.

A few days later Miss Mansfield called and wanted to meet with Jonathan, she said the court had heard his case, and she was ready to come over to the hospital to let them know what the court had decided. Jonathan was scared, they met her the following day, and he couldn't concentrate on anything. Barry and Janice tried to lighten the mood, but they too started to worry for him. They had a miserable evening even though Barry suggested they watch an episode or two of 'Friends.' For a while, it did get them to forget about the verdict they would finally get from the court tomorrow. They all knew the next day would change their lives, especially for Jonathan.

The following day Miss Mansfield came to the hospital with Detective Superintendent Brown and arranged to see Jonathan with his mum and Dr Rao. Barry for once stayed away and let Janice go into the interview room with Jonathan. He wished him good luck saying, 'no matter what she says, your mum and I will always be there for you. Stay strong!'

'I will.' Jonathan mumbled, 'and Barry…'

'Yes?'

Jonathan said nothing, he walked over to Barry and gave him a tight hug. Janice looked at the two of them trying not to cry. She needed to stay strong for Jonathan.

When he let go, Barry said, 'Good luck.'

He nodded and went into the room with his mum. Janice looked at Barry who was still watching then mouthing a silent, 'Thank You'.

Barry smiled feebly. He felt helpless. Jonathan's fate was now in the hands of the law.

25

When everyone was seated in the room, Jonathan looked at Miss Mansfield to see if her face gave anything away. It didn't; she smiled at his mum. Detective Superintendent Brown was also hard to read, and Jonathan didn't think Dr Rao knew. He will also have to hear it first hand from Miss Mansfield.

She looked over at Janice and said, 'glad you could make it Mrs Rice, you had something of an ordeal. The court had time to take into consideration your statement so thanks for that.'

Janice was too nervous for Jonathan's sake to speak, she nodded her head and smiled. She looked over at Jonathan who was silent, she knew when he got like that he was scared, all she wanted was this to be over and done with.

Miss Mansfield then spoke to everyone. 'Good morning to you all and thank you for making the time to see the detective and me so quickly. I knew that you would want to find out what they decided. We only got the verdict yesterday evening, and it was too late for the detective or me to come over, as we had prior engagements to deal with. Jonathan and

Janice, you both have said you said you are happy to proceed without Jonathan's counsel being present, as he is in court today. Are you definitely ok for me to proceed without him?'

'Yes, Miss.' he said.

When Miss Mansfield looked at Janice she said, 'Yes please, go ahead.'

'Very well, I got some favourable news for you, If I didn't, I would have insisted your counsel be present, and we would have postponed for a suitable day. However, I realise you have been waiting a while for the verdict, and I have talked to your council who agrees for me to pass on the verdict to you. Your council pleaded 'Diminished Responsibility' as the defence for the murder of your dad Mr Niraj Rice. In your case diminished responsibility was successfully pleaded, it had the effect of reducing your murder conviction to manslaughter. The court accepted your plea after they looked at the statements given by the police,' she looked over at the detective, 'Crown Prosecution Service and your council.

Furthermore, there was the question of whether the defendant: you Jonathan, were suffering from an abnormality of mental functioning caused by a recognised mental condition bipolar disorder. The jury considered your medical statements given by Dr Rao and also looked at your medical history. The medical opinion given suggested that you were also suffering from schizophrenia which means that you have schizoaffective disorder. Your abnormality of mind substantially impaired your mental functions in the killing of your dad. A satisfactory psychiatric report from Dr Rao concluded that you fulfilled the criteria set out in section 2(1) of the Homicide Act 1957.

Another factor that the judge considered was your ability to save your mother being killed by your father. The court decided that you acted with speed and without fearing for your life to save Mrs Janice Rice, your mother. They agreed that you were put in a vulnerable position in a household that had regularly suffered emotional and domestic abuse by Mr Niraj Rice. The statement from your mum and her diary given to her employer was handed in as evidence as well.

Because the murder had been committed by a minor living in an emotionally and domestically abusive household to protect another life, the judge and jury have shown you leniency. The court had to weigh whether you would benefit the most by sentencing you to either youth prison or to hospital, such as this one. Due to your character references and considering the unique conditions of this case, with the bonus that you have never committed a crime in the past, the court gave you a conditional discharge.'

She finished awaiting questions from them, and Dr Rao had a small smile on his face. Janice then said, 'this is quite complicated, what does that mean? He won't need to go to prison?'

'Correct, he won't go to a youth offender's prison but...'

Janice looked over at a stunned Jonathan, 'Oh my god did you hear that, I can't believe it!'

Janice smiled at them and leaned over to hug her son. Jonathan didn't know what to think, for all this time he hoped that he could stay with his mum. He then pushed her gently away to address Mrs Mansfield.

'You said but... but what? Won't I be able to stay with my mum? Will I have to be kept here in the hospital?'

'Well, the conditional discharge means you will receive no punishment provided that over the next two years no further offences are committed. This does not mean you are exonerated, it means you are free from court. However, if you re-offend, then your sentence would be activated, and you may face prosecution for any new crime you commit.'

Jonathan looked at his mum with a huge grin on his face, he was feeling faint, and the blood drained from his head.

She continued, 'There are however some conditions you will need to abide by.'

Janice answered apprehensively, 'Oh like what?'

'The court has given Jonathan a 'Community Treatment Order or CTO in short. With conditions,' she said.

'Meaning?' Jonathan asked.

'You will be given supervised treatment for your mental health problems when you are out of the hospital, but if your psychiatrist sees fit, he can return you to the hospital for immediate treatment. There are also certain conditions you have to follow like; you have to reside in a certain place, and make yourself available for visits or medical treatment and examination by the medical care workers or your doctor. You will also have to go to regular counselling as agreed by your doctor, in this case, Dr Rao.' She said looking over to the doctor who nodded in acceptance. 'This agreement has to be put in place by Doctor Rao before you leave the hospital.' She continued, 'The order will last for the two years of your conditional discharge.'

The detective who was sitting quietly letting Miss Mansfield do all the talking then said, 'Do you fully understand what she said Jonathan?'

He nodded and said, 'Yes, she said the judge looked positively on the fact I saved my mum and I was living in an abusive house. They took my age into consideration and that I had no previous convictions. Because of this, the judge reduced my sentence to manslaughter due to diminished responsibility.' He looked over to Miss Mansfield for approval.

'That's correct.' She said.

'Because of that, they gave me something called a 'conditional discharge' so I won't go to prison and will have to get regular treatment at the hospital for at least two years.'

Miss Mansfield smiled saying, 'you are definitely a bright young man, aren't you?'

'But not bright enough to have stopped what happened at home!' he said sarcastically.

'Jonathan!' His mum scolded.

Dr Rao then said, 'It's ok Mrs Rice, be grateful for the verdict.'

Janice remembered and said, 'yes of course we are, aren't we Jonathan?'

Very formally addressing both Miss Mansfield and Detective Superintendent Brown Jonathan said, 'I am very grateful for your help and kindness to me detective and Miss Mansfield. I am just glad this is over and sorry, but if there's nothing else can I go now? I don't want to think about this anymore, and my head is starting to hurt. Please don't be offended by my rudeness.'

They all looked at him in surprise, except for Janice who knew he was good at articulating his thoughts. She was proud of how he had turned out and how well he was dealing with it all.

Detective Superintendent Brown and Miss Mansfield realised it was their cue to leave, she then said, 'When you put it so sweetly of course. Detective, can we leave now?' She turned to the detective.

'Nothing else from me, I am just glad I can finally close this case, not that I didn't like seeing you, Jonathan.' He said giving him a wink.

They both stood up, Dr Rao showed them to the door and

asked Barry who was waiting outside to escort them out of the hospital.

Barry was glad when the door opened, but he was none the wiser on Jonathan's fate seeing the faces of Dr Rao, the detective and Miss Mansfield. He didn't ask them anything and quickly showed them out. He ran back to the room and knocked gently before going in without being asked.

All three of them still sat around the table looking drained and tired. Fearing the worst, he went over to Jonathan who was holding his head in his hands. Jonathan didn't hear Barry come into the room, and he forgot he was waiting outside for the news.

Barry said, 'Jonathan mate, don't worry I will be with you every step of the way. And you're mum too. Won't we Janice?'

Jonathan lifted his head to look at him in confusion, realising that nobody told him any of the news yet he said with a big grin on his face, 'you can't get rid of me that easily!'

'What? What do you mean?' Barry shouted in excitement looking at Janice and Dr Rao.

The doctor calmly told him to take a seat, so he could fill Barry in on what the court had decided. Before Barry sat down, he hugged Jonathan who stood up to leave and whispering in Barry's ear, 'I'm free to leave Barry. Thank you for being there for me.'

When they pulled back from their hug both had tears in their eyes, Janice said, 'Barry I will take him to his room for a nap and get a headache pill for him.'

'I will do that don't worry, I can hear what the court decided later. All that matters is he isn't going to prison.'

'Don't be silly, you stay here and let Dr Rao fill you in on everything, and I will catch up with you once Jonathan is asleep.'

Addressing Jonathan Barry said, 'Ok mate, go get some well-deserved sleep, and we can talk later.'

Jonathan just nodded his head gently. Barry smiled at both as they left the room, then he went over to the doctor to hear what the court's decision was.

After hearing what Dr Rao said he sat back on his chair and sighed heavily. He then said, 'I am so glad doctor, that boy has been through so much.'

'I am too, now the hard work begins. Jonathan hasn't been on proper medication until now, and I will monitor him closely, so he can lead a normal life from now on.'

'I will miss him when he leaves the hospital. Do you have any idea when that will be?'

'Maybe not for a day or two, plus they need to find somewhere to stay before they leave so until then, I guess. I have some formalities to sort out to make sure he adheres to the court order, and until that is done, I don't think I can discharge him.'

'Maisy, Janice's employer, has been coming to see her when she was in the coma and also whilst she has been out. She is a dear old lady. Maybe she knows about somewhere they could live until they sort out their permanent residence and until Janice works out what she will do with the house.'

'Good, ask Janice to have a word with her.' Then the doctor smiled and said, 'a little birdie tells me that Maisy wasn't the only visitor that Janice had whilst she was in a coma!'

Barry stilled his breathing and calmly asked, 'oh, who else visited her?'

'Someone sitting in this room.' The doctor teased Barry.

'Of course, I went to see her, I took Jonathan there every day, we spent hours with her.' Barry said defensively.

'I know about those, I mean the late-night visits.'

'Oh, that!' Barry said admitting defeat. 'I hope that was ok doctor. I just went to encourage her to come out of the coma for Jonathan's sake. How did you find out?'

'Well, let's say the nurses had placed bets on how long you stayed each night.' He said laughing at Barry's shocked face.

'You mean they all knew?'

'They gave you a wide birth, so you weren't disturbed. Didn't you think it was strange that you encountered nobody whenever you went to visit Janice?'

'Yeah but I thought during the late shifts staff were thin on the ground.'

'They are, but you got caught in the act one night, a nurse was about to go into Janice's room and heard your voice, so she stayed by the door to listen. You were very sweet to her, so I hear. They all said you always kept the door slightly ajar for fear someone might think you were there to do something untoward.'

'Good god, now I am a laughingstock amongst the staff.'

'Well not really, they think you are a soft romantic!' He said laughing at Barry. 'So, the million-dollar question is, are you into her, and more importantly does she like you back?'

'Really, doctor!' Barry said a little loudly. 'I didn't peg you as the office gossip!'

'Don't be silly Barry, I am teasing you. I am so fond of you, make sure professionalism and your private life don't mix for now. Not till Jonathan is out of your charge anyway.'

'I will for sure, doctor. I love my job and wouldn't want to jeopardise it at all.'

The doctor nodded in agreement. When Barry left the interview room, he was still in shock, he wanted to hide somewhere and not face the staff. He didn't know they were all speculating about Janice and him. He didn't want Jonathan to find out anything either, he should have realised that as big as the hospital was, the gossip that went around it was even bigger. 'That's just hospital life, I guess' he surmised!

Barry bit the bullet and went into Jonathan's room in search of Janice. He found her reading a book with a sleeping Jonathan in his bed. They both left the room soundlessly and headed for the canteen. He didn't care who saw him speaking to Janice. Soon she will be gone from the hospital, and they will have to gossip about someone else.

When they got to the canteen, they found a nice private spot by the window. Janice said how happy she was that Jonathan was not going to prison and that she would keep a close eye on him from now on. He suggested that Jonathan was growing up quickly, and soon he would have to keep an eye on her instead! She laughed at that suggestion, he couldn't help watching her expressions. Her eyes lit up when she talked about Jonathan, and she smiled a lot more now that they knew he was out of the woods.

'On a more serious note Janice, where are you going to stay once you leave here?'

'Yeah, I have been thinking about that, I first thought we could check into a cheap hotel for two or three weeks. I have savings that I was going to use for the deposit for the flat. But then I spoke to Maisy about it, and she wants me to stay at her place. She has got a spare bedroom. Either Jonathan or I could sleep on the couch, that would do temporarily I guess.'

'But for how long? That sounds difficult for all three of you.'

'Yeah, it will be. For as long as it takes to sell the house, pay off the small mortgage left on the house and buy something with the left over money that is at least two bedrooms. A flat will do if we won't be able to afford a house. But the one thing I know is, that there will be enough money to buy outright, I want to be mortgage free. I might even have to move out of the area to get something cheaper.'

'Oh well, I will do anything I can to help, and I hope you don't mind me asking, but once the dust is settled and I have days off, I was wondering if you would allow Jonathan to stay overnight with me. I have a spare room, and we could do things I promised him after he left the hospital.'

'Gosh Barry, that is so sweet of you. I would allow it, but I suspect Jonathan has his own mind and would overrule me even if I said no!'

'Thanks, and that will give you some breathing room in Maisy's house. You are welcome to come too, for the days out I mean.'

'I know what you mean, and yes I will.'

Then she looked seriously at Barry and said, 'I hope I don't lose you as a friend, once I leave here.'

'No way, I am here for both of you.'

She smiled happily. 'Because it's nice to get adult companionship and to discuss Jonathan without someone always demeaning us.' She ended sadly.

'You mean his dad.'

She nodded and looked out of the window. Barry wanted to hug her, but he knew he couldn't. They didn't speak to each other for a while. He let her wander off in her thoughts, and he knew one thing, he wouldn't leave them unless they specifically asked him to. He always wanted to be with them and hoped they felt the same way about him.

The next ten days were a blur for everyone, Jonathan and Janice would see Dr Rao often to get counselling and advice on how Jonathan should take his medication. Janice was busy making phone calls and occasionally going out of the hospital to visit Maisy. Janice visited estate agents, so she could sell their house and hired professional cleaners to get the house ready to sell. She knew she would have to drop the price of the house by a few thousand, due to the murder but luckily for her it was in a good area and houses in that area didn't stay on the market for long.

Barry missed the routine he had with Jonathan and Janice, but it was something he would have to deal with. He moved out of the doctor's quarters and went back to his flat, he had to get it ready for Jonathan's visits and overnight stays. He suggested Jonathan stay over at his place for three nights a week until they found permanent accommodation. Janice was reluctant and didn't want to impose, but Jonathan thought it was a great idea. Eventually, she relented, to Jonathan's delight.

The day finally came for Barry and the hospital staff to let them go. They gave Jonathan and his mum a nice send-off. The staff that helped with them did a little collection and presentation. Maisy took them home, and Barry got leave that day to see they settled into Maisy's house. They all gathered at the canteen to wish Janice and Jonathan the best of luck. Janice got a huge bouquet which had a lot of lilies, her favourite flower. Maisy knew all about Janice's preferences and was paid to get the flowers from her shop. Because Maisy was so kind, she doubled the order so that Janice would get twice as many flowers. Jonathan got special edition comics and a hundred pounds worth of iTunes voucher from the staff. Barry got him a new iPad, so he could download and watch all the 'David Attenborough' programmes he wanted.

Janice couldn't believe their generosity, she cried hugging Maisy who also had a tear in her eye. Dr Rao looked like a proud father sending his children off to university. Barry wanted to cry too but decided to 'man up', hard is it was for him. Jonathan didn't care that he promised Barry he wouldn't cry, he hugged him for his very generous gift, and said, 'I don't care, Barry, I want to hug you and cry like a girl!'

Barry didn't know whether to laugh or cry. He hugged Jonathan back saying, 'remember mate, you will be staying at mine most days, so what's yours is mine.'

'Don't even think about it! That iPad is all mine!' Jonathan said smiling through his tears, then seriously, 'Barry I don't know how to thank you. You have been like the dad I should have had!'

Barry was so touched, 'I will never stop seeing you unless you ask me to. Until then you got me ok? Now stop this right now mate, what the hell are you doing? Do you want me to cry in front of all my colleagues?'

Jonathan nodded whilst crying and smiling with the scolding he got for trying to make Barry cry. They left the hospital in a flurry of goodbyes from the staff.

Dr Rao went to his office, picked up the phone and called the detective. He whispered, 'They have gone.'

There was silence for a second or two. The detective then said, 'And are you ok, doctor, shall we meet up for a drink later, just to pat ourselves on the back?'

'Yes please, I will miss Jonathan a lot. You knew how professional I had to be with him. But he has become my favourite patient.'

'I know, shall we let our hair down tonight with a drink or two?'

'A drink sounds perfect, god knows I need one!' Dr Rao said laughing.

EPILOGUE

S ix months after leaving the hospital, they moved into Jonathan's grandfather's mansion. Jonathan knew his mum had left him because of his controlling behaviour and wanted to make her own way in life. However, whilst Janice was in a coma, her father passed away leaving his only daughter his various businesses, and all his assets, including the house they were moving into.

At first, Janice didn't want to live in her father's house, but when Jonathan went to see it, he fell in love with the house. She didn't have the heart to deny him something she took for granted growing up.

'He deserves it', she said to Barry one evening when she was questioning her reasoning on trying to justify whether moving into her old house was something she should do.

Barry was so glad for them, knowing they never needed to worry about money again. Janice left the running of the business to the managers, she decided checking on the business once a month would be more than was necessary.

She did, however, want to continue to work at the florist and bought the shop from Maisy. Their family home was still on the market, but Janice was in no rush to sell, so she put it up for rent. Niraj's family never spoke to her again, and she was glad of it.

Despite living in the new house, Jonathan still stayed some nights at Barry's house, and in turn, they invited Barry to stay over at their place.

One night when Barry came over, Jonathan made himself scarce by feigning a headache and went to his room to give Barry and his mum time alone.

When he got there, he put on some music, suddenly he heard a voice behind him, 'You didn't think you could get rid of me that easily did you JR?'

He couldn't believe Peter was there, Peter Parker - Spiderman, his fictitious, imaginary friend!

'I hope you didn't believe all that hype from Dr Rao and Barry about me. I am your friend now and forever. I will never let you down JR, you will never live without me. We will be friends forever, just you wait and see.'

———

"Sometimes the hardest part isn't letting go but rather learning to start over.
- Nicole Sobon"

———

ENJOYED DARE TO IMAGINE?

If you enjoyed this book, I would love for you to leave a review.

Reviews are incredibly valuable to an author. They help spread the word to other readers so they too can discover and enjoy the story.

I thank you for your readership and I hope to bring you many more exciting books for you to read.

Don't miss a thing…
Subscribe to my mailing list

www.nilzaelita.com

ABOUT THE AUTHOR

Nilza Elita is an author that is unafraid to push the boundaries to explore the human mind, she likes mixing real life situations with her fictional characters and can bring out empathy and compassion in her readers.

Nilza was born in Bombay, a city now called Mumbai in India, and has lived in several countries that has given her a global perspective, ultimately making her the author she is today.

She spent her childhood years in Dar es Salaam in Tanzania, her teenage years in Lagos, Nigeria. Her late teenage and early adulthood was spent in a beautiful little town in the Borders region of Scotland called Jedburgh.

Nilza studied and got a Bachelor Degree in Business Administration from the Herriot Watt University in Edinburgh, Scotland.

In her spare time she can be found at the gym attending several group fitness classes.

Nilza lives in London England, enjoying the fast-paced excitement of city life with her two children.

For more information about her
book launches, behind the scene information
and author news visit:
nilzaelita.com

<u>Nilza Elita Social Media Platforms</u>
Pinterest: Nilza Elitas Pins
Instagram: Nilza Elita Instagram Posts
Facebook: Nilza Elita Facebook Page

facebook.com/Nilza-Elita-189273191926640

instagram.com/nilza.elita

pinterest.com/pinterest.co.uknilzaelita

ACKNOWLEDGMENTS

It has been said, that being an author is a solitary profession, but in the making of this book, I have been supported by an invisible team behind me, without whom this book wouldn't exist, they are:

My children - Jay and Sasha, who have been supportive and patient with me during the writing of this book. On many occasions they have told me they are proud of me which amazing to hear. My son Jay has been exceptional in the help he has given me whilst I researched the Marvel characters featured in this book. He has guided me in choosing the right Marvel character to fit in with my story, and I am very grateful for his love and dedication towards this book.

My partner Vasco who has been my guiding light, he has never for a moment doubted my abilities to write this book. I thank him from the bottom of my heart for giving me the patience, understanding and devotion, unconditionally. Vasco, I am so grateful to not only have your support but to have you in my life too.

The Vilaportuguesa Team in Portugal - For giving me the most beautiful and serene place in the world to write. For giving me copious amounts of freshly squeezed orange juice and (English) tea. For giving me the space and time, undisturbed. I may have been concentrating on my laptop, but I noticed all the support your team has given me. Thank you Vasco for allowing me to write in all your Vilaportuguesa establishments - Restaurant, hotel and boat, https://www.vilaportuguesa.pt

My editor Shari who has been patient with me. She took my book and made my words beautiful, and for that I will forever be grateful. She adopted and loved this book as if it were her own - nobody could ask more from an editor. Her professionalism shone through. Not only have I found an editor that have my readers and book's best interests at heart, I have found a friend I can confide in the writing of my future books.

To the SPF community and Facebook groups - Genius, Mastery and SPF. I have learned so much from Mark Dawson's groups, podcasts, and all the authors that support this community. They are positive and help in ways I can't even describe here. Only they will know what I mean when/if they ever get to read this acknowledgement. I couldn't have done it without their supportive author's arms around me.

And finally... I would like to thank you the reader. Without you buying and reading this book there would be no reason for me to write.

FURTHER INFORMATION

In writing this book I invented Jonathan's legal scenario based on outcomes of legal cases in the UK. At present, there is no case in UK law that has dealt with a minor who committed a murder in self-defence and saved a life whilst suffering from a disorder like schizophrenia. Therefore Jonathan's sentencing has been created using UK law as the basis for his sentencing.

This book has touched on a few subjects you may not be familiar with. I have gathered some facts on the subjects for you to read if you so wish. None of the characters in this book are real, all characters, their flaws and strengths have been created by my imagination however, the scenarios that they have dealt with are real.

HYPNOTISM

In this book it transpires that Jonathan has in fact hypnotised himself to find out what memories he had repressed. In his hallucinations, he heard the voices of his 'friends' who suggested hypnotherapy and he acted on those suggestions.

In reality you may question whether one can actually hypnotise themselves. The answer to that is: yes they can. Self-hypnosis is completely possible because our perspective of this type of therapy is: 'all hypnosis is self-hypnosis'. Hypnotherapy is like talking therapy, and if you aren't prepared to listen and accept the messages and suggestions, then you will not hypnotise yourself.

Self-hypnosis can be taught by hypnotherapists (in the case of Jonathan, he learned it from reading books and the internet). Hypnotherapy is taught by including simple affirmations, points of pausing from one behaviour to adopt another, and by getting the student to get themselves in a different mindset, so that they can operate in a more useful way independently.

The Facts

Hypnosis is akin to meditation or relaxation, of which it resembles. Nobody has ever been harmed by hypnosis. It is a real phenomenon, although there are still some disagreements over its precise nature and function.

There are hundreds of research studies that have demonstrated the effects of hypnotherapy in the treatment of anxiety, pain and psychosomatic illness. The benefits of hypnotherapy have been recognised by the British and American Medical Associations.

Some people respond better than others to hypnosis, with only 5% of people being unresponsive to this type of therapy. In other words, research indicates that virtually everyone can be hypnotised to some extent.

Hypnotherapy has no professional standards at present.

SCHIZOPHRENIA

Schizophrenia isn't split personality unlike popular belief. Many people think that schizophrenia makes people violent. In this book Jonathan did not turn violent until he had to protect Janice. In addition, he was encouraged to act on his anger by his hallucinations.

The Facts

• Violence in a patient that has schizophrenia is an exception, not the rule.

• People with schizophrenia are more likely to be victims of violence by others. Hospital admission is often not needed, many people with this condition live a stable life and have relationships.

• It is true that a combination of factors can cause this disorder like genes, brain damage at birth or during pregnancy or childhood abuse. Family tensions and stress will make it worse.

• During a lifetime, 1 in 100 people will suffer an episode of schizophrenia. It occurs in all countries and societies of the world and affects both sexes alike.

• Sufferers have a 5 to 10% chance of dying by their own hand within ten years of diagnosis.

• Schizophrenia strikes most often in late teens and early twenties and slightly later in women.

• There is now some evidence that suggest using street drugs especially cannabis may increase your chances of suffering an episode of schizophrenia.

• About 25% of people who suffer from schizophrenia will go on to recover completely without further problems in the future. Modern medications effectively reduce the risk of relapses to about 10%.

If you know someone that needs further support or you would like to find out more, visit:

UK - www.mind.org.uk

US - www.schizophrenia.com

DOMESTIC ABUSE

Domestic abuse is described as an incident or pattern of incidents of controlling, coercive, threatening, degrading and violent behaviour. This can include sexual violence, in the majority of cases by a partner or ex-partner, is experienced by women and is perpetrated by men.

This type of crime is deeply rooted in societal inequality between women and men. Women are more likely to experience multiple incidents of abuse.

Anyone can encounter domestic abuse regardless of race, ethnic or religious group, sexuality, class or disability.

Identifying Emotional Abuse

This type of abuse can go unnoticed, the indicators are:

You have been made to feel guilty, insulting remarks at you like name calling, overprotection, jealousy, making decisions without consulting you, your abuser becomes more demanding, they lack empathy or compassion, financial abuse, they undermine you, your friends disappear, you prefer to be alone, they turn you against your family and many others.

To get help or find out more please visit:

UK: www.nationaldomesticviolencehelpline.org.uk

US: www.thehotline.org

Printed in Great Britain
by Amazon